ANNA SPARROWS

His Prodigal Alpha

Shifters Sanctuary Book 2

Cover design by Ky at Blue Brolli Graphics

First edition

This book was professionally typeset on Reedsy.
Find out more at reedsy.com

For my husband. The grumpy to my sunshine. It's about time I dedicated a book to you.
Here's to a HEA!

Contents

Preface

This is Book 2 of the *Shifters Sanctuary* series, however it can be read as a standalone.

His Prodigal Alpha is a sweet, instant attraction (fated mates vibes) romance. It **IS** an **mpreg** romance, and it does contain **violence, threats, infertility, surprise pregnancy, kidnapping/abduction of small children/infants** (I promise it's brief and has a HEA), **anxiety/allusions to an emotionally abusive upbringing, a birthing scene,** and some **mild angst**.

This book contains elements suited to readers over the age of 18.

I am still a firm believer in not yucking someone else's yum, so if the above isn't for you, don't force yourself to read it.

Life's too short to read something you don't enjoy.

Acknowledgement

A HUGE thank you to Ky Abbey. My alpha reader. My PA. My cover designer (Blue Brolli Graphics is *awesome*). You've done so much to help me get this book to print, I don't even think I have the page space to explain it all. Thank you for being you.

I'd also like to thank Cindy for being an amazing alpha reader and friend. You helped take this draft from something I honestly kind of hated to something I'm once again proud of. Without your specific and in-depth feedback, I can't imagine what would have happened to this book.

Similarly, thank you to Claire for talking me through far too many 'I'm a fraud' rants as these characters refused to follow the plot I had set out for them. Damon was determined to be difficult from the start.

Finally, thank you (yes, *you*) for reading this. I am beyond warmed by the fact that you picked up one of my books when I know just how many other potential reads are out there begging for attention. It means more to me than I can properly express. I genuinely hope you enjoy the book, but even if you DNF, thank you for giving it a chance.

Prologue – Damon

The Christmas festival was in full swing when I parked off the main drag of the now-infamous little town. Shifters Sanctuary had become notorious in shifter circles since the news of an alpha had begun circulating. According to rumor, he was the only one of his kind, but I knew that to be untrue.

How did I know he wasn't the only alpha in the world?

Well, the obvious swell of my belly wasn't from indulging in too much pie.

There was another alpha out there somewhere, but fuck if I knew where he had run off to. He hadn't taken his body changing mid-orgasm very well and, the second his knot had deflated, the fucker had run out of the bathroom stall in which we'd had our anonymous tryst without so much as a backwards glance.

Apparently my being a shifter hadn't bothered him, but the idea that he wasn't human had been too much to handle. I supposed I couldn't blame him for that.

I'd been too mystified by the entire encounter to consider the fact that I, an omega, had been knotted during unprotected sex until the vomiting had started six weeks following the experience. Then I had been in denial for a while after that. It wasn't until my stomach started to curve outwards in a very telling way that I accepted what had happened.

I'd unknowingly found an alpha in a random bar. We had been incredibly interested in each other. I would even go as far as to say that we were inexplicably drawn to each other. I had begged him to fuck me hard right then and there, desperate for him to fill me and claim me.

And the asshole had knocked me up and vanished.

Okay, okay; he obviously hadn't realized he was an alpha any more than I hadn't realized that he wasn't human, but I still felt as though I had the right to resent him a teeny, tiny bit. After all, I was the one left holding the baby: figuratively and literally.

Unable to hide my condition from my not exactly pro omega rights pack, I'd gotten together as many of my belongings as possible and had made a run for it. As far as I'd known, I was the only pregnant omega in a long-ass time, and I had no idea how I was going to make it through the following months, let alone the birth.

And then, while I'd been staying in a small shifter town in Nebraska, I'd heard the whispers.

There was an alpha with a pregnant mate. They'd started to build a pack in Bumfuck Nowhere, Iowa. Word was, they believed there were others out there like them. Like the alpha. Men with dubious backstories who didn't know their family histories, or those who came from shifter lines but presented human, who needed to find a compatible omega to unlock their inner alphas.

Was that what had happened to me? It sure as fuck sounded like it.

I'd sidled into the conversation as nonchalantly as I could, needing more details. Namely how the fuck could I find the town and were they looking for twenty-five-year-old college dropouts who were happy to earn minimum wage in exchange for any kind of job at all?

A couple of months and a fuckton of effort later, and there I was: Shifters Sanctuary.

I didn't know why I had thought that early December in Iowa wouldn't be cold, but I wasn't prepared for the blast of chilly air that hit me as I climbed out of my beater of a car. It had been all I could afford to buy with the meager savings I'd stashed away over my teens, and I'd only been able to convince my parents to allow me to buy it because I'd been going to college and needed it for the commute. I was glad that I'd bought it in my own name, because nobody could accuse me of stealing it when I ran away from the pack with what few possessions I owned tossed haphazardly into the trunk.

It had once been white, but was rather a mottled mass of scrapes and rust marks and had been since I'd bought it. But I had taught myself a thing or two about mechanics, so the engine ran well, and the heater worked just fine. It was better than having no car, and Ol' Betsy and I had been through a lot together since I was eighteen.

Wrapping my too-thin coat tighter around myself, I made my way towards the central source of the festivities. The street was lit up with fairy-lights and multi-colored Christmas lights both. The ten or so storefronts on either side of the main street also had their windows illuminated and decorated in

Christmas cheer. Loudspeakers played Christmas carols and there were stalls set up selling anything from cookies and hot cocoa to knitted beanies and dolls.

My throat tightened involuntarily as I brushed my index finger over one of the crocheted toys. It was only a few dollars, but I couldn't even afford that for my unborn child. Not while I was homeless and jobless.

"Can I getcha anything, honey?" the lady staffing the stall asked. A delicate sniff revealed her to be a hedgehog shifter. The cat living inside my soul relaxed at that.

Well, I called it a cat. I was actually a puma shifter, but I mostly felt like an oversized house cat.

Shaking my head, I decided that if I had any chance of staying in the town as part of their pack, I might as well start trying to make nice with the locals. "No. I...I'm actually looking for the Alpha. Is, um, is he around here somewhere?"

Her nose, red from the cold, twitched. Her eyes narrowed and she looked me up and down. With my oversized coat closed, she couldn't see my bump. I preferred it that way.

"Why are you asking?" she sounded less friendly at that point and more defensive, as if a diminutive omega like me could really be a threat.

I wondered if that meant the Alpha was a good man so his pack cared about his well-being and wanted to protect him from potential threats, or if it meant that he was a bad man who ruled them all with an iron fist.

"I, um, I kind of...I..." A lump lodged in my throat and I cursed my hormones for making me cry at the drop of a hat. But it had the benefit of giving away just how pitiful I was, because Hedgehog Lady's demeanor slipped right back to empathetic and maternal.

"Oh, sweetie, I'm sorry. We're just real protective of our fledgling pack is all. Here, come sit," she ushered me to walk behind her table of knitted goods and sat me down on the plastic chair she'd had sitting in the corner of her stall. "I'm gonna get you a cup of cocoa, and I'll get the Alpha. Stay right here, okay?"

At the point of sniffling and fighting my stupid hormonal response, I could only nod.

She returned a few minutes later with the promised cup of hot cocoa and a tall, broad-chested man with dark hair and deep brown eyes. At his side was another man, shorter and slender, with flopsy light brown hair and green eyes.

The taller man called for my attention without even having to speak. I could scent the difference in him on the air. It buzzed and tickled my nose. *Alpha.*

My lower lip quivered and I ducked my head.

Having guessed that the man standing next to the Alpha was his mate, I was overwhelmed with a moment of irrational jealousy. How come that guy had been enough for the man who had mated him, but I wasn't enough for the guy who mated me?

The Alpha cleared his throat and I forced myself to look up at him with watering eyes. Both men scented like wolves but, strangely, my inner cat had no complaints about that. Perhaps it realized they weren't a threat to me.

The Alpha smiled back at me softly. "Hi," he greeted me casually. "I'm Beck. Jazz said you were asking for me?"

My eyes darted between him, his mate, and the hedgehog lady. Jazz.

Weird name, but okay.

I nodded and tried to swallow around the lump of emotion

in my throat. "Yeah," I croaked out. "I, uh, I heard about this town. This pack. And I, um, I was wondering if I could join it. The pack, I mean. I...I ran away from my pack. I couldn't stay. If they found out..."

"Whoa," Beck held up his hands to stall my babbling. "Let's start with your name first, huh? And maybe we'll head inside somewhere and get out of the cold. You're shivering."

I hadn't even noticed. I nodded again, dumbly. Then, after a beat of silence, I realized they were still waiting on my name. *Stupid baby brain.* "Damon," I finally blurted, then blushed. "My name is Damon. Damon Richards. I'm sorry. It's...it's been a really long trip to get here and I'm...I mean, I know I shouldn't just expect that you'll let me join the pack, but I have nowhere else to go and—"

"It's okay," this time it was Beck's mate who spoke. He also smiled kindly at me. "Shifters Sanctuary is supposed to be just that: a haven for outcast shifters and people who don't have a pack or family." He extended his hand. I took it. "I'm Ollie," he said, shaking my hand and then gently tugging me upwards. Standing next to him, I realized he wasn't as short as he looked. In fact, he was at least two inches taller than me. "Come on, let's head inside. Have you eaten? The diner here makes the best burgers."

"You'd think you would be sick of them by now," Beck teased his mate as they guided me back out of the stall and towards the town's diner. "Considering how many you ate when you were pregnant."

The child in my belly rolled over, as if summoned into action by that word. It was a word I hadn't spoken out loud to anyone yet, but Beck and Ollie used it as though omega pregnancies were totally normal.

Having lived through one, I supposed for them they had become as much.

I let their banter wash over me until we were inside the warm building. It was a long, narrow space, with one wall lined with back-to-back dining booths, and the other with a kitchen and counter. Three stools lined the counter space next to the cash register. It looked as though it had been decorated in the 80s to resemble the 50s. The Formica counter tops were chipped and worn, and the bright red vinyl seats of the stools and booths had also seen better days. But it smelled so good. My stomach rumbled audibly and the baby inside me kicked up a storm.

"Come on, let me take your coat and you can take a seat. It's sweltering in here." Ollie was bright and cheerful and he had no idea what kind of anxiety he'd just set off with his request.

I swallowed and turned to face him and Beck, reminding myself that they had been through what I was going through. If I was going to be safe anywhere, it would be with them. They would understand. I needed them to understand. If they didn't, I really was out of options.

"Before I do, there's something else. The reason I ran from my pack. I…um…I…" God, why was it so hard to say aloud? With a growl of frustration at myself, I said. "How about I just show you?"

Giving them no time to respond, I removed my coat.

The threadbare sweater I wore beneath it was stretched tight over my unmistakable baby bump, and the jeans I was wearing were baggy around my legs but growing ever more snug around my waist. I'd found them in a Goodwill during my travels, and the sales lady had looked at me strangely for buying a pair so much larger than I had visibly needed at the time. Standing in that diner, I thought they wouldn't be big enough for much longer.

"Holy shit," Beck breathed, before turning to Ollie with startled eyes. "I swear, I didn't do it."

Ollie just rolled his eyes at his mate. "I know that, dumbass," he sassed, but the affection in his words was more than obvious. "But you know what this means."

Beck nodded, his expression becoming serious. "He's definitely joining the pack."

"Well, duh," Ollie sighed. "But that's not what I meant." He turned back to me, his eyes roving over my swollen, gravid form. "We were right: there's at least one other alpha out there somewhere."

Chapter One – Damon

It had all started in a run-down bar in the middle of nowhere, Texas.

"Well, now, what's a pretty young thing like you doin' in a place like this?"

The voice drawling the question sounded just as sleazy as the pickup line itself. I hung my head over my margarita glass for a moment before I sighed and turned to face the owner of the voice.

To be fair, he wasn't quite as gross as his voice had led me to believe he'd be. Yeah, his dirty blonde hair looked like it was slicked back with way too much product, and yeah, his teeth were yellowed and crooked, but he had an otherwise pleasant enough face. Still, he'd already rubbed me the wrong way and I wasn't interested.

"Sorry," I told him, my voice pitching high as I raised it above the general din of the bar I'd found myself sitting in, "I don't speak English."

He stood baffled for a moment, his jaw slack and eyes

squinting with confusion. "But…"

"Really sorry," I repeated, gesturing for him to move along.

Laughter, rich and deep, came from my right as the spare stool beside me was suddenly pulled back and occupied.

"That's a new one," my new companion said with a smile in his voice, his thick forearm reaching out in my peripheral vision, summoning the bartender with a 'come hither' gesture formed by two thick, masculine fingers.

Who knew fingers could be masculine? I sure hadn't until then.

Taking another swallow of my out-of-place drink, I turned to give the newcomer my attention.

Holy fuck.

To say the guy was easy on the eyes would be like saying the Grand Canyon was an interesting little hole in the ground.

He was big and broad. Not gym muscled, but his biceps and forearms looked like he was no stranger to manual labor. His skin was a deep golden color, and his hair looked to be sun-bleached in artful streaks through light brown waves. I couldn't see his jaw beneath a well-kept, thick beard in similar shades to his hair, but it was the blue of his eyes that really caught my attention, bright and sparkling with mirth. And when he smiled they crinkled at the corners, helping to cement the deep laughter lines that made him seem so warm and friendly.

I startled as I felt my body react to his proximity, with slick threatening to dampen the seat of my dark jeans. And that was to say nothing of my dick suddenly standing to attention within its confines, either. I was surprised by how rapidly my arousal hit me, and how intensely. That had never happened before. I guessed I was hornier than I'd first thought.

"I'm gonna have to remember that line," he said once he'd ordered his beer, adding, "not speaking English?" for clarification when I blinked blankly back at him.

I felt heat rise to my cheeks and I dipped my chin. "It was kind of an asshole move, I know. But guys like that take 'I'm not interested' as a challenge."

He nodded and raised his bottle to his lips. "Men like that do tend to think with their dicks. And, really, 'I don't speak English' is still much more polite than 'fuck off', right?"

Was he flirting with me? We weren't in a gay bar (I'd checked, because I would have been way more comfortable visiting one of those), so what was the likelihood *two* men had set their sights on me in a sexual way? I knew my presence screamed twink, both in build and mannerisms, but this was still Texas, and I was trying to keep a low profile. I wore jeans and a plaid shirt, and I'd done my best to fit in with the crowd.

My pack would kill me if they knew I'd sneaked away just to blow off steam. Sadly, out in the middle of this small town, there weren't a lot of places a flamboyant omega like me could scratch the kinds of itches I had. I'd been prepared to settle on a few drinks and time away from the pack, but now my body had taken notice of the guy to my right and I was suddenly *very* aware of my needs.

As I chuckled and agreed with him, I took in his scent. Clean sweat, sunshine, grass, and a hint of faded cologne ignited a fire inside me. I clenched my ass as a wave of desire hit me hard and fast. When was the last time I'd reacted like that to someone so quickly? I didn't think I ever had.

"What's your name, kid?" he asked, gesturing to the bartender to bring us both another round.

I swallowed roughly, not bothering to correct him on my

age. At barely twenty-five, I was probably at least a decade his junior.

Did I mention that older men did it for me? Well, they did. And even though late thirties/early forties wasn't *that* old, it was good enough for me.

"Damon," I told him, offering him my hand. "Damon Richards. And you are?"

Beneath that lush beard which glinted with gold and hints of amber, his wind-chapped lips pulled into a genuine smile as he took my hand. His palm and the pads of his fingers were calloused. The feeling sent tingles of electricity up my arm. "Rex," he introduced himself. "Rex Murphy. It's nice to meet you, Damon."

The way he curled his deep, Texan drawl around my name made my stomach flip and my cock twitch. I swore that my skin burned with the flush of arousal he ignited.

"Just so you know," I said, picking up the glass the bartender set in front of me, "for you? I'll speak any language you want."

Rex threw his head back as he laughed and I knew that, without a doubt, I'd be getting my itches scratched after all....which was a damn good thing, because I was hornier than I had ever been before.

Chapter Two – Rex

"Mmm," Damon practically purred as I manhandled him into the only ladies' bathroom stall in the building, sucking light hickeys into the skin of his neck, "there's, uh, there's something I should tell you before we…oh, *God,* your mouth…your *beard…*"

I chuckled and delighted in the way he seemed to shiver at the sound. "Hmm?" I asked him once the door was locked, tugging at his shirt, trying to free the hem from beneath the waistband of his sinfully tight jeans. "What have you got to tell me, darlin'?"

"Fuck," he muttered, rubbing his face into my beard in an almost feline way, "I never have to do this." He was blushing so hard, it felt like his cheek was on fire. I could feel it through my beard.

"Do what, kitten?"

He huffed out a little laugh and then swallowed audibly. "It's funny you should call me that. I'm, um," he took a steadying breath and then stepped out of my hold, putting barely a foot of space between us as he leaned against the opposite wall.

He eyed the door behind me before setting his beseeching gaze on mine again. His brown eyes were wide and flecked with gold. They were so mesmerizing; it was what had drawn me to him to begin with.

"Don't freak out, but…I'm a shifter. A puma shifter, to be specific. And if that's too weird or it's a deal-breaker, I'll just—" Damon moved, edging around me towards the door, but I looped my arm around his waist, tugging him back into position in front of me. I stifled a chuckle as he blew out a breath to clear away the lock of dark hair that had fallen over his eyes.

"Shifter, huh?" Theoretically, I knew they existed, but I didn't think I'd ever met one before. Well, not one who had come out and told me what they were. There had been a lot of news about shifters reappearing in society after a freaking dragon had brought a building down in Manhattan. That had only happened a few months earlier, and sensationalism was still running rife in the media. Nevertheless, I didn't buy into the rhetoric that shifters couldn't be trusted. I figured they were like most people: there would be both good eggs and bad. "That's neat."

Damon didn't reply.

I cocked my head at him, smiling as gently as I could, considering the way my jeans were tented obscenely. All I wanted to do was get inside him. I couldn't care less that he wasn't entirely human. With long, dark hair and those gold-flecked eyes, he was as pretty as he was witty, and his lips tasted like ambrosia. In the moment, that was all that mattered. "There a reason why you had to tell me? I wouldn't have known if you didn't."

"Yeah, you would have." He squirmed on the spot. "I'm what shifters call an omega. It's like a secondary gender, I guess. I…well, to cut to the chase, my body produces slick to assist with…" His blush deepened and he cleared his throat, tucking his hair back behind his ears. He was adorable, especially when he refused to meet my gaze any longer. "Anyway, when I get really horny, I get wet."

I blinked. "Wet? Like—"

"—I've prepped with *way* too much lube?" he finished for me, nodding as he laughed nervously. "It doesn't normally happen with humans…or often, really…but I, um, it's been a while, so I must be more worked up than I thought." He cringed. "I get it if it's too weird. I can just leave. Just…just don't freak out and beat me to a pulp or anything, okay?"

My heart clenched. Just what kind of men had he been associating with if he had to ask me such a thing? "No, kitten. I wouldn't ever hurt you like that."

It was a stupidly intimate thing to say when we were only going to hook up and part ways, but I couldn't say nothing, could I?

"So, um…" Damon finally looked back up at me. His cheeks were still bright pink, and his eyes were still blown wide with lust. My dick, which had started to flag under the more serious tone of the conversation, bounced right back into action at the blatant need in his eyes. "Are you still in? Or should I go?"

"Oh, I'm definitely looking forward to being *in*," I replied playfully, offering him a wolfish grin.

He rolled his eyes, but the flush of his cheeks and the way his Adam's apple bobbed as he swallowed gave his excitement away.

The bathroom stall we were in was a narrow, closed room,

with a toilet on one end of the space and a wall mounted sink on the other. It was cleaner than the men's room, potentially because it wasn't used as frequently, but it was still kind of dingy.

I closed the space between us and kissed him again, my body demanding contact. I'd never felt quite as desperate to be with someone before, even though I'd had my fair share of one-night stands and impromptu bar hookups over the years. This felt different. I didn't think I could walk away from this opportunity if I tried.

Damon melted into my renewed embrace, as though he felt the same relief from reconnecting. His fingers scrabbled at my belt buckle, and I chuckled into his mouth.

"Need help with that, kitten?"

He nodded and rocked his hardness into mine. "Please. I can't wait a minute longer. *I need…*"

The sheer desperation in his voice went straight to my cock. When was the last time anyone had wanted me so badly? It did wonderful things to my ego, and I was determined to reward him for making me feel so damn vital.

"I've got you," I promised, getting my pants unbuckled and unzipped in what had to be record time. I moaned as he took my exposed cock in hand and stroked me without a second's hesitation. There were some perks to going commando at times like these. "Easy, sweetheart. I'll take care of you. Gotta get your jeans off, too."

"Hurry," he begged, rubbing his face in the crook of my neck. His skin was still feverishly heated with arousal and perhaps a hint of that earlier embarrassment. It was adorable.

I squeezed his denim covered ass before I reached between us to fumble with his button and fly, trying not to be too distracted by his hand still working my dick. "You're gonna have to help me get these painted-on jeans of yours down, kitten."

He whined with frustration, an almost mewling sound, but released his hold on me to do as I'd asked. I watched him hook his fingers into the material and then shimmy the pants over the slight curve of his hips, then further still down his slender thighs. He turned around in the tight space of the room and bent over, easing the jeans all the way to his ankles. My mouth watered when I discovered the jockstrap he was wearing, practically delivering access to his waiting hole on a silver platter.

Unable to resist, I reached out to squeeze the perfect, lightly fuzzed peach he had presented to me, trailing my fingers between his cheeks, unsurprised to find him slicked up for me. He'd told me to expect as much, after all.

I groaned and teased at his hole with the pad of my index finger, my cock dribbling to find him opening for me with almost no resistance.

"Yes, please, get inside me..." Damon begged and pushed back onto my probing digit, practically sucking the finger into his body with a pleased sigh. He was hot and wet inside as promised, almost like he'd been prepping with copious amounts of lube. He wriggled and squirmed, seeking stimulation. "Rex, please!"

I startled at the sound of my name falling from his lips. Nothing had ever sounded so right before. Suddenly, I was overwhelmed with a matching sense of urgency to be inside him.

"Bend over. Brace yourself on the sink."

My kitten scrambled to obey, leaning on the sides of the

wall-mounted porcelain bowl with each of his forearms. He spread his legs as far as the jeans around his ankles would allow and his enticingly dusky-pink hole glistened with the evidence of his arousal. I used two fingers to breach him this time, testing his limits. They slid inside with the same ease as the first.

"Fuck," I growled out, delighting in the way he thrust back onto my fingers with abandon.

"Now, Rex. Now. Please. I can't handle the emptiness…" Damon babbled, already sounding wrecked.

With my other hand smoothing down his spine, I caught his gaze in the chipped, rust-speckled surface of the mirror. His youth-rounded face was bright red, his eyes wide and gleaming. Sweat plastered his hair to his forehead and the sides of his cheeks. He looked debauched already, even though we had barely started.

"Please!" he begged again, rocking back onto my fingers. "I can't explain it, but if you don't fuck me, I….*fuck*…I'll combust."

A similar need was building in my gut, causing my dick to ache. It strained towards him like a divining rod.

"Shh, kitten," I assured him, withdrawing my fingers and wiping the remaining slickness from them over my cock before I gripped its base and brought the flushed, weeping head to his hole, "I've got you, remember?"

"Yes, fuck, yes!" Damon bounced his hips backwards, encouraging me to sink inside him, and when I did, the sensation almost overwhelmed me.

"You feel amazing," I told him, gripping his hips as I pulled out and then dove right back into the welcoming warmth and slickness of his body. "So tight. So hot. So wet."

With the way his inner walls gripped my cock, it felt like he was made for me.

In the mirror, I watched as Damon closed his eyes and tilted his head back, his lips moving soundlessly. He was beautiful; a wrecked vision of pleasure and all-consuming need.

Looking down to where we were connected, I enjoyed the sight of watching my cock slide in and out of his ass for a few more thrusts before I realized just how selfish I was being. Hell, I hadn't even helped tug his dick free from the front of the strap!

Moving to correct my mistake, I leaned forward to do just that, unsurprised to find the material covering his straining erection damp from his precum.

"Yes!" Damon cried out as I slid my hand inside the waistband and stroked him in time with my thrusts. "Yes, just like that. I'm so fucking close."

Releasing his shaft, I allowed my hand to drift lower, finding his balls and fondling them. They had drawn up tight and I knew it wouldn't take much to push him over the edge. Rolling them in my palm before I let them go again, I returned my attention to his leaking length and then squeezed the base before my next upstroke. I shifted my hips, attempting to find just the right angle and then—

"Oh, *fuck!*" Damon squeezed his eyes shut even more tightly as I hit my mark. I repeated the action, my breath hitching as the channel of his ass convulsed around my cock. "Oh my God. I'm coming. *Fuck.* I'm there, Rex, I'm there. I'm…*nnnngh.*"

Warmth coated my hand and the inside of his underwear as he rode my fist through his orgasm, but it was the clenching and spasming around my cock which undid me, too. I threw my head back and practically roared as my own orgasm barreled through me, waves upon waves of unexpectedly intense bliss rolling through my body. I came in jets, filling him up with—

Oh, fuck.

My hips stuttered as I continued to empty my load inside him, while my already erratic heart squeezed with panic.

I hadn't worn a condom.

I'd gone bare with a stranger I'd met in a bar. A shifter stranger, at that. Who knew what kind of risks I'd just taken.

I was so distracted by the panic of being unsafe that I didn't register the weird tingling at the base of my cock until it was too late. "What...?" I asked at the same time Damon ground down on me and moaned, inexplicably making me come *again,* my dick more sensitive than I could ever remember it being.

"Holy fuck!" Damon raised his head to meet my terrified gaze through the mirror. His expression was blown wide with shock. "Y-you're *knotting* me."

I tried to pull out of him. Jolts of equal parts pleasure and pain rippled through my cock. I yelped.

"Stop!" Damon cried, and I stilled. He softened his tone, realizing that I was in the middle of a pretty significant panic attack. "Stop trying to pull out. You'll only hurt us both."

"What's happening to me?" I demanded, gritting my teeth when he pushed himself up from the sink to look at me over his shoulder. The movement sent more bolts of sensation through my cock, forcing me to come again, however weakly. This was definitely not normal.

"I don't know," he admitted. "This has never happened before. The only people who can knot an omega are alphas and—"

"I have no idea what that is, but I ain't it."

His lower lip quivered and he bit down on it. I felt a little guilty for being so antagonistic while I was still inside him, but the situation was so far from normal, I didn't think standard social etiquette applied anymore.

"Well, no, you…you scented completely human," he finally replied when I had nothing else to offer him. "A-and alphas are extinct. This…this is some kind of anomaly…*ohhh*." He went stock still and the pink flush returned to his skin. "Fuck. I'm sorry. But you feel so *good* and I need…" Swiveling his hips, he groaned, and my voice joined his as he stimulated my…whatever the fuck he wanted to call it.

My legs were beginning to feel like jelly from the multiple (paranormal?) orgasms. I cast a quick look around. My gaze landed on the toilet. Scrunching my nose, I figured it was that or wind up in a heap on the questionable floor.

With a brief warning that I was moving us, I held him upright and shuffled backwards until I felt the cold surface of the toilet bowl hit the back of my calf muscles. I shuddered and came through numerous tugs to my body's newest feature as I shuffled my jeans down my thighs and then sat on top of the closed seat, bringing Damon with me onto my lap.

He shouted in surprised ecstasy as the landing brought him down hard, pushing my cock impossibly deeper inside him. I was convinced I was going to pass out from the intensity of the pleasure that caused. Then he experimentally bounced in place, not seeming to care that my fingernails were digging into the exposed flesh of his hips.

"Yes," he whispered as he moved, exhaling the word with every bounce. "Yes, yes, yes, *yes*."

Despite being freaked out, I couldn't deny that my body craved every single jerk to my…knot? Was that what he'd called it? It was as though every nearly painful bolt of pleasure cooled the burning ache to fuck him hard and raw just one fraction at a time.

"R-rex," Damon moaned my name, practically hissing the 'x' into six sibilant syllables. "I can't...can't get enough."

I knew how he felt. Some part of me demanded that I fuck him and fill him over and over again, and it wouldn't be satisfied until...*until*...

Whatever thoughts had been on the edge of my consciousness fled me as Damon let out a keening cry and I felt the tell-tale convulsions around my cock. I bit back another gravelly bellow as his body milked my balls until they ached.

Damon slumped back against me, his head rolling into the crook of my neck. He nuzzled the underside of my jaw and I fought back the instinct to kiss the top of his sweaty head.

"So...we just wait it out?" I asked into the strangely tense silence that descended.

"Yeah, I guess. Your knot should deflate after a while. At least, I would assume so." He yawned. I tried not to focus on how cute the squeaking sound that accompanied the yawn was. "Alphas and omegas couldn't possibly stay tied together forever."

With no other alternative than to try and relax and let the whole bizarre situation run its course, I just nodded.

An hour later, after another short, impulsive, irresistible burst of fucking and coming, we were separated. I hastily cleaned myself up and ignored the sounds of Damon doing the same behind me. I'd never experienced a more awkward parting than that one. I wished him well, ignored his attempts to try and discuss what my being able to knot him meant, and I fled the bar as though the hounds of hell themselves were at my heels.

Some inner part of my soul whined to turn my truck around and head back to him, a voice in my head telling me that I would regret my choice to run away. I ignored those instincts.

Whatever that had been, I had no intention of repeating it.

That didn't stop him from becoming the only thing I could think of day in and day out, though.

* * *

My senses changed over time. It happened so gradually that I barely even noticed it. But, one night, sitting in a roadhouse bar in Mississippi, I realized I'd been listening in on a conversation being held clear across the crowded room.

My ears pricked at words I hadn't heard spoken aloud in months.

"...shifters. Potential alphas, they said," one man was murmuring lowly as he nursed his beer. His companion was seated across the booth from him, a worn Stetson on his head and a dubious expression on his face.

"Come on, now. That's gotta be just another fairytale," the second guy said on a sigh. "I know that mess in New York was shifter related, but I reckon the alpha thing is just a story they're making up to save face."

The first guy shook his head. A lock of thick, red hair fell across his forehead. He pushed it away impatiently. "No. My cousin...you know, Mindy? Anyhow, she's got a friend who lives in Iowa, and *they* said that there really is an alpha. Startin' a whole new pack 'n everything." As though he could sense me listening, the guy looked over both of his shoulders cautiously. I lowered the brim of my own hat and pretended to fiddle with my phone. Seemingly satisfied, the first guy spoke again.

"They're spreadin' word that there might be more alphas out there like him. Guys who didn't know they were shifters until they started to change."

The second man snorted. "Please," he rolled his eyes and sat back against his seat, chewing on a toothpick. "These ain't nothin' but urban legends, Beau."

Beau huffed impatiently. "But what if they ain't? What if these potential alphas are out there? It could mean that we omegas might start bein' treated right again. We'd have value again."

I sat up a little straighter, frowning. In my bid to forget that night, I had studiously avoided all talk of shifters and their secret societies. I hadn't Googled. I hadn't read any of the news articles that were still circulating following the mess in New York. I hadn't gone on a deep dive to find any of the shifter communities or packs that I suspected were littered across the country.

But, in that moment, I realized avoidance had been a mistake.

What did Beau mean when he said that omegas would have value again? The implication that they didn't have value as things stood was upsetting. They shouldn't need these mythical alphas in order to be treated as equals. They were people, damn it. All people had value.

The thought that omegas weren't treated right among their own damn species because of something outside of their control made me feel sick. It came too close to reminding me of the way I'd felt when I'd come out to my adoptive parents and they had told me they didn't accept it. Over two decades later, it still stung like hell.

Was that why Damon had been so skittish when he'd told

me what he was? When he had asked me not to hurt him? Was he so used to being considered little more than an object that he had expected me to treat him poorly?

I wasn't proud of the fact that I'd essentially panicked and run away after my own body had changed, and after hearing Beau's words, I felt worse. Guilt ate away at my insides. Had I treated him any better than his own people had? Than other men had?

He'd been just as into our little-more-than-anonymous hook-up as I had, but then shit had gone down and I hadn't even stopped to ask if he was okay. I mean, sure, my body had changed, but he had been just as stuck as I was, his ass stretched and impaled on my knot, experiencing something that —if the conversation I was overhearing was to be believed— was completely unexpected for him, too.

And I just ran away with my tail between my legs.

I didn't even get his number so I could check in on him after I'd calmed down.

If I ever saw him again, I would apologize for that. He'd deserved better treatment. Hell, even now, months after our encounter, I couldn't shake him from my thoughts, and that had never happened with any of my previous hook-ups before. Sure, some of the focus could be attributed to the fact that it had literally changed my life —and body— but it was more than that. I couldn't quite explain it, but there had been a spark between us. A connection. I'd been drawn to him, determined to make him mine, if only for twenty minutes.

Courtesy of the knotting thing, it had been longer than that.

Not wanting to linger too much on those thoughts, I tuned back into the conversation across the bar. The room had become more crowded, and a band was setting up on the little stage at the back of the room. I doubted that I'd be able to listen in for much longer, even with my recently advanced hearing.

"…still think it's all a tall tale," Beau's companion sounded like he was trying his best to talk him down from his escalating hopes.

"It's not!" Beau thumped the table between them with his fist, causing the glasses accumulated on its surface to clatter against each other. "Bessie told Mindy she even saw the alpha and his mate. She said the mate, the omega, was *super* pre—"

I winced as the drummer chose that moment to give an impromptu solo fill, his sticks hitting every drum on his kit with rapid double strokes, creating a loud but pleasant cascading effect from one end of the kit to the other. When the guitarist also started riffing, ostensibly double checking the tuning of his bright red strat, I gave up on being able to eavesdrop any longer.

Draining my glass, I set it on the worn timber tabletop in front of me and then eased out of my seat, sliding my leather jacket back on over my shoulders. I'd come to a split-second decision: I was going to head to Iowa and see if there really were other men like me. If nothing else, they might have the answers I had spent so long trying to avoid.

Chapter Three – Damon

"So," Ollie sauntered in through Eric's front door and sat on the edge of the reception desk, swinging his long legs childishly, "this alpha of yours…"

I sighed. The pack had been kind enough to take me in, allowing me to stay in one of Ollie and Beck's guest rooms while Eric organized a studio apartment in town to be, in his words, 'spruced up' for me. I'd only just moved into the cozy space the night before. I would have happily slept in a barn if need be, but nobody in the pack would allow it. Instead, I'd been offered a roof over my head and a part-time job in Eric and Brandt's doctor's clinic.

I had been surprised to learn that the big, buff omegas in question were dragon shifters, and even more surprised still to learn that they were brothers. Eric appeared to be the younger of the pair, with golden blonde curls and a heart shaped face, where Brandt was all long, dark hair and even darker eyes. They had another brother, Sage, who also looked completely different to the two of them, with red hair and bright blue eyes, freckles, and a jovial disposition.

From what I had gathered over the week or so I'd been living in Shifters Sanctuary, Eric owned the majority of the properties in the little township, having purchased them over the course of a number of decades. He had all but gifted a large farmstead to Ollie and Beck when they had moved here, and they seemed happy enough for him to live and work out of the small grounds-keeper's cottage on the same property. The living room in the cottage had become a makeshift reception room, and the two smallest bedrooms were converted into consulting rooms for Eric and Brandt. Because all the clientele were shifters, Eric had had soundproofing installed in all the rooms to preserve doctor-patient confidentiality.

With Ollie turning up to discuss 'that alpha of mine', I was glad that the soundproofing worked both ways.

"He's not *mine*," I argued, even though I knew the remonstration would fall on deaf ears. Ollie, I had discovered, was an eternal romantic. He had this idea in his head that what he and Beck had experienced was some sort of 'fated mates' deal and that the same thing had happened for me and Rex.

Only my surprise alpha hadn't bonded with me when he'd knotted me in that gross bathroom stall. He hadn't sealed our souls together with a mating bite like the legends —and Ollie— spoke about. He'd put a baby in me and fled. If that was fate's idea of an ideal mate for me…well, I supposed I should be glad the asshole hadn't bitten me, shouldn't I?

That was unfair. Rex wasn't an asshole. He had been nothing but sweet to me, and even though he had obviously been surprised by the changes to his body, I had never felt as though he was going to flip out on me. Additionally, it was as much my responsibility as his to think about protection, and neither one of us had. No, I hadn't realized that he was an alpha —not when he had scented human— but it was still best practice to be safe, even if shifters were immune to most human STIs. Even after he had knotted me and filled me up at my begging, he had no reason to suspect the rules had changed. I should have thought about it at the time, but I had also been blindsided by the fact that my sexy human cowboy was an alpha.

So, no, he wasn't an asshole.

Fate could still suck my dick, though.

Imagine dangling an alpha in front of me and then whisking him away again, only for me to discover the consequences months later, and with no way to contact the alpha in question! Didn't I deserve the happiness that Ollie and Beck had? Didn't my cub deserve its alpha father? Where was fate in all of this mess, hmm?

"Even so," Ollie waved off my protest, "was he, oh, I don't know…about yea high," he gestured about a foot taller than himself, which was a mild exaggeration, "broad shouldered, sandy-colored hair and a hot AF beard, with a thick, sexy Texan accent? Real fondness for cowboy attire?"

Midway through the cutesy way he was describing the alpha who had left me in the ladies' room of a roadside bar, I stiffened. "He's *here*?"

Ollie nodded, a Cheshire Cat smirk spreading across his face. "Turned up on Main Street asking questions about Beck. Jazz called because he scented like alpha and puma. Beck told her to bring him up to the house." I watched as Ollie smiled absently and rubbed at his chest, a far-off look in his eyes before he gave himself a shake and cocked his head at me. "Wanna come see him?"

I gaped at Ollie as if he had lost his damn mind and gestured to the very obvious baby bump I was sporting. "Because I should just waddle on up there and be like 'surprise!'?" I completed my sarcastic line with a timeless display of jazz hands.

Honestly, what were the chances Rex had come looking for Beck's pack right then, when I had only arrived a week earlier?

Fate was determined to fuck with me, I just knew it.

Ollie seemed to be thinking similar thoughts, but with a much more positive bend to them. "Yes! I mean, if this doesn't prove that you're fated, I don't know what does."

"Or," I grizzled and pushed aside a notepad containing messages for Eric to follow up on so I could drum my fingers on the desk's timber surface, "he heard there was someone else like him in the world and came looking for answers the same way I did."

"But within a week of each other?" Ollie's green eyes gleamed and he clasped his hands in front of his chest. "It's a Christmas miracle!"

I groaned. I'd been doing my best to ignore the rampant holiday cheer my host was attempting to ram down my throat. The guy was obsessed with the festive season. He had turned the entire town into what basically amounted to Santa's village without the height-challenged minions. Eric had thankfully drawn the line at having his living room bedecked in too much tinsel, though he had found one of those damnable 'Elf On The Shelf' things hiding in his consulting room's storage cupboards. The toy was now shoved inside my desk drawer, not that Ollie would know about it.

"It's not a miracle and it's not fate," I huffed, rubbing my belly as the little boy inside rolled over.

Learning that I was having a son was pretty neat, I had

to admit that. Eric had all but demanded that he give me a thorough checkup when I confessed that I hadn't seen any medical professionals since discovering the little womb usurper's existence.

He and Brandt had gone all out with the practice they had set up in Shifters Sanctuary, complete with a proper ultrasound machine and all. He'd told me that not only did he anticipate Ollie and Beck would likely require the use of such things again, but half the beta couples in the town would probably appreciate not having to travel an hour away for OBGYN services as well. Blood tests and major issues were still sent off to the nearest hospital, but the basics could now be handled right there in town.

So, I'd found myself on Eric's exam bed staring at the monitor screen as he pointed out my son's fingers, toes, and penis. The kid in my belly had not been shy about showing off his goods, that was for sure, spreading his little legs as he wriggled about inside my belly while the transducer wand caught it all on film.

To be honest, I was just relieved there was only one of him. I couldn't imagine having twins like Beck and Ollie had. Especially not on my own.

"What do you call it, then?" Ollie arched an eyebrow at me.

I shrugged. "Predictable? I mean, Beck said the same thing that I'm feeling: he was thrown for a loop when his body changed and, after the panic receded, he wanted answers. Eric's been working double time with half the town to get word out there about the whole sanctuary thing, which is why so many people are turning up and hoping to join now; myself included."

There was even another farmhouse they were calling the

Frat House on account of the number of potential alphas who were living there — men who had heard on the grapevine about Beck's background and thought there were enough similarities that they might also be alphas and unaware of it.

I'd met one of the new guys on my second day in town, when he had come to get the results of some blood tests he had allowed Eric and Brandt to run on him. He had been hot as sin and, were it not for the upheaval I was going through, I would have happily volunteered as tribute for him to try and coax out his potential knot. The fact that he reminded me of a younger, darker haired and darker skinned version of Rex meant nothing.

Six months into my pregnancy, my hormones were demanding sex, and the presence of hot men was not helping.

Damn these men and their sexy southern drawls.

"Well, even so," Ollie scowled back at me, clearly disappointed that I wasn't going along with his 'Christmas Fairytale' ideals, "what are the chances you'd both be here now? Like, within days of each other? That, my friend, is kismet."

I fought the urge to chuckle at his triumphant smirk. He meant well, but I was still feeling bitter and jaded. "No," I reminded him with a shake of my head, "*that* is the effect of having the old-school shifters and their nutty religion spread all sorts of bullshit about you all as well."

I'd heard a lot of rumors about the pack as I had road-tripped my way there, and not all of them had been pleasant. At one of the packs I'd stopped in, carefully concealing my growing belly, the local diner TV had shown shifter preacher Joe Morstein sermonizing about the evils of the 'Neo-Shifter Movement', as he had dubbed Beck's pack. I didn't think it would be long before they gathered enough support to try and overrun Shifters Sanctuary. I could only imagine the things they thought they could achieve if they had the hierarchical weight of an alpha or two at their disposal.

I'd always felt that the Moonmusic church was more cult than religion. I found their views on omegas downright chauvinistic and cruel. Listening to the sleazy looking, pinched-faced man on the screen prattle on about the risks of allowing omegas equal rights in a pack had only cemented my belief that finding Shifters Sanctuary was the right choice for me and my cub. Older shifters in the diner, though, had been sympathetic to Morstein's lecture. They had eyed me warily. Not only was I an outsider, but an omega to boot. I hated to think what they would have done if they'd caught sight of my pregnant belly. I'd merely mumbled something about being a college student driving back to my pack and then hightailed it out of there as soon as my bill had been paid.

"More and more people are coming to see it our way," Ollie argued back, but I just nodded.

"Exactly. Which is why so many shifters are fleeing their oppressive Moonmusic-based packs in search of a better life here. I was one of them."

Well, there was that and the fact that I had no idea how else to conceal my pregnancy or how I was expected to give birth, so finding the only other documented pregnant omega had been my best bet.

"We're gonna have to agree to disagree on this," Ollie eventually conceded with a sigh. Then he pinned me with a much more serious stare. "It doesn't change the fact that Rex deserves to know he's going to be a dad in a few months."

He had me there, I had to admit it. My shoulders slumped

in resignation, and I looked down at my hands, twisting my fingers together. "I know. I do."

"But you're scared, right?" Ollie's voice had softened into sympathy. Before I could answer, he continued, "Beck and I both freaked the fuck out when we found out I was pregnant. I told him he could run for the hills…and I was so afraid that he would take me up on that."

"But he didn't." I did my best not to sound resentful. Beck had knotted Ollie and stuck around, which was more than I could say for Rex, not that our situations were anywhere near the same.

For one thing, it sounded like Beck and Ollie had been talking about a relationship before shit went down. For another, they'd bonded when they first knotted together, and it sounded like there was an emotional tie between them after that. Both of those things would have enticed Beck to stay, even while he was freaking out.

Rex and I didn't have that. We'd agreed on a quick bathroom fuck, that was all. We hadn't bonded, or even exchanged phone numbers before the fact. I couldn't have expected him to change his mind about that after being with me had changed his body so unexpectedly, could I?

"No, he didn't. But he could have, and that was terrifying." Ollie's reply brought me back to the moment. I looked up at him, unsurprised to see the genuine empathy in his green eyes. "Day, you've got to tell Rex. But if he does flip out, you're not alone in any of this anymore, okay? You've got me and Beck, and the dragons," he added, nodding at someone over my shoulder before looking back into my eyes, "and the whole damn pack, really." He smiled as Mrs. Potter, an elderly rabbit shifter with a sharp tongue, made her way past us towards the front door. "Bye, Dottie! See you at bingo next Friday?"

"I'll be whoopin' your ass as usual," she agreed, then let herself out, leaving Ollie to chuckle.

"Did I miss something?" Eric asked, circling in from behind me to rest his hip on the side of my desk next to where Ollie had perched himself.

Ollie grinned, tilting his head in my direction and giving it a little jerk. "Damon's alpha has turned up."

Even though Ollie was right about Rex deserving to know about our kid, he was wrong about one thing. "He's not *my*—"

"He's up at the main house," Ollie kept talking over the top of me. "Beck told me to come grab you while I gave Damon the heads-up."

Eric actually rubbed his hands together as he grinned. "Excellent. An unbonded male alpha. I've got a number of tests I want to run. Let me grab my bag."

"Yes, please do remind me of just how very unbonded I am!" I called at his retreating back.

Ollie snickered. "You'll have to forgive Eric. This research has been his focus for…well, forever, really. You should have seen him when he found out about Beck. It was like all his Christmases had come at once."

"You and your fixation on Christmas," I shook my head. "I've been here all of five minutes and I know that you'd be more than happy to celebrate it every day of the year."

The fact that it was early December wasn't helping dim his obsession at all.

"Don't tempt me. I'm still trying to get Beck to pitch my 'Christmas In July' idea to the Council."

Despite the anxiety that was building inside me now that Rex was in town, I couldn't help but laugh.

Chapter Four – Rex

Shifters Sanctuary was not the town's official name. Or, at least, they didn't have any signs declaring the place as such. I supposed that might garner them attention from humans and, even though humans knew shifters existed, it seemed smart to try and lie low anyway. At least until human society felt less threatened by their —*our*— existence.

I was still struggling with my own identity as a shifter, what with not actually having shifted yet. I hadn't had the balls to try. I could just see myself getting stuck as an animal and living out my days eating rodents or something.

No, thank you.

Anyhow, when I parked my car on the main street (unsurprisingly called 'Main Street', if the lone street sign was anything to go by) and meandered into the tiny convenience store, I was not expecting the short, frumpy woman behind the counter to react the way she had. She scented the air, her button nose twitching, and she regarded me with wide, surprised eyes.

"Hello, ma'am," I pasted on my friendliest smile, "I was

wonderin' if you could point me in the direction of—"

"Our Pack Alpha?" she finished for me, already reaching for her phone.

I cocked my head. "Could you tell me a little about him first?"

She firmed her lips and regarded me with suspicion. "You're not plannin' on challenging him, are you? Because Beck's a good Alpha. We don't need any trouble around here."

I could feel my lips twitching in amusement at the idea of this short, matronly woman giving me a talking to. Schooling my features, I held my hands up in the universal sign of surrender. "No, ma'am. No challenge, no trouble. I'm actually hopin' to find some answers about this whole…alpha thing."

There was no sense pretending she couldn't scent what I was. I'd encountered a few shifters on my journey to Iowa, and the ones I had spoken to had all sniffed the air and looked at me with wide, curious eyes. Somehow, I had known that they knew what I was, but thankfully none of them had given me any trouble.

The shopkeeper's eyes narrowed as she clearly assessed the veracity of my claim. "You promise no trouble? Not even with D…" she paused, seeming to rethink her phrasing, "any of the omegas?"

Placing my hand over my heart, I assured her, "I swear on my birth mama's grave, I'm not here to stir the pot with anyone. I really do just want answers."

I decided it was a good sign that she was such an enthusiastic gatekeeper for the town, not that I thought she could do too much damage if I did have nefarious intentions. But her defense of the Pack Alpha had to mean that the rumors I'd heard were true: he was a nice guy and was trying to build a safe space for people like him. People like me.

"Well then," relaxing marginally, she stuck out her hand, "welcome to our little pack. I'm Jazz."

"Rex," I introduced myself, bending to kiss the back of her hand and smirking as she giggled lightly.

"Oh, you're dangerous," she accused, then pulled out her phone.

Within minutes, she was shutting up shop and hustling me towards my truck, inviting herself along for the drive. "I'll direct you," she'd insisted when all I'd asked for were directions to the Alpha's home, to which I'd apparently been summoned. Her eyes had gleamed with what I could have sworn was mischief. "I'm not missin' this show for the world."

"Show?" I asked as I climbed into the driver's seat.

She grinned. "You'll see."

The drive to the large farmhouse took less than ten minutes and, as we drove up the long driveway from the street to the house proper, I couldn't help but smile to myself. The crunch of gravel beneath my tires, the scents and sounds of a working farm, the crisp, clean country air…it was all so familiar to me. Familiar and calming.

I was a country boy through and through. I'd grown up on a ranch just outside of Fredericksburg, Texas. While my adoptive parents had mostly raised cattle, the property had also grown crops and had a large copse of peach trees. It had been idyllic and, if not for my parents' rampant homophobia, I would have wanted to visit again, just for old times' sake.

I parked my pickup next to a similar vehicle, its paint white where mine was red, and tilted my face up towards the sun as I climbed out of the cab, enjoying the warming rays in the cold December air.

"Come on," Jazz urged from the other side of my truck. I could barely see the top of her thick, brown hair through the window, "Beckett and Ollie are waiting for us."

I nodded and made my way around to her, then followed her up the front steps of the farmhouse. The wrap-around porch was freshly painted, as was the front door. Jazz gave three firm raps on the glossy white surface and, barely ten seconds later, the door swung inwards to reveal a willowy young man with a baby on his hip.

He smiled warmly at me, extending his free hand. "Hi," he beamed, his green eyes sizing me up from my toes to my hair, "I'm Ollie. And this," he bounced the baby at his side, "is Duke. Come on in. Beck's just changing Rory." The look he shot towards my companion was almost plaintive. "Jazz, could I trouble you to make us all some coffees?"

I shook his hand as Jazz bustled past me, declaring his request was no trouble at all. "Rex," I introduced myself, then wiped my feet on the welcome mat and moved inside as I'd been instructed to, "it's nice to meet you." I looked around the cozy timber-hewn living room and smiled at the worn floral couch, so much like the one we'd had back in Texas. "You have a lovely home."

"Thanks," Ollie replied, still making absolutely no secret of his curiosity in me. He cocked his head. "So, an alpha, huh? Bet that came as a shock. It did for Beck." His lips curled upwards. "Especially with the way it happened."

"Oh?" I arched an eyebrow at him. I didn't know much about the Pack Alpha's backstory, only that he'd thought he was human…until he wasn't anymore.

"Popping a knot mid-orgasm is understandably unnerving," Ollie shrugged.

"Oliver! *Honestly.*" I turned my head at the sound of the exasperated admonishment, watching as another guy —older than Ollie, but he had to be close to a decade younger than me— came down the stairs, holding a dark-haired baby to his shoulder. He was about my height and broad shouldered, with short dark hair and dark eyes. He held himself straight, even while his smile softened and became almost conspiratorial as he turned his attention to me. "Sorry," he said, his gravelly voice deep and more mature than I'd anticipated. "Ollie likes to overshare. I don't think the word 'boundary' is in his vocabulary." He came to a stop in front of me and extended his hand. "Beckett Smith," he introduced himself easily, but there was a subtle power about him that told me he was an alpha. *The* Alpha. Even though I hadn't met another alpha before, my instincts told me he couldn't be anything else. Hell, even his scent seemed kind of electric, so different to the other shifters I'd encountered so far. "But you can call me Beck. Everyone else does."

I shook his hand. "Rex. Rex Murphy."

"Come sit down, Rex," Beck gestured to the couch. He waited for me to sit before he chose the matching armchair positioned on the other side of the timber coffee table, then he extended his arm out to Ollie. "I'll take Duke if you want to head down to the clinic and get Eric or Brandt. I'm sure they'll have questions for Rex, and answers to any of his questions, too."

Ollie nodded and carefully maneuvered the baby he was holding onto Beck's lap, where Beck secured him with his free arm. He paused to smile at the way the boy reached for the other baby, making gurgling sounds. Then he cocked his head back at Beck. "What about D—"

Beck cut him off with a shake of his head. "One step at a

time," he cautioned, then leaned his head back for a quick kiss. Ollie obliged. Beck's smile was warm. "Thanks, babe."

Ollie nodded and then bade us goodbye as he headed back out the front door.

"He won't be long," Beck told me when a few moments of awkward silence had passed. "Eric and Brandt are the town doctors and researchers. Eric's been researching alphas for years: long before I kind of magically discovered I was one. He's been a huge help through all of this."

One of the babies —the darker haired one; Rory, was it?— squawked in his lap. He bounced his knee and gave Duke a soft pet on his back. "Be nice to your sister."

I hadn't even noticed that the little guy's hand was squeezing the other baby's arm, no doubt causing the sharp complaint.

I jutted my chin at the pair. "Looks like you've sure got your hands full."

Beck chuckled, and he sighed in that tired way that all new parents seemed to do. "They're not easy, no," he agreed. "But I wouldn't trade them for anything."

"How old are they?"

"About four months," he answered. "They're way easier to handle now that they can support the weight of their own heads. I was terrified I'd break them when they were all fresh and new."

I blinked at him and did some quick mental math. *When did the whole mess in New York happen? About a year ago? Assuming babies cook for about nine months...*

"Hang on," the words were out before I could remind myself that his relationship was none of my damn business.

I took a closer look at the babies in his lap. One looked a hell of a lot like him, not that I thought I was any good at being able to see resemblances between squidgy baby faces and adults. It wasn't exactly something I often found myself in a position to do, and it wasn't as though I spent a lot of time with kids. I definitely had no plans for any of my own, either.

"I mean…" I trailed off and shook my head, holding my hands up apologetically. "Sorry. It's really none of my business."

There were a number of plausible explanations for the situation, really. He might have already gotten a woman pregnant prior to being with Ollie. He and Ollie might have had an open relationship. He might have hired a surrogate before meeting Ollie. They might be his sibling's kids.

It was none of my damned business.

Except he spoke about them like they were his own and… *nope.* I didn't know the story and it wasn't my place to poke around asking about it, either. I was there to get answers about the whole 'surprise alpha' thing. No sense getting derailed by my natural curiosity. That had always been my downfall.

Beck's dark eyes were locked on mine as he sat in what felt like contemplative silence. He hummed in thought to himself, then sighed. "How much do you know about shifters?"

I blinked. "Pardon me?"

"Like, there's the basics we learned in history back in school," he continued, back to bouncing both his legs to the contented babbles of the babies in his lap, "but that didn't really cover the whole alpha/omega/beta thing at all."

I nodded. "No, I'd never even heard the terms until…"

Flashbacks of that night with Damon blinked through my mind.

Beck lifted the corner of his lip in a wry, knowing smirk. "Yeah, I've been there. Bought the t-shirt and everything."

Was it my imagination, or did he dip his chin towards the kids when he said that?

"So," he forged on, disrupting my curious thoughts, "there's a whole old-school hierarchy that comes with the alpha thing. Not that we really follow it here. Well, except for the whole town's insistence that an alpha should be Pack Alpha…but I'm working on trying to change their minds. Biology shouldn't determine leadership status, you know? Even though I can do this weird thing where I can momentarily compel them to do stuff. But I don't like to do that because it's totally an abuse of power and…I'm rambling."

"Okay…" I replied slowly, trying to follow his point. "So it's just a hierarchy thing? Which doesn't really matter unless you're part of a pack?"

Beck shook his head and his expression turned uncomfortable. "The whole belief system when it comes to alphas being superior to betas and betas to omegas is fucked," he said bluntly, then cringed and looked down at the babies in his lap. "Shit. Ah, damn it. I mean…*ugh.* Sorry. Just don't tell your Papa I cursed, okay?"

The infants gurgled back at him, and I chuckled. "I think you're safe for now. I don't know much about wrangling small humans —small shifters?— but pretty sure it takes most of 'em a while longer to start repeating the stuff they're not s'posed to. Or," I added, cocking my head, "telling on you to their Papa."

"Yeah, well, their Papa may look sweet and harmless, but I'd rather not find myself in his bad books, or in the doghouse, if you'll excuse the pun."

I arched my eyebrow at him, and he snorted. "Because I'm a wolf shifter. Not that wolves are dogs, but I'm taking creative license here."

"Right…"

Beck cleared his throat into the stilted silence that fell between us. "So, anyway, the whole power structure is dumb. But there are other, um, differences between each secondary designation. Biological ones."

I sat up a little straighter, all ears again. "Like the slick thing? And the knotting?"

He nodded and bit his lip. "Eric, Brandt, and Ollie can explain it better than I can, and I'm sure they will when they get here."

"Give me the summarized version," I demanded, not having the patience to wait. This was what I'd come here for, after all. To learn about what I was and *why* I was like this. To learn what my body was secretly capable of. The details could come later.

Beck's expression twisted uncomfortably again, but he nodded. "Okay, well, betas are the closest to human in terms of their biology. They can shift, but…that's about it in terms of anything special or different about them. They're born unmarked, or so I'm told."

"Okay…" I rolled my wrist at him, hoping he might speed it up a little.

"But omegas are born marked from birth. They get a mark in the shape of a crescent moon somewhere on their bodies." His handsome face contorted into a scowl. "So, even though it makes no damn difference until they hit puberty, they get whacked with the label that they're omegas and, without alphas, aren't good for much except slave labor, and they're usually raised without a whole lot of self-worth."

The news wasn't really a surprise to me, not after what I'd heard back in that bar in Mississippi, but it still got my metaphorical hackles up. "But why?" I demanded, leaning forward to jab at my own knee with my index finger as I spoke. "Why does their value rely on the presence of alphas?"

Beck shifted the babies in his lap and couldn't quite meet my eye. "Without alphas, they can't help grow the pack."

I knew I must have looked a hell of a lot confused, 'cause I sure felt it. "I don't follow."

"What, um, what did Da…" He stopped himself and started again. I was beginning to wonder what people around here were trying not to say. "What did the omega you were with tell you about his slick?"

"That it helped with…" I tried to recall his words and frowned. Having gone over that night so many times in my head, I couldn't forget it even if I wanted to. However, I'd never realized that my sweet kitten hadn't actually said *why* he got slick. I'd inferred it was to make having sex easier for his kind. Self-lubrication for the win. "You know, he didn't say. He got flustered." Despite my mixed feelings about the events that had followed, I couldn't help but smile at the memory. "Then we, uh, got distracted."

Beck snorted and raised a knowing eyebrow. "I know how that goes." He looked back down at the babies, his expression softening. "Worth it."

The logic didn't compute.

Suspicion began to niggle at the back of my brain, willing me to make some sort of connection between my experience and what was in front of me. But, try as I might, I was at a loss.

"What do you mean?"

Steeling himself, Beck began, "So, the slick is to help with mating, for lack of a better term."

Feeling my shoulders relax, I nodded and chuckled, "Well,

yeah, I got that part."

"No, I mean—" Whatever he was going to say was interrupted by the unmistakable sound of one of the infants filling their diaper. Loudly. It was followed by a drawn-out moment of stunned silence before the baby in question began wailing. Beck sighed. "Really, dude? I *just* changed your sister. Can you two not, like, get into sync or something?" He looked over at me, chagrined. "Would you mind holding her? I've gotta take care of this."

Before I could agree or protest, the other baby was thrust into my arms and Beck was heading towards the stairs. I blinked at the startled baby, and she blinked back at me.

"Uh," I said stupidly, "hi."

Her lower lip quivered and turned down.

Panic flooded me.

At forty-two, I'd had very little experience with small children, and even less with babies. I'm pretty sure the tiny creature could sense my unease because she started to whimper and squirm.

"Oh no," I muttered, repositioning her into the crook of my arm and tucking her in close to my chest on instinct. "It's okay, little darlin'. We're cool. *Shh*," I rocked from side to side in my seat. "Hush now. Your Daddy's comin' back in just a few minutes, I swear."

"Not if it's another diaper explosion," Jazz's amused voice almost had me jumping out of my skin. She entered the room from the rounded archway that seemed to lead into the kitchen and dining area of the home. In her hands, she carried a tray containing an eclectic assortment of mugs and a French press coffee maker full of the dark brew, which smelled delicious. She set it down on the coffee table in front of me as she continued, "Beck's notoriously bad at dealing with those. But Ollie insists he's gotta get used to it, so…it may be a while." She gestured down at the tray. "Cream and sugar?"

"Yes, please. Two sugars, ma'am."

The infant in my arms had stopped grizzling, clearly just as surprised by Jazz's abrupt entrance as I was. She reached up a chubby hand and smacked my bearded jaw with a surprising amount of force for such a tiny, uncoordinated little thing.

Jazz chuckled and set my coffee down on the table. She straightened and, with her hands on her ample hips, observed, "You look good with a baby."

"I…what?"

Lips curling upwards, her smile seemed kind of secretive. But she jutted her chin towards Rory and repeated, "It's a good look. There's somethin' about a handsome man holding a baby that makes my ovaries ache."

I had no idea how to respond to that.

My cheeks burned. "Well, this is probably the second time in my entire life I've done it, and it will probably be the last for a long while, so get your fill while you can, I s'pose."

"Now, honey," Jazz's smirk was suddenly unsettling, "you don't know that, do you?"

"Know what?"

"That this'll be the last time you hold a baby for a while."

I didn't like the way she cocked her head or the way her dark brown eyes glinted with humor. It set off all kinds of internal alarms and my instincts were usually right.

"What are you not sayin', Jazz?"

Eyes widening with exaggerated innocence, she held her hands up in surrender. "Nothing, nothing! Just that you'll probably be staying close to Ollie and Beckett for a while, won't you?" Before I could refute that, she stuck those same hands out towards the baby. "Here, let me take the little princess so you can drink your coffee before it gets cold."

I leaned back, holding the kid a little closer to my body. Not that I thought she was a threat to Rory or to me, but I didn't want to be distracted, and I certainly didn't want her to have an excuse to wander away while I was trying to not-so-subtly interrogate her.

"Jazz," I said her name with my most charming smile in place, deciding that it would be easier to catch flies with honey, "what have I missed around here, hmm?"

She bit her lip. I could see her resolve wavering. Nevertheless, she shook her head, wisps of brown hair flying about her head with the motion. "I think it's best to wait for Beck to come back. O-or Doc Weldman. Er, Weldmans? Docs Weldman? Whatever, there are two of 'em now, and one of them'll be able to explain."

"Explain *what*, though?" I was getting frustrated.

"Me," a new voice answered in her stead, and my heart leapt into my throat.

I *knew* that voice. It had haunted my dreams and memories since the day I had fled that roadside bar in Texas.

"Or, more to the point," Damon continued, sounding tired and wary as I heard him get closer. I couldn't bring myself to turn my head and face him. I was still a damn coward where he was concerned. Still ashamed for having freaked out and left him the way I had. "*This*."

The last word was spoken as he rounded the couch and stood in front of me. He was every bit as beautiful as I remembered, though his face was a little rounder and simultaneously more drawn as he stared me down in Beck and Ollie's living room.

But that wasn't where my vision focused.

No…my gaze was drawn to his hand resting on his swollen belly.

The clues *finally* snapped together inside my head with an almost audible click. Beck and Ollie. The babies. The dancing around what omegas and alphas meant to each other. Jazz's weird commentary.

My throat went dry, and I lifted Rory, pushing her blindly towards Jazz, my eyes not leaving the very obvious bump beneath Damon's clinging gray woolen sweater. "On second thought," I heard my own strained voice say, like I was having an out-of-body experience, "I think you'd better take her."

Chapter Five – Damon

So, there's a scene in one of my favorite movie-musicals where the two protagonists are thrust together by their respective social circles after not having expected to see each other again.

Now, I'm not saying I really fit the reference entirely, given that I knew what I was walking into, but the stunned expression on Rex's face as we reconnected reminded me of that moment in the movie.

I just hoped that he wouldn't do what the guy in the movie did and act all cool and aloof, breaking his one-time fling's heart in front of their gawking audience.

Not that Rex could break my heart.

For one thing, I hadn't been in love with him after that quick romp in the bar's bathroom. For another, I had no plans to pursue a relationship with him, no matter what Ollie kept on saying.

But I was anxious about his reaction to my condition, and for what it might mean for the kid inside me. His kid. *Our* kid.

"Sorry, that took a little longer than I…" Beck's voice trailed off as he descended the stairs with Duke held securely against his shoulder. "Well. Shit."

As if he was being woken from a trance, Rex gave himself a little shake and swiveled his head around to glower at the other alpha. "You don't think you could have led with 'alphas can knock omegas up' by any chance?"

For his part, Beck had the grace to look sheepish and apologetic. He cuddled his son a bit closer to him, as though using the tyke as a shield. "I was trying to deliver the information tactfully."

"Well, I'd say that ship has sailed," I cut back in, and all attention moved back to me again. Rex's blue eyes refocused on my belly.

"I'm gonna assume that's mine," he drawled, then finally directed his gaze up to my face.

Under the scrutiny of our audience, I snorted. "I haven't been knotted by any other alphas, so…yeah."

"Jesus Christ," pinching the bridge of his nose, the father of my unborn child winced. "*Fuck.*"

I did my best not to flinch and reminded myself that my reaction to realizing what the changes to my body meant had also been less than ideal. Holding my head high, I affected a nonchalant smile and threw a slightly too-casual thumb over my shoulder. "Pretty much. So, now that that's out of the way, I'm going to head home."

In the safety of my little apartment, I would be able to cry into a pint of ice cream without anyone knowing about it. Thank God I'd already moved in! Now *that* is what I would call fateful timing.

"Day…" Ollie tried to reach for me, his concern palpable. I shrugged him off as I made my way past him. He tried a different tactic. "How are you even planning on getting home?"

"My car's at the clinic," I reminded him. "But, even then, this town is freaking tiny. It wouldn't take me that long to walk back to the apartment."

"In the freezing cold at six months pregnant? I don't think so." He folded his arms across his chest and arched his eyebrows haughtily.

"Lucky I don't have to, then, huh?"

"Well…I don't like the idea of you walking back to the clinic on your own, either. What if you hit a patch of ice and slip?"

Pursing my lips, I tried to remind myself that Ollie had taken me into his home and let me stay there for the better part of a week. He meant well, as meddlesome as he was being. "I'm not an invalid," I gritted out from between my teeth. "I'm pregnant. I'll be fine."

"Can we please stop saying 'pregnant'?" Rex looked a little green around the gills when Ollie and I turned to look back at him. He was gripping the armrests of his chair tightly, his grip white-knuckled.

I supposed shock could do that to a man.

Ollie just scoffed at him. "You'll get used to it," he sniffed dismissively, before looking me over in concern again. "Are you really okay?"

"I'm fine." I wasn't. "I promise." I crossed my fingers behind my back.

For all my macho, independent omega, 'I can do this on my own' bullshit, some part of me had hoped that Rex would take one look at my rounded belly and declare that he'd always wanted kids and that he'd be the best mate and father ever.

That part of me had clearly spent far too many years sneaking romance novels and watching musicals.

Now I felt rejected in a worse way than I had when Rex had pulled out of me, done up his jeans and run away with his non-existent tail between his legs. Worse still, I felt as though my baby had been rejected by his other father and that was what had the tears threatening to start.

My father had died before my fourth birthday, so I'd never really gotten a chance to know him. I had fading memories of him being an affectionate man, and I knew that he had adored me. It wasn't until after he'd died that Mom had moved us down to her cousin's pack in New Mexico. There, she'd remarried another beta, and I'd soon learned that being an omega meant I needed to make myself useful to the pack any way I could, because I wasn't going to be able to help grow it like the betas could. As if a person's value was tied to their fertility. It was archaic and gross, but it was how a lot of the old-school packs operated. Not that it was actually about being able to have kids — it was about power and control, and the pack-minded betas enjoyed having both.

I'd always wondered if things might have been different if Dad had lived...but he hadn't, and I'd missed out on feeling a father's love during my formative years.

While I was determined that my son would always feel valued and loved regardless of his designation, I had hoped that he'd also know the love of his other parent, too.

It didn't seem like that was in the cards, though. I felt guilty about that, like I was already failing him...and he wasn't even born yet.

Those thoughts brought a lump to my throat, so I motioned

towards the door. "Anyway," I croaked out, not bothering to spit an 'I told you so' in Ollie's direction, "I'm going to go."

I ignored Ollie's repeated calling of my name as I bustled out of the door and into the crisp afternoon air. I wished I'd had the forethought to pick my coat back off the hanger before I'd stormed out, but I wasn't about to head back inside the house for it.

It was only a half mile walk down to the clinic and I could handle the cold for that long. Besides, it distracted me from the more emotional thoughts I'd been having only moments earlier.

"Damon," Brandt's deep voice followed me. Having made it to the beginning of the path which would lead me down through the small orchard of apple trees and to the clinic, I turned to watch the tall, dark-haired man close the distance between us in long-legged strides. He held my coat out towards me as he approached.

"Catching your death isn't encouraged," he said drolly. "Especially not in your condition."

"Jesus, not you, too," I grumbled, snatching my coat from his outstretched hands.

Brandt arched a bushy eyebrow while I angrily struggled into it. "I am a doctor. If you're going to listen to anyone about such things, it should really be me." He smirked and the sunlight glinted off the few streaks of silver in his hair.

From what I had gathered, he was the oldest of the Weldman siblings, but considering the guy was a dragon, I couldn't begin to guess how old he was. His accent had a European lilt to it, which seemed to make him more distinguished than his younger brothers. But, at that moment, the smugness made him seem almost adolescent.

"You're not still practicing medicine from the Middle Ages, are you?" I snarked as I began my way back down the pretty tree-lined path. "Because, while I highly doubt I'll manage to catch a cold in the ten minutes it will take me to walk from here to my car, leeches and shit aren't going to fix it anyway."

He was silent for a moment before he asked, "Does this mood of yours have anything to do with the new alpha?"

"Wow, you have *such* an analytical mind. What gave it away?"

Brandt snorted at my sarcasm, but he had the grace to apologize. "Sorry," he fell into stride with me, "that was a silly thing to say. Of course you're unhappy with this alpha's reappearance. Especially when his reaction to your pregnancy was—"

"I was there," I reminded him, still a bit snippy. Then I sighed. "Let's just change the subject, hmm? How's moving to Smalltown, USA working out for you?"

He shrugged. "When you've lived as long as I have, you experience everything in various iterations multiple times over. This is not my first small town experience, in America or otherwise."

"I got that from the accent, big guy. How come your brothers don't sound like movie villains from the nineteen-eighties?"

Brandt snorted again and shook his head. "They're significantly younger than I am. Our clan moved here when they were still in their formative years."

"Ah," I inclined my head in understanding, "so you kept the accent from the Old Country," I enjoyed the wry twist of his lips at my subtle teasing, "and they grew up American."

"That about sums it up, yes."

"Well, that makes about as much sense as anything else."

Companionable silence fell between us for a few minutes as

we walked. Then, as the cottage came into view, Brandt asked, "Are you going to give him a chance? Your alpha?"

Gods, give me strength.

I shook my head. "He made his feelings perfectly clear. And, y'know, I'm totally fine with being rejected myself, but I'm not giving him another opportunity to reject our son."

"If I might play Devil's Advocate…"

It took all my willpower not to grit my teeth and scream. *Brandt's technically a very old man,* I reminded myself, *he grew up at a time where people setting their own personal boundaries was unheard of.*

Nevertheless, Brandt was well adapted to modern society. He really should have known better. Especially when his next words were, "He's one of two known alphas in the country, Day. Potentially in the world. Maybe give him a chance to process the news that you just dropped in his lap before condemning him?"

"What about me getting a chance to process, huh?" I spun on my heel to demand, giving in to my burst of temper. "*I'm* the one going through all of this, not him. He can walk away! But not me!"

The complaints spilled over before I could stop them, all the feelings I'd been keeping to myself finally bubbling over, like a pot left to boil for too long. My hands shook and I stuffed them back into my pockets, but the tremble only made its way into my voice.

"He gets to stay every bit as hot and handsome as I remember, while I'm freaking *waddling* everywhere. And don't get me started on the heartburn, or the swelling in my ankles and feet, or the hormonal acne which keeps popping up in places where acne should *not* exist. And that's not even mentioning the hemorrhoids which keep coming and going!"

I left out the random bouts of uncontrollable horniness, the cravings for foods I couldn't financially afford to satisfy, and the fact that I couldn't sleep in my preferred position (on my stomach) which meant I was struggling to sleep at all.

I'd lost the battle against my emotions and tears trickled down my cheeks while Brandt looked at me with genuine dismay. I pointed back in the direction of Ollie and Beck's house angrily. "Why should I be taking *his* feelings into consideration? He thinks he's had a shock? He's not the one living this!"

"Day…" Brandt was apologetic, but I didn't want to hear it.

"It's fine," I sniffed and shook my head, pulling one hand out of my pockets to wipe my face. "I'm fine."

"You're not," he insisted, "and had I realized how much you were struggling with your pregnancy, I wouldn't have empathized quite so easily with the new alpha." He reached for my elbow and tugged me gently towards the cottage, rather than towards the little lot where my car was parked. "Come inside and let us see if we can't do something to ease some of your discomfort. We should at least be able to treat the hemorrhoids."

My face flamed. Of all the complaints to have blurted out! Doctor or not, he didn't need to know that part. "I don't have them *now*. They just…come and go."

Honestly, the next person who told me that pregnancy was a magical experience would get a foot lodged firmly up their ass.

"What about your ankles swelling? Is Eric aware? It can be a sign of pre-eclampsia."

My irritation at him began to fade almost as swiftly as it had built. I refused to acknowledge that my sudden mood swings might also be related to my condition. I was not a slave to my hormones, damn it! Instead, I told myself that I was just being appreciative of Brandt's genuine concern.

"He is aware, and I'm fine," I replied. "But he is keeping an eye on me just in case, I promise."

While both doctors were tracking my pregnancy, Eric had made it very clear that omega fertility and births were his specialty, even though he had only attended one birth — Ollie's. Given that it was the only one anyone in the world had seen in hundreds of years, that made sense. But Eric had been researching shifter evolution and omega biology for decades before he'd even met Ollie, so he was still my primary physician. Brandt assisted him during the ultrasounds and to check blood work, but otherwise left Eric to do his thing, and seemed to only assist in the background doing research.

Brandt looked like he wanted to argue with me but bit his tongue. "Are you having any other difficulties which Eric is not aware of?"

I thought again of the cravings I didn't have the funds to quench, of hating sleeping on my side, of being so horny sometimes that it almost hurt.

"Nope," I shook my head. "I'm okay."

"Promise me that if you do, you'll say something." The look Brandt pinned me with seemed to pierce right through me. "You're a friend now, Damon. Not just a lab rat for my brother's research."

That was kind of him to say, I had to admit it. But, as I opened my mouth to acknowledge as much out loud, my stomach growled audibly. I glowered down at the bump while Brandt chuckled.

"Come on; Sage has been on a mac 'n cheese kick. There was a vat of the stuff in the refrigerator last time I checked."

My stomach growled again. I rubbed it and smiled softly when the little womb usurper did a somersault. "Well, I'd be stupid to turn down carbs and cheese."

"Good," Brandt guided me towards the cottage door. "And I'll locate something to combat the potential heartburn, too."

I snorted. I guessed he wasn't completely backing off about my complaints after all. But it was nice having someone care about me, though my traitorous brain wished that it was someone else doing the caring. Someone with blue eyes and a sexy Texan drawl...

Nope.

I was better off without Rex and that was the end of it.

"Lead on," I told my dragon companion, and I hoped that the cheesy goodness would distract me from my woes.

Chapter Six – Rex

Watching the dark-haired man with the goatee hustle out the door with Damon's coat in hand, guilt settled like a lead weight in my belly. I was well aware of the others in the room staring at me in silent condemnation and I couldn't blame them. Not really.

It was obvious that they cared about Damon. That my kitten was one of them. One of their pack, if I was using the terminology right. And my reaction to his…*condition*…had hurt his feelings.

I wasn't exactly proud of myself for that, either.

However, in my defense, I wasn't expecting to ever see Damon again. And even if I had hoped that I might, I certainly wouldn't have considered that I might have left him with a parting gift of that magnitude.

I mean, seriously, where I came from, men couldn't generally knock up other cis-presenting men.

Alright, so where I came from, men's penises didn't change shape and lock them inside their lover mid-orgasm either, so

I supposed my logic might have required reevaluation.

Nevertheless, I thought I could —and should— be forgiven for floundering a little under the circumstances. Riding a building wave of self-righteous indignation off that thought, I turned back to Beckett. "*Tactful*, huh?"

"I was getting there," he protested, appearing chagrined. "I was trying to ease into it. I know it's jarring, so…" He trailed off, rubbing his free hand over the back of his head. "I didn't realize they'd be bringing Damon with them." Turning to face his lover, he arched an eyebrow. "What happened to one step at a time, babe?"

Ollie remained completely unrepentant, shrugging his shoulders. He gestured blithely in my direction. "What was I supposed to do? Keep Day in the dark about Matthew McConaughey here arriving on our doorstep?"

For his part, Beck just cocked his head and waited in silence.

Ollie huffed. "Fine," he practically whined. "I *may* have pushed the issue to get him up here. But you know how I feel about keeping secrets. Put yourself in Rex's shoes: how would you have felt if you were…I don't know…being given a tour of the town and you saw the guy you knotted with a huge baby bump and you realized you were the *only* person in town who hadn't put two and two together, hmm?" He folded his arms and tapped his foot impatiently. "Do you really think that was the better alternative?"

"Well, no," Beck acknowledged. "But did you have to spring him on the poor guy without any warning at all?"

"*You're* the one who was supposed to give him the basic warning about alpha/omega biology. If you'd done that, I'm willing to bet he would have been smart enough to think back to knotting an omega and consider the possible repercussions."

Beck snorted. "Like we did, huh?"

A chill that had nothing to do with the December weather descended. Ollie's cheeks flushed and his pretty face lost all signs of mirth.

Understanding that he had quite obviously stepped in it dawned over Beckett's expression. He reached towards Ollie. "Shit, baby, I didn't mean—"

He was silenced by Ollie's hand being held up, palm outward, the hurt in the younger guy's green eyes enough to make even me feel guilty. "Just don't, Beckett. You know how *stupid* I felt…"

Beck closed the space between them within a couple of long strides, carefully repositioning the baby in his arms so he could pull his young partner against him for a hug. He murmured low apologies and reassurances into Ollie's ear, and I averted my gaze, feeling awkward.

This was not the kind of moment I should be intruding on.

The other man who had entered the room with Ollie and Damon made his way past the couple, hardly paying them any mind. He was tall and blonde, blue eyed and buff. I rose from my seat and extended my hand towards him, considering he was already reaching his out towards me.

"Doctor Eric Weldman," he introduced himself as we clasped hands, and I noted that we were roughly the same height, though I was lankier than him. His handshake was firm, but not in that macho, posturing way. Similarly, his smile was kind while his eyes contained an analytic gleam.

"Rex Murphy," I replied.

His nostrils flared. "Mountain lion," he declared, then cocked his head. "Interesting. There goes my theory about alphas taking on the species of their mate post-bonding…so perhaps the compatibility and fated component is genetically predisposed."

"Fated component?" I asked, blinking in surprise. "You tryin' to tell me this whole mess was meant to be?"

Eric wasn't shaken at all by my sharp, incredulous tone. He just tilted his head from side to side, explaining, "It's a possibility we're considering. Not fate in the sense that you're likely assuming, but that there are specific mates out there who are so compatible with you that meeting triggers a mating heat —or, in your case, a mating rut— and unlocks your previously hidden alpha designation and shifter abilities." He sighed and shook his head. "What we obviously don't know, given that you and Damon are only the second known case of this happening, is how to determine that compatibility ahead of time. It seems to be an instant, unpredictable connection, likely predetermined by pheromones and genetic factors."

"Genetic factors?"

"It's our belief that you surprise alphas likely have at least one shifter parent. I don't know your personal history, but Damon said that you scented human before you mated."

I cringed, both at the reminder of Damon storming out only minutes earlier, and at the word 'mated'. "That's what he told me after I…" I gestured down towards my crotch. "Y'know."

"Knotted him," Eric supplied clinically. "Yes; it was the same for Beck and Ollie. Beck didn't begin to scent as shifter until after they'd mated and bonded. However, you didn't bond with Damon, and you still scent like shifter, so it's likely the bond itself plays no part in bringing out one's alpha after all." He brought a hand up to stroke his hair-free jaw. "Fascinating, really."

I frowned. "What's the difference between bonding and

mating?"

"Mating is just his fancy science-y term for the sex and knotting and breeding," Ollie supplied as he wandered over and joined the conversation, bending to pick a pink mug from the tray Jazz had set down earlier. He poured himself half a cup from the coffee press and then added creamer and sugar while he chatted casually, "Bonding is where shit gets really weird." He paused while stirring his spoon in his cup, the metal tinkling pleasantly against the ceramic. "Whoops. Sorry," he looked over at the two babies in Beck's arms, "don't repeat Papa's bad words, kids."

I shared a conspiratorial glance with Beck and smothered a snort. But then what Ollie had been saying caught back up with me and I prompted, "What do you mean bonding is where it gets really weird? Because my cock changing shape? Kind of what I'd call *really weird*."

"Did you have the urge to bite Damon when you achieved orgasm?" Eric prompted and I was glad I wasn't drinking my coffee, because I would have spat it all over him.

"What?!" As it was, I was choking on my own spit. "What kind of fu—er—fudged up question is that?"

Ollie cackled gleefully. "Oh, you're kind of vanilla, huh?"

If only he knew.

"*Oliver…*" Beck warned.

The youngest man in the room held his hands up in surrender. "Sorry, sorry," he was still giggling to himself, so I didn't think he really meant the apology. He cleared his throat. "Anyway," he tugged at the collar of his sweater and tilted his neck, showing off a shiny scar in the shape of a bite mark. "*This* is what happens when an alpha bites an omega when they're mating. Beck's got one, too. It, um, it kind of tied us together in a magical kind of way. Like…a mystical connection."

"A mystical connection?" I tried not to sound too dry when I repeated his words.

"I know how it sounds," he took a sip from his coffee and then sat on the armrest of Beck's chair, one hand draping behind Beck to toy with the hair at the back of his head, their earlier disagreement forgotten, "but we can feel each other's emotions, sometimes physical sensation," his cheeks pinked a little as he admitted that, "and proximity."

"That sounds…" Invasive. Frustrating. Terrifying.

"Yeah," Ollie agreed, nodding. "But we've been working on controlling it so it's not constantly 'on', you know? It's all hit and miss, but…yeah. That's what we call bonding."

"Well, I didn't feel inclined to bite him, no," I shook my head.

"I wonder if other conditions need to be met, then," Ollie mused as he looked towards Eric. "I mean, Beck and I did it on instinct, but we were so far gone with the mating heat…Do you think the weeks between meeting and finally satisfying the heat and rut cycle contributed to the spontaneous bonding?"

"Possibly," Eric said with consideration. "Then there's the fact that you bit each other, so the physical position must play a part in it as well." He glanced at me. "When you and Damon—"

"Nope," I held up an index finger, already guessing where his question was heading. "That's taking things a bit too far."

"We'll circle back to it," he shrugged, then asked, "would you mind if I conducted some tests? I just need some basic samples. Hair follicles, blood, semen: the usual."

"Semen?" I backed up a step. "Why? Isn't Damon's condition proof enough that everything down there's in working order?"

"Well, I'd like to compare your semen to Beckett's. Comparing a bonded alpha to an unbonded one. It may hold the answers to questions we have about inter-species breeding."

"Inter-species breeding?" My voice pitched higher with the question as my head swam.

"He's not going to use your sperm to impregnate any other omegas," Ollie said, but the words did little to reassure me.

"*Other* omegas," I repeated.

The fact that I'd knocked up anyone at all was still freaking me out.

I sat down heavily in the armchair I'd started in and ran my palm over my face. "Christ, this is actually happening, isn't it?"

"Let's steer away from talking about pregnancies for now, yeah?" Beck suggested. The comment itself was laughable coming from him, given that he was bouncing two babies in his lap. Babies that he had put inside Ollie.

"Here, hon, drink some more coffee," Jazz suggested, pushing my mug into my hands, and I startled at the sound of her voice. I'd forgotten she was even in the room. "Don't go passing out on us now, okay?"

I drank because it was easier than talking. Who would have thought that at forty-two years of age, I'd be panicking over knocking someone up? Plus the whole 'I'm not human' thing, but I'd pretty much already come to terms with that.

"Have you shifted yet?" Beck asked me gently after I'd taken a few deep gulps from my cup.

And maybe I haven't come to terms with not being human after all, I thought to myself.

In response to Beck, I just sighed and shook my head. "I wouldn't know how, and it'd be just my luck that I'd get stuck in my animal form or somethin'."

To my surprise, Beck didn't laugh at me. He nodded and hummed his agreement. "I had the same concerns. But after I shifted that first time, it was just instinct." His brow furrowed. "Of course, I kind of followed Ollie's example through the bond. You don't have that."

Ollie giggled and then clamped his hand over his mouth when everyone turned to frown at him. "Sorry," he offered sheepishly. "That just reminded me of earlier, when Day..." Expression falling, Ollie looked to his feet. "Never mind."

"Anyway," Beck redirected, "you should consider trying to shift. When I shifted, it was like...like missing pieces had all been put together inside me. I stopped freaking out about being a shifter because it felt natural, like it had been a part of me all along."

"Technically," Eric interjected, "our running theory is that it *was* a part of you. Just hidden, or locked away, or whatever analogy you'd like to use."

"About that," I said, allowing my mind to go back over the conversation so far, "you said something about having a shifter parent? How would I even go about finding out if that's the case?" When they all looked back at me blankly, I sighed. "I was adopted when I was three. My birth mom died from a suspected aneurysm, and I didn't have any other biological family. My father was never in the picture, he's not even on my birth certificate." My brain-to-mouth filter proved itself inactive as I turned to Eric and asked, "How do birth certificates work for alpha and omega pairings?"

"The same as any others," he answered easily. "Ollie's listed as Rory and Duke's mother, Beckett as their father."

"Right," I stretched the word out as his answer tumbled about in my head. My stomach clenched at the thought of my kid —or was that possibly kids? I hadn't even thought to ask Damon— having a blank space on their birth certificate.

"Okay."

"So you didn't really know your birth parents?" Beck asked, shaking me from the dangerous path my mind was traveling down. I shook my head and he offered me a small, commiserating smile. "Me either. I grew up in foster care."

I winced. "I'm sorry to hear that."

"I survived," he brushed my words off, but I didn't think it was because he didn't appreciate them. "But it only seems to back up the idea that our parents, or at least one of each of our parents, could have been shifters."

"Anything's possible."

I didn't think I'd spoken truer words that day. I'd gone searching for answers about what I was, already uneasy with my body being other than human, and I'd walked into even more impossible surprises.

Speaking of which...

I cleared my throat. "I, uh, I think I should talk to Damon."

Ollie sat up straight and glared at me. "Why? So you can hurt his feelings some more?"

"Ollie," Beck nudged his side with his shoulder, his hands still holding their gurgling children in place on his lap, "that's not fair. Do you remember freaking out about the twins? 'Cause I sure as hell do."

"You weren't an ass about it," Ollie muttered, still sounding a little petulant.

"Damon didn't really give Rex much of a chance to talk, though, did he? And I'm not saying his feelings weren't valid, because they totally are, but I do think giving him and Rex a chance to talk privately about everything might help more than us meddling any more than we already have."

Ollie leaned his head back and remained silent for a long

moment before he eventually exhaled and nodded. "Fine. You're right."

He climbed off the armrest and set his half-empty mug back on the coffee table. Jazz bustled about, collecting the rest and taking them from the room.

Ollie reached down and plucked a baby from his lover's lap. "How about I take this pair to their aunts, and I can show you how much I appreciate your level-headedness?"

Beck's cheeks flushed and he looked at me with apology written across his features. "Sorry. We, uh, don't get a lot of childfree time."

"Don't forget," Eric told him before I could say it was fine, "we're still monitoring Ollie for signs of a heat cycle starting again. I'm estimating he'll be fertile again any time now. It's been just over four months since he gave birth, so—"

"Lalalalala," Beck clenched his eyes shut and shook his head. "Nope. No. We're using condoms."

Eric sighed heavily. "Beckett. How will we know that the birth control we've developed will even work if you don't allow us to try it?"

"I have four-month-old twins, Weldman. Could you imagine throwing more babies into the mix?" He shuddered. "Hard pass for now."

"As offended as I think I should be," Ollie added, "I'm with Beck on this one. When the kids are a bit older, we might risk it, but for now…" He booped the kid in his hold on the nose with his free index finger, grinning at the baby gurgle the action elicited. "I love them, but they're enough for us."

"We'll see if you're still saying that during your next heat," Eric snarked back at him, but the smirk on his face, as well as the answering exasperated smile and eye-roll from Ollie, told me that this wasn't the first time they'd had this conversation.

Eric turned his attention back to me. "Come with me. We'll head to the clinic, I'll get those samples, and then you can go and make amends with Damon."

My heart hammered in my chest at the thought of *that* conversation, but I followed the doctor out the door anyway.

Chapter Seven – Damon

I wasn't completely surprised when a knock sounded at my door an hour or so after I'd dropped onto the soft brown couch. It was the kind of couch that you sink into. The kind I was convinced was half cloud, determined to swallow me up.

It was ridiculously comfortable and appealed to the big cat inside me.

Sadly, when the knock sounded again, I knew I had to haul myself out of my squishy cocoon of warmth and actually talk to the person on the other side of the door. I had a feeling I knew who it was, and my stomach tightened with nerves. I grunted as I managed to heft myself up and then grumbled all the way across the room (the whole four steps between the couch and door), steeling myself for the confrontation to come.

"Hey there, kitten," Rex greeted me quietly and with liberal contrition, his big blue eyes soulful and locked on mine. "Can we talk?"

For all that I thought I'd been prepared for that moment, I wasn't. Just looking at the man —the *alpha*— who had upended my world had me tongue-tied. Even pale-faced and shocked stupid sitting on Ollie and Beck's couch, the man had made my heart race. But now? Looking down at me with a gentle smile and apology written all over his face? He was drop dead gorgeous.

Heart beating so hard and fast I thought it was going to burst right out of my chest, I could only nod and step aside, shutting the door carefully behind him. He was taller than I remembered, still just as broad shouldered and golden-skinned. He seemed to command the tiny little studio apartment as he stood at the foot of my twin bed, surveying the space.

It wasn't much, but it was all I needed. A bed, a wardrobe, a couch, a TV, a kitchenette and a bathroom. Cozy and slightly cramped, but private and warm.

The walls had been painted two days before I moved in, so it was bright and clean, too.

"Nice place you've got here," Rex said when his gaze finally settled back on me. "Reminds me of my first apartment back in Houston…only you don't seem to have a drug dealing downstairs neighbor." He frowned. "Right?"

"I'm pretty sure the little old tortoise shifter who lives downstairs is not a drug dealer," I couldn't help but laugh, imagining the frail older man living the stereotypical thug life. "Poor Mister Keogh."

"Tortoise? How does that even…you know what? Not my circus, not my monkeys."

"Or tortoises," I supplied helpfully.

Rex snorted. "Still a smartass, huh?"

"I seem to recall that you liked that about me."

His blue eyes sparkled with amusement. "I still do, kitten."

Danger, my brain blared as my heart lurched, *danger!*

I would not be stupid enough to go mooning over this man when, barely a couple of hours earlier, he'd looked at the life we'd accidentally created together and had…had…um…he'd…

Well, okay, he hadn't actually reacted badly, had he? He hadn't rejected the baby or me. Not in so many words, anyway, and I hadn't given him a chance to say more.

He'd freaked out, that was all. I'd also lost my shit when I'd worked it out. Maybe Rex deserved a little leeway.

Damn Brandt and his rational logic getting to me.

Nevertheless, I decided to put the brakes on our flirting. I turned my head and scoffed, "Coulda' fooled me."

The second the petulant complaint was past my lips, I regretted it.

I didn't *want* Rex to want me. I was *fine* being single. I didn't need to behave like a sulky teenager.

Was it possible to blame my hormones? Not just for the outrageous mood swings, but for how desperately some part of me did ache for his affection? I was going to blame the hormones.

Rex exhaled slowly. "Damon, c'mon now. Give me a break. I wasn't expectin' to see you again, let alone…" I turned back to face him, arching an eyebrow at the vague hand gesture towards my belly.

"Pregnant?" I offered, taking a sadistic thrill from the way he flinched. Then the anger I was trying so hard to hold on to melted into bone-deep exhaustion. Sadness warred with apathy, and I huffed a miserable little laugh, stomping over to the bed so I could sit on the edge of the mattress wearily.

"Don't worry, Rex. You're off the hook. I don't want anything from you."

Why did my heart ache when I said it, though?

Stupid, traitorous body.

"Hold on just a minute," he groused, carefully coming to sit beside me, making the mattress dip and creak. "I never said I wanted to be off the hook. Don't go puttin' words in my mouth."

My throat felt tight and my eyes burned with unshed tears. "Don't act like it isn't a relief."

"Now, I'm lettin' that go on account of you goin' through a hell of a lot more than I can even imagine right now."

His gentle chiding made me feel a little bit guilty. However, I still snorted inelegantly and accused, "Brandt got to you, didn't he?"

After a short pause, Rex said, "Maybe. But, hey, you know what he told me?"

My mind whirred, worried that Brandt had told Rex about my multiple pregnancy complaints, but I knew my new friend wasn't the type to do that. Plus, he was a doctor; surely he believed in doctor-patient confidentiality. "What did he tell you?"

"He pointed out that gettin' eaten by a dragon is far scarier than any baby ever will be."

I blinked, struggling to process that sentence. "He...he threatened *to eat* you?"

"Yeah, and Eric backed him up. You maybe wanna warn a man that your town is filled with ornery dragons next time?"

I'd only been in Shifters Sanctuary a week, so I hadn't seen any of the Weldman brothers shift. I had seen footage from the mess in New York the previous year, though, and if that was the kind of damage one dragon could manage on his own, I wasn't going to push any of the dragons living in town to that kind of anger. The fact that Eric and Brandt had threatened to eat Rex as a way of defending my honor was sweet, though, in its weird-ass way. They barely knew me, but they'd told an alpha they'd eat him!

The giggle burst out of me without warning, followed by unstoppable laughter. Inside my belly, my son (*our* son) seemed energized by my buoyed mood, kicking up a storm. I placed my hand to my belly, no longer finding the alien-like tapping from the inside quite as strange, and rubbed the spot his feet were abusing, trying to control my unruly amusement.

Rex's gaze followed the movement of my hand. On his thigh, his fingers twitched. "I know I don't have the right, but…may I?"

Giggles evaporating into quiet hiccups, I swallowed and nodded, pulling my hand away from its spot. My heart rate increased, and it was like the moment extended into slow motion as Rex tentatively reached out to splay his palm over the curve of my belly, right where my hand had been.

The kid inside me seemed to sense that the touch was coming from someone other than me, because he only seemed to kick harder, the *tap-tap-tap-tap* of his feet suddenly feeling less ticklish and bubbly and more like the tyke was trying to break down the wall of flesh separating him from the outside world.

"Sweet Jesus," Rex breathed shakily, sounding awed and terrified all at once. He tore his gaze from my stomach to look me in the eye. "You really are…I mean, not that I thought you were lying, but…shit just got *really* real."

My lips twitched and the giggles threatened to overwhelm

me again, but I managed to smother them. "Yeah, I thought I was going to re-enact a scene from *Alien* the first time I felt him move. But I'm getting used to it now. It's even kind of comforting sometimes."

"Him?" There was a quiet reverence in Rex's voice, his palm pressing just a bit more firmly on me, as if he was trying to get even closer to the kid inside my belly. "Did you say 'him'? A boy?"

Realization dawned on me. He hadn't known that.

Of course he didn't know, I scolded myself. *It's not like you got a chance to tell him.*

"Yeah," I replied softly. "A boy. Well, unless he says differently when he's old enough to tell me I was wrong. But, y'know, I'll love and support him —*them*— no matter what. Alpha, beta, omega…girl, boy, genderfluid…None of that matters to me."

"No, of course not, but," Rex's expression turned soft, "a son. Not that a daughter wouldn't…I mean…*shit*, I'm messin' this up."

It was such a far cry from the utter panic and refusal I'd seen on his face earlier that I didn't rush to reassure him at first. I was too dumbstruck by the perceived change in his attitude and how quickly that had happened. Were a few hours really all he'd needed to wrap his head around his, no — *our* impending fatherhood? Because I'd needed a hell of a lot longer than that.

"I'm sorry, kitten, I didn't mean to imply that I'd be any less amazed if we were havin' a girl, I just…"

That got my brain working again, my thoughts snagging on his use of the word 'we'.

"Whoa, cowboy," I held up a palm towards him, halting his

rambling. "What's this 'we' business?"

Blue eyes blinked at me, a flash of hurt visible before it was hidden behind a more cautious expression. His big, warm palm left my cotton-covered flesh and I swear the kid inside me threw a tantrum about it going away, rolling and kicking up a storm. I rubbed at the spot, hoping to soothe my son and myself.

"Well," Rex began slowly, as though he was weighing his words before he spoke them. "It is my baby, right? I mean, you didn't come across any other alphas six months ago, did you?"

My heart started hammering again, but this time in fear. As an omega, I didn't have the kind of social standing or rights that he did. "It's *my* baby," I barely refrained from wrapping my arms around myself protectively. "All you did was knot me. I'm the one growing him. *I'm* the one…" Emotions clogged my throat as the words from my breakdown in the apple orchard threaten to overwhelm me again. Shaking my head, I tried to push them away. "It's my baby," I repeated fiercely. "And so help me, if you even think of trying to take him…"

The scowl that had taken up residence on his face shifted swiftly to shock and he held his hands up in surrender. "No, darlin', no. I'm not gonna take him. I wouldn't know the first thing about lookin' after a baby, for one, and for another thing…you're right. You are doing all the hard work right now. But," the mattress beneath us shifted as he straightened his spine, "I'm no deadbeat, Damon. And I'll be damned if my kid grows up not knowin' me."

The vehemence in his statement made me pause. Had a little chat with Brandt and the *minor* threat of being eaten really caused such a turnaround in Rex's attitude? And why the hell did I think it was so freaking hot? That had to be my constant horniness kicking back in; not something I wanted to deal with at that moment.

"Okay," I responded calmly, grabbing a pillow and hugging it to me. It had the benefit of hiding my growing arousal as well as providing comfort. "So, you've changed your mind, then? You want to be a dad?"

Rex let out a little growl of irritation and I hated that the sound went straight to my dick. "I never said I didn't," he huffed. "Sure, I didn't exactly jump for joy when you turned up at Beck's, but I was in shock! Still kinda' am, if I'm bein' completely honest."

"I'd appreciate complete honesty."

Instead of getting annoyed with my haughty response, my baby daddy —dear God, I was *never* going to think that phrase again— chuckled lightly and spread his arms wide. "That's why I'm here, kitten. I'm tryin' to do the right thing. We're gonna have to get to know each other, 'cause we're gonna be in each other's lives from here on out."

"Don't you have a life somewhere? A job? Friends? Family?" I didn't have any of those things, but I didn't imagine that he would also just be able to uproot himself and move to a tiny town in Iowa, of all places.

He frowned. "Even if I did, I'd argue that bein' here for my son is more important. That bein' here for *you* is more important."

My stupid, evil, traitorous heart squeezed again.

"Besides," he continued, ignorant of my internal battle with my hormones and daydreams, "I came here looking for answers on the whole shifter thing. I'd already planned to settle in if the...pack...would have me."

His hesitation over the word 'pack' was also ridiculously

endearing. I cocked my head. "So, you're staying here, then?"

Staring at me with obvious caution, he nodded. "Yeah. Beck and Eric are gonna show me the ropes, teach me to shift—"

"You still haven't shifted?!" My voice pitched high with incredulity. "It's been six months!"

"And I had no intention of gettin' stuck as an animal, thanks." It was his turn to tilt his head to the side, observing me. "Can you shift while you're…uh…"

"Pregnant?" I offered again, and he winced.

"Yeah. That."

Unlike before, this time I could only find his discomfort with the word kind of cute.

I was going to kill whoever invented hormones.

Chuckling, I nodded. "I can, yeah. The last time was really draining, though. I only ran with the others for a little bit before I went back up to the main house to curl up and sleep. I also felt super ungainly, which is weird because animals are built to have litters, not just a single cub. But," I shrugged, "shifters aren't really animals, I guess. And we're not really human. Eric said Ollie had the same complaints, so I'm guessing the baby doesn't shift with me or something."

Although how that logic would work with a smaller animal, like a hedgehog or a bunny, I had no idea. There was some sort of magic at play, I supposed. That was the only way we could shift between forms at all, really. I didn't think there was a scientific explanation for it, after all.

Rex's expression twisted, his nose scrunching adorably. "That's just plain weird."

"I don't make the rules."

He snorted. "I know, kitten. But I'm still havin' some trouble gettin' my head around all of this stuff. Men having babies, me being able to turn into some kind of animal…it's gonna take a little gettin' used to."

"A puma."

"What?"

"You should be able to turn into a puma. A mountain lion." I clarified. "That's, um, that's what you scent like now. Back when we met, you scented human. But now…now it's puma and alpha."

Rex got up and paced the length of my apartment, rubbing the back of his neck. "I remember you sayin' I smelled human at the time. And, hey," he stopped mid-pacing, his eyes wide. "You said you were a puma. It made callin' you kitten even more appropriate."

I thought back to that day and smiled to myself. Even if it had completely upended our lives, being with Rex had been a revelation.

Most men before him hadn't shown me half the respect or even affection that he had. But Rex had been kind. He had seemed to care about my feelings. He hadn't been rough with me (until I had begged him to) and he had respected my boundaries. Before him, the guys I'd slept with had seen me as little more than a willing hole, especially the beta shifters who had looked down on me for being an omega. But, even if I'd only been a quick one-night stand to Rex, he'd been sweet about it.

In addition to that was the way he'd made me feel. I had never been as horny and desperate to be fucked as when I'd been with Rex. It was like my body had known how compatible we were, and it had begged to be filled and sated.

Ollie described feeling something similar when he'd met Beck, but he had been able to deny those feelings during their first meeting. Then he said that when they met again two weeks later, it triggered a super intense weekend fuck-fest (his words, not mine) that he and Eric hypothesized was a full-blown mating heat.

I wondered if my short but intense desperation to be fucked stupid by the big, gorgeous cowboy had been something similar. I'd needed him to fill me, to knot me, to *breed me*…and he had. But the desperate urge hadn't returned after he'd driven away. To hear Ollie tell it, his heat had come in waves over the weekend he had mated and bonded with Beck.

But Rex hadn't bonded with me, either. It was entirely possible that bonding during that first heat might make things more intense. I would never know, not unless another alpha and omega pair turned up in town.

My thoughts had veered wildly off track. What had Rex been saying? Oh, yeah. I was a puma.

I nodded. "I am, yeah. It makes sense that you are, too, if you buy into Eric and Ollie's fated —or, at least, compatible— mates propaganda."

"Do you?"

"What? Buy into the theory?" I shrugged. "It makes about as much sense as anything, I guess. I mean, Beck and Ollie are both wolves, and you and I are both pumas, so the logic tracks."

"Eric mentioned testing the possibility of mixed matings," Rex said, sounding a little awkward when it came to the last word.

Cocking my head, I wondered, "How does he plan on doing that? Parading other omegas in front of you and seeing if you can knock up a bunny or a hedgehog?"

The horrified look on Rex's face made me laugh. "Nuh-uh,

he's promised me no more babies. It'll all be test-tube lab stuff."

Ignoring the sting of his anti-baby protest, I nodded and shifted on the mattress, wincing at the ache developing in my hips and lower back. "Eric did seem pretty excited to have a new lab rat…and it would be nice to have answers about all of this, too."

"Anyway," Rex said, frowning at me as I rubbed at my sore spots. I was either going to have to move back to the couch or sit at the head of my bed, propped up against the wall and a mountain of pillows. "I'm gonna be stayin' put and—are you alright?"

The concern in his voice as he swerved mid-sentence was sweet. I offered him a reassuring smile.

"It's nothing, really. My back just gets a bit achy lugging this guy everywhere." I smoothed my hand back over my bump for emphasis, adding fondly, "The little freeloader."

"Should charge him rent," Rex joked, but he was still eyeing me warily. "Can I help?"

"I just need to get my back supported and I'll be fine."

"Lie down on your side." He crossed the room and gestured to the bed. "Maybe put a pillow under your…" he hesitated, his throat working, "under your belly."

"I don't need—"

"Just humor me?" He paused then softened his tone. "Please?"

With a sigh, I did as he asked, feeling ridiculous stretching out on my bed while he loomed over it. That didn't compare to how I felt when he walked around to the foot of it and then started crawling up to stretch out behind me, though. "What are you doing?" I all but yelped.

"Shh," he murmured soothingly, which didn't help to calm

my racing heart at all as his large, warm body made the mattress dip at my back. "I'm just gonna work out some of the kinks for you."

I knew he meant the pain in my back, but I couldn't help thinking about other kinks we could explore together. How was he with bondage? I mean, the guy was a cowboy. Surely that meant he had a knack with ropes.

My dick took that thought as an invitation to spring all the way back to life, reminding me that my hormones demanded satisfaction that my hand and dildo alone couldn't give. If that wasn't embarrassing enough, I became more than aware of my slick beginning to flow and pool. My cheeks flamed.

"This is okay, isn't it?" Rex asked quietly, his big hand rubbing soothing circles over the small of my back, having located the source of my earlier discomfort with precision. "I just wanna help."

As long as my slick doesn't seep through my pajama pants, it's fine, I thought in reply, but could only nod mutely as he carefully worked away the knot of tension he'd found. I groaned as the pain eased, both because the over-the-clothes massage really was relaxing and also because his touch was only encouraging my dick to make its bid for freedom.

"You okay?" he asked again, and was it my imagination, or had his tone gone a little husky there?

It had to have been my imagination. Stupid hormones.

"Mmhmm," I agreed, keeping my eyes firmly shut. My back hadn't felt so good in weeks. "Oh my God, that's magic."

His resulting chuckle was throaty and so close to my ear that I could feel the warmth of his breath skirting across my skin. Goosebumps erupted over my skin and I shuddered.

"Cold?" he asked.

I shook my head, praying that he wouldn't lean over and spy the obscene tent in the front of my soft pajama pants.

He lowered his voice to a gentle murmur, his fingers still easing the discomfort in my lower back. "Talk to me, kitten. Let me help you."

Desire was pulsing in my veins. With every careful, deliberate movement of his fingers, my body was coming to life. I'd only felt this desperate once before: the night we'd conceived our son. It was like flames were licking along my nerve endings.

My hormones had been making me feel horny since the early days of my second trimester, but never quite like this. It was as though Rex's proximity and touch had flipped a switch inside me, triggering the same instant connection that I'd felt that night in the bar.

A needy whine rent the air. It took a moment to realize that the sound had come from me.

"What's wrong?" Rex asked, his hand moving from the small of my back to run over my baby bump, his concern flaring. "Does it hurt? Are you—" he cut himself off abruptly when he brushed the dampened fabric concealing my insistent cock. His hand withdrew quickly and he rested it on my hip. "Oh." A beat. His fingers flexed, gripping my flesh through the soft fabric I was wearing. "*Oh.*"

Mortification flooded me. I still couldn't bring myself to open my eyes. "It's hormones," I explained, even though I suspected it was more than just pregnancy hormones. There had to be something to Eric and Ollie's theories about the whole fated mates thing, because my body's insane need for Rex was unlike anything I had experienced before. "Y-you were touching me and they lit up like the fourth of July."

He was silent for a long moment. My throat tightened and my heart thumped hard and fast inside my ribcage.

"Can I help with that?"

I jolted at the cautious, quiet question, my eyes flying open. I turned my head to peer over my shoulder at him, knowing that I must look completely blindsided. "What?"

Rex's blue eyes were darker now, the irises inside them blown wider with lust. But his tone was steady when he repeated, "Can I help you with that? With your...*discomfort*?"

I almost whimpered as I felt slick trickling out of me at the mere suggestion. Swallowing roughly, I tried to remain rational. "You don't have to." My cheeks felt like they were on fire and I averted my gaze. "I'm not...I mean, my body's not the same, and—"

"You think I find you less sexy like this?" He sounded incredulous as he swept his hand over my distended belly again. "You think takin' care of you, of your body's needs, will be a chore for me?" His tone told me that those assumptions, should I be making them (which I was) were wrong. "Kitten, I might still be freaking the fuck out over havin' a baby, but you're just as hot to me as the day we met. I want you just as badly now as I did then, but I don't wanna push you. I wanna reconnect at your pace."

My heart, which I had already established was a traitorous asshole, squeezed at how earnest he sounded. "We..." I started, then paused to try and calm my jumbled thoughts, wading through the mantra of *'fuck me, fuck me, fuck me'* which had started to drum on in the background of my mind, "we need to talk properly. To...to...take things slow. Having a baby isn't a reason to jump into a relationship."

"I agree," he soothed, still rubbing big, arching circles over my abdomen. "But I also want to help make this as easy for you as possible. If your hormones are drivin' you nuts, let me take the edge off. We can take things slow and have sex on the side. Friends with benefits style."

I was tempted to argue that we weren't even friends yet, but my body was screaming at me to just say yes.

"It…it wouldn't mean that we're together," I told him, though some part of me wished I could have the fairytale happily ever after that I saw Ollie living. "It's just sex. Sex because you put a baby in me and now my body is demanding your knot again."

That urge terrified me, though. It was one thing to have a quick fuck in a bar bathroom, not thinking I'd ever see the guy again. It was a whole new issue to want to sleep with the man who had put a baby in me and who was talking about sticking around.

As horny as my hormones were making me, I knew I'd regret giving in to those urges so soon.

"Whatever you need, baby." Oblivious to my inner turmoil, Rex's voice was low and full of promise. "Just tell me what to do."

"I want…" I swallowed roughly. "Fuck, I want your knot. But…I can't. I'm sorry. I can't." I was on the verge of tears, frustrated by my body's demands and my brain's corresponding opposition.

"Hey," he soothed, "I'm sorry, kitten. I wasn't pushing. I just want to help you, and you said your hormones…"

"Hormones are the worst," I all but sobbed, still torn between giving in and getting some sort of relief and holding off until our relationship was in a more stable position. "I'm sorry. Mood swings and epic horniness must make me seem unhinged."

I *felt* unhinged.

"Just tell me what you need. Anything, Damon. I want to help." He was so earnest that it brought a lump to my throat. "If you want me to leave—"

"No," without realizing it, I grabbed at his wrist as I protested, "I don't want that."

I didn't. Even if letting him fuck me again was a bad idea, it didn't mean I wanted him to leave, either.

"I'm sorry," I sighed, feeling guilty for the mixed signals I was sending. "You didn't ask for this."

Splaying his hand over my belly, Rex's voice rumbled at my back, low and gentle, "You didn't ask for this, either."

"We're going around in circles now," I told him. "Besides, I'm kind of happy about him. I mean, I freaked out when I realized I was pregnant, but that was more because I grew up thinking I couldn't have kids of my own, and I knew that being a pregnant omega in my old-school pack was dangerous. Especially with no alpha to show for my condition, y'know? They'd know that I snuck out. That I broke the rules. That I didn't drag you back to the pack the second I realized what you were."

"I—"

"Don't. It wasn't like either of us knew you were really an alpha. And, I guess, even if I had known it, my body was so determined to have you, I probably still would have forgotten that you could knock me up. All that biological imperative or whatever the hell Eric chirps on about."

He was quiet for a moment. "But now that I'm here, we're gonna do this together, right? Raise this kid together?"

I'd been completely prepared to be a single dad, but I wasn't ever going to be the kind of guy who kept a kid away from his other parent, not when that other parent wanted to be involved. "Yeah," I answered softly. "But once you're in, you're in. There's no coming in and out of his life."

Rex didn't even hesitate. "I wouldn't dream of it."

We continued to lie there in my bed, fully clothed, my arousal fading out again, even though a low thrum of my ever-present horniness remained. It should have felt awkward, but it didn't. It felt...nice. Outside of a few short relationships in college, I had very little experience with this kind of contact, snuggling in comfortable silence. Being an omega in one of the Moonmusic-based packs was a lonely existence.

Cuddling was nice, I decided, even though we hadn't really broached *how* we'd go forward from that point. We'd taken a step in the right direction, at least.

Regardless of what we were going to label our relationship, I couldn't deny that it felt like we were heading towards *something* monumental....which was crazy, right? We'd only known each other for a few hours in total.

Rex's hand drifted over my belly in slow, lazy circles, pausing as our son rolled and kicked out in the direction of his palm.

"That's never going to get old," he muttered, pressing a little more firmly, seeking out more contact with the child inside me. "I am really sorry I freaked out on you. I mean, back at the bar...and then also at Beck and Ollie's place, too. I'm...well, let's just say I don't always deal well with change."

A snort escaped me before I could rein it in. "Stop apologizing, we're good. Otherwise, it makes what we're doing now just plain awkward."

Because we were still cuddling. He'd given me a massage, he'd talked me through a weird, hormone-fueled semi-meltdown, and now we were cuddling as though we were *together* together.

He let out a bark of surprised laughter. "It feels good, though, right? Just being close. Not even sexual. Just…close." His voice lowered and turned soft and contemplative. "It's been a long time since I've done anything like this with anyone."

I couldn't deny that I was on the same page as him. The big cat living inside my soul was practically purring at being so intimately connected with his mate.

No. Nope. Not mate. It's too soon to be thinking of him that way.

I could picture my inner omega rolling his eyes at my refusal to agree. Even though it was all in my head, I struggled against my instincts sometimes. Logic and rationality should trump biological imperative, shouldn't it?

"Can I take you out on a date?" Rex's question startled me out of my thoughts. "I know we just agreed to raise our kid together…but, I mean, I want to see if we can be somethin'. A family. We can take it slow," he hurried to add, as though knowing that his huge declaration would otherwise send me running for the hills, "as slow as you need. But…could we try dating?"

Would it really be all that different to this new strangers-who-cuddle arrangement? We'd already agreed that we needed to get to know each other better, and he was also insisting that he was going to stick around for our kid. My heart beat a little faster at the idea, but I reminded myself that I wasn't going to make rash decisions anymore.

"Can…can I think about it?" I asked, feeling guilty when he tensed at my back. "I'm not saying no, I just…I need some time to process. And you should really do the same."

His palm smoothed over my belly again, and his lips brushed

the spot behind my ear. "Of course you can, kitten. I'm gonna be here for you either way."

Well, how was I expected to keep up my rational front against sweetness like that?

In no rush to end our impromptu snuggle session, we chatted about other things. He stayed true to his word, not pressing his desire to pursue a romantic relationship as he fed me snippets about his life. I'll admit, I was surprised to hear that he was forty-two, considering he barely looked a day older than thirty-five...maybe thirty-eight at a stretch. When I told him I was twenty-five, I'm pretty sure he had a mild conniption.

"Twenty years," he breathed.

"Uh, no," I corrected playfully, "seventeen. I guess I'll be teaching our kid math, huh?"

"I mean, I knew you were younger, but..."

"Hang on, are you trying to tell me I look *old* for my age? I'd advise you to think *real* carefully about your answer." I was enjoying teasing him, finding the banter came just as easily to me as the night we met. "Next you'll be saying I look fat, too."

"No, no, I...I just...I mean, the lighting that night..." Rex trailed off as I cackled with mirth. His fingers twitched where they still sat on my belly. "You're trouble, you know that?"

I grinned. Even if he couldn't see my face, I was certain he could hear the smile in my voice. "I'm pretty sure we established that the night we met."

He hummed in playful contemplation, "Hmm, I'm startin' to like your particular brand of trouble."

Chapter Eight - Rex

A son. I was having a son. Despite my thoughts whirring about like crazy, and my anxiety over sudden, unexpected parenthood making me dizzy, I was strangely excited by the news. And, as I'd told Damon, I would have been equally happy if he had said it was a girl, too.

It was like learning that extra information had made it all the more real. Having just held Beck's kids, I could vividly imagine cradling my own in my arms. While I'd never thought it was something that I wanted, I couldn't deny that I was rapidly warming to the idea. Then the little critter had started kicking, and Damon had allowed me to feel it, and my conviction to stick around had cemented.

Yeah, I was doing it because I wanted to cowboy up. I wanted to do right by my kid, and also the man carrying him. But it was more than just the feeling of obligation that made me want to stay. It was instinct. Something deep inside of me yearned for it…and for *more*.

Damon was right, though: we didn't know each other. We

might have been connected for the rest of our lives through the kid we'd made, but even if my new urges said otherwise, that wasn't any reason to try and initiate one of those bond things I'd just learned about. In fact, to do so without talking it through would be crazy. To do so without trying to date first would be even crazier.

I hadn't meant to put the idea out there so soon after just agreeing to take things at his pace but cuddling him so intimately seemed to make my inhibitions disappear, and that urge inside me to make him mine was becoming more and more insistent.

I needed to get a handle on that. Feeling possessive unnerved me. But that was my baby in his belly and the thought of him potentially moving on to someone else —not that there was anyone else in the picture at the moment— made me want to hiss and growl. *Literally.* That had to be the shifter thing manifesting, right? I wasn't *actually* going insane.

Oh, God, I really hoped I wasn't going insane.

Eventually, Damon started to drift off to sleep in my embrace.

"I'm gonna go," I told him, ignoring the voice at the back of my head which demanded I stay and snuggle with him all night long. "But," I picked his phone up from where it sat on the lone bedside table and passed it to him, "unlock it so I can put my number in. Just in case you need anything. And I mean *anything.* You wake up at some ungodly hour craving pickles and ice cream, and I'll bring 'em."

"You've changed your tune pretty quickly, haven't you?" he asked, his voice slurred with sleep, unlocking his phone and handing it to me as requested. "It's okay. You can still be freaked out. It took me a while to," he paused to yawn, blinking rapidly, "to, um, to get used to the idea."

"I'm sure I'll go back to panicking when I'm alone again," I admitted lightly, "but it doesn't change the fact that this is happening. You're…you're pregnant," I swallowed roughly and forced myself to continue, "with my kid. I wanna take care of you. Both of you."

"You're sweet," he yawned again, closing his eyes.

"Looks like I'm not the only one changin' his tune quickly, hmm?" I mused, more to myself than to him. He made a vague, muffled sound of agreement and rolled onto his side, facing the window with his back to me. Once again, I had to fight the urge to crawl back into bed beside him and spoon against him like I had just been doing for God-only-knew how long.

Be patient, I told myself, *it'll come.*

It was a pity that I'd never really been good at being patient.

Setting Damon's phone back down on his bedside table, I pulled his blankets up over him and then made my way to the door, twisting the lock on the handle before I shut it behind me. I tested that it was locked properly before I made my way down the hallway and the narrow flight of stairs which led to the ground floor.

Leaving the building, I just about had a heart attack when the shadows moved and spoke in a low, dry voice, "Well, it didn't take you long to patch things up, did it?"

Clutching my chest, I glared into the darkness, Beck's shape coming into focus as my eyes adjusted to the lack of light. "Please don't tell me you've been sittin' out here for the past couple of hours. That's creepy, man."

He chuckled and stepped forward, shaking his head. "I promised Ollie I'd check up on Damon. He's new to the pack, but he's one of us now. And with his condition…"

I bristled at the idea of someone else watching out for my pregnant mate, then did a double take at my own inner monologue. *Mate?* I wondered, concerned at how natural the word felt when, even as late as this morning, I never would have thought it part of my vocabulary. *Mine?*

I'd been in this tiny town for less than twenty-four hours and I was being confronted by more shifter instincts than I had in the six months I'd spent avoiding even thinking about what I really was deep down inside.

"He's fine," I replied gruffly, trying to be grateful that my… *no*, that *Damon* had someone else looking out for him. "He's sleeping."

Beck nodded, seemingly unruffled by my curt response. "Ollie slept a lot, too. Growing whole other people inside them takes a lot of energy."

I didn't know what else to say other than, "Mmhmm."

Beck's lips twitched and he observed me knowingly, tilting his head to the side. Instead of asking any probing questions about my feelings on the insanity of the day's events, or even about my intentions with Damon, he asked, "Wanna try shifting?"

"Uh…"

"I just figured it might be easier for you without an audience."

His statement reminded me that he had been in my shoes not all that long ago. Even though he seemed so at ease with being a part of this strange new world, there had been a time where it had been new to him, too.

Nevertheless, I shook my head, ignoring the voice inside me that begged to try. Some part of me felt trapped, restrained, inhibited. I was terrified of what releasing it might mean for me. Would I lose the sense of who I was? Would I become more animal than man? Where did the line between the two beings begin and end?

"Can we talk?" I asked instead. "About when all of this happened to you? I just…" I paused, licking my lips as I considered my phrasing carefully. "I just need some answers. Reassurance, even. I know that you're happy with Ollie and you seem settled into life as a shifter, but…"

"It's scary," Beck finished kindly. "I get it. Not to mention, I had nine months of lead-up before the kids were born. You're only getting three or four."

"Yeah…" Panic, which had receded while I was in a happy, relaxed bubble with Damon, made my heart thump wildly. It had been so easy to get lost in a fantasy of domestic bliss when I'd been in Damon's bed, locked away from the outside world. But now, reality was setting back in.

It was like my brain was on a roller coaster, dipping and swerving and doing loop-de-fucking-loops over the subject of my impending fatherhood. I was giving myself whiplash.

The fantasy was all well and good, but in reality? I knew nothing about raising babies. I was a forty-two-year-old perpetually single gay man who had never planned to settle down. I didn't have a house, let alone a crib or any other baby-related items. I'd never even gotten a dog because it was too much responsibility!

Suddenly, I realized that I would need to organize somewhere to live with the space for a small boy to grow. There would be education to consider, too. Clothing, food, social activities…pets?

Did shifters even bother owning pets when they were able to turn into animals themselves? And, hey, did any of 'em ever moonlight as pets? Like, say, if they were house cats or regular dogs?

Fighting the urge to pull out my phone and Google 'how do I know if my cat is a shifter?', I got the feeling I was overthinking things. Or maybe I was just trying to distract myself.

Three months didn't feel that long. How was I supposed to brace myself for fatherhood in such a short amount of time? God, I'd only just told Damon that I wanted to date him, to see if we could work towards being a family, but now I was feeling the urge to run again. To flee and not look back, just like I did the night I met him. The night we conceived our son.

No.

No, I was not going to be a coward. Not again.

While I hadn't planned on seeing Damon again, I'd gone crawling back to him the second I'd gotten a chance. Instinct had told me to, just like instinct was telling me to grow up and accept the changes coming my way.

"Come on," Beck led me to where his truck was parked behind mine on the street, "let's head back up to the house and we can talk, alpha to alpha."

* * *

Sitting at Beck's dining table with a plate full of homemade spaghetti and meatballs and a tall glass of ice-cold beer, I felt strangely at home. I hadn't felt that way since my teens; before I'd come out to my adoptive parents. And, even back then, I'd never felt as though I fit in properly. But in Shifters Sanctuary, at Beckett Smith's dining table, I honestly felt like I belonged.

He'd just begun regaling me with his thoughts on discovering he wasn't human when Ollie entered the room, dropping into his fiancé's lap. Beck rubbed Ollie's back and nuzzled his face into the crook of his neck, over Ollie's mating mark.

Quickly avoiding being caught watching, I looked back at my half-eaten dinner and twirled my fork in my pasta, watching red flecks of sauce spin off the strands of tasty goodness.

"Kids asleep?" Beck asked, and Ollie hummed in answer.

"Yeah. Duke fought me on it, but he eventually went down."

"You should get some sleep," Beck murmured, his voice filled with a mixture of emotions that made my chest ache. "I'll take the first wake-up call."

I cast them a sideways glance, feeling like an intruder on their intimate moment.

"Don't be too late coming to bed," Ollie instructed. "You know I sleep better when you're with me."

I was going to get cavities from all the sweetness.

Beck chuckled softly. "I won't, baby. I promise."

I looked back down at my plate as they kissed chastely, vaguely registering Ollie sliding back off Beck's lap. Ollie ignored me as he left the room, and Beck sighed.

"He'll come around," he told me, even though I hadn't said anything. "He's just protective of Damon. They're close in age, and he feels like he could have been in Damon's situation, you know?"

I winced. "It's not like I knew I could knock him up." Swallowing roughly, I gave up the pretense of continuing with my meal. What little I had eaten was sitting heavily in my gut. "Sure, I should have used a condom anyway, but—"

"I get it. The whole mating heat and rut thing is no joke," Beck grinned wryly. "Your instincts take over and, hey presto, instant family."

"But you stuck around with Ollie. I ran the second my knot went away."

"True," Beck shrugged and sat back in his seat, fiddling with the edge of the cork coaster that sat beneath his empty glass. "I was scared out of my mind, though," he confessed. "I do wonder if we hadn't accidentally bonded, whether I might have made a different choice."

Considering how deeply in love he and Ollie seemed to be, that admission surprised me. "Really?"

He nodded. "I thought about running and not looking back. But I could feel his emotions. His proximity through the bond. That's what stopped me. I was freaking the ever-loving-fuck out, but I didn't know how to sever the bond —or if we even could— and I didn't know what would happen, or if it would hurt either of us if I ran away."

It might have made me a really shitty person, but I felt better hearing that. It made my own decision to turn tail feel less cowardly.

"How does that bond stuff work, anyhow? Doesn't it get tiring or confusing feeling two lots of thoughts or emotions or whatever?"

Beck nodded and swirled his glass, watching the dregs of foamy amber spinning around. "It took a lot of getting used to. After I got used to shifting, I found it easier to manipulate the sharing of the emotional and physical sensations. We, uh," his cheeks turned pink, "we've had some fun with that, too."

It took me a couple of seconds to cotton on before my jaw dropped. "Hold up. You use it for sex?"

"Sometimes." Beck cleared his throat. "There have to be some benefits, too, right? But that all came over time. It...it's kind of like the bond is sentient, I guess? It evolved with our relationship. Now, it feels as natural to me as shifting. Like an invisible limb or something."

"And shifting feels natural to you?" I struggled to wrap my head around the concept. "Even though you've only known you were a shifter for…what? Just over a year?"

"I can't explain it, but the first time I shifted, it felt like I was coming home. Like my body and my mind just knew that I was always meant to have a wolf form." He cocked his head and looked me up and down seriously. "Haven't you felt the urge to try it?"

Shaking my head, I answered, "Nope."

Except that was a lie. The longer I left it, the more the little voice at the back of my thoughts demanded that I needed to try. I'd done well to ignore it in the months on the road, working odd jobs in every town I stopped, keeping myself as physically exhausted as possible. But coming to Shifters Sanctuary had seemingly given those shifter urges a shot of adrenaline, and it was getting harder to silence the nagging voice that told me to embrace who I really was inside.

You're going to have a son, it said. *A shifter son. You'll need to be ready for that.*

The voice wasn't wrong. How would I be able to properly raise my own kid if that kid had the ability to turn into a mountain lion? It sounded ridiculous, but I was suddenly afraid that my kid would turn himself into a big cat and run away or, in a tantrum, maul me. Images of a rebellious little boy with Damon's hair and my eyes manifested in my head, rapidly followed by a vision of that same little boy turning into a large cat and climbing up a very tall tree where I had no hope of reaching him.

Taking another long sip from my beer, I asked, "When do kids start shifting for the first time?"

Beck smirked as if he knew exactly what I was thinking.

Considering he had been in a similar position, albeit with more time to wrap his head around the concept, maybe he did. "Apparently it's not until they're about five or so. Ollie said something about nature taking over once they're mentally ready for it? I don't know. I'm just glad I'm not going to walk into the nursery to find my kids are suddenly wolf cubs. I have enough trouble diapering them as they are."

The petulant grumble he ended on had me chuckling. The mental image of big, broad Beckett trying to wrestle a diaper onto a bundle of fur was too much for my overloaded brain, and I found myself laughing harder than the situation warranted.

"What's so amusing in here?" a new voice asked as I calmed down and caught my breath, and I turned to face the newcomer.

There was a petite woman leaning against the timber archway that separated the kitchen/dining area from the hallway that opened out into the grand staircase and living room. Her hair was cut into a pixie cut, colored bright red, and she was wearing a plaid mini skirt over thick black leggings, as well as a warm-looking black sweater.

"Hey, you're back," Beck greeted the newcomer with genuine affection, pushing from his seat to gather the much smaller woman into a hug. "You've been missed."

"I was gone for less than a week," she chuckled, disentangling herself from the embrace. "Micah says hi, by the way."

Beck's smile dimmed a little. "He's still not interested in coming out here?"

The look the woman shot him asked if he was crazy. With her eyebrows almost at her hairline, she said, "You really think the country life is the life for him?" She turned her attention to me and explained, "Micah's a makeup artist and a bit of a glambot. His whole life is fame and fashion."

"I…have no idea who you're talkin' about," I responded. Then, remembering my manners, I also pushed my chair back and stood, turning to face her with my hand extended. "Rex Murphy, ma'am."

"Sandy," she replied, taking my hand and giving it a shake. Then she sniffed the air and blinked in surprise, turning her attention back to Beck. "Another alpha?" More blinking and a small gasp, followed by a perfectly manicured red fingernail aimed at my nose. "You're the one who knocked Damon up?"

Jesus, did everyone in this town know my business?

"You'll have to forgive my sister," Beck cut in before I could tell this Sandy woman to get back in her own lane, "she's also protective of our newest pack member."

"Yeah, well, we've established the fact that I made some piss-poor decisions when my entire world got upended," I grumbled. "And if I'd known that I'd left Damon in a…uh… *delicate* situation, I'd have made things right a long time ago."

Sandy snorted.

"Sandy," Beck's tone had turned into one of warning. There was a tingle of *something* in the air. It was undefinable, but it made the hairs on the back of my neck stand on end.

Sandy sighed and gave her brother an incredulous look. "Really? You're going to *Alpha* me?"

"I thought we were calling it compelling?" Beck shrugged off the question.

"That sounds like something out of a nineties vampire novel," she shot back, rolling her eyes. "Anyway, whatever we're calling it, you're going to use those powers on me?"

"Rex is our guest," Beck stood firm. "You remember how panicked I was when everything happened with Ollie?" Sandy's expression softened and she nodded. Beck relaxed as well, gesturing in my direction as he continued, "Good. So then you'll have a bit more compassion for someone else going through the same shit."

His sister sighed and conceded, "You're right. I just can't help it. Damon's been through a lot and I—"

"Collect strays, yeah, I know." Beck laughed softly. "But Rex is also a stray, San. Give him a chance before you get all growly, okay?"

"Fine." Sandy agreed, then turned her attention back to me. She had the grace to look mildly sheepish. "I apologize, Rex. I tend to get a little defensive of the people I care about."

It made me smile to think that Damon, who had only been in town a week or so, had already made such a strong connection with these people. I couldn't blame them: I'd been just as drawn to the feisty younger man when we had met. He was unintentionally charismatic. Hell, the fact that I'd gone from panicking to wanting to date the guy within a few hours was clue enough that it was nearly impossible to dislike him.

"It's all good," I told her with a thankful grin. "I'm glad he's got a whole town looking out for him."

"Well, I'm glad you give a shit," she replied.

I couldn't help but appreciate how direct she was. In that moment, despite the rocky start, I decided I liked her.

Having diffused the tension, Beck reached out and clasped my shoulder, giving it a reassuring squeeze. "Finish your dinner, then turn in for the night. Try to get some sleep. Tomorrow, we'll talk about shifting."

I nodded, even though I was still anxious about it.

But I guessed I couldn't put it off forever. Especially not

if I planned on settling in Shifters Sanctuary…and that was looking more inevitable with each passing minute.

Chapter Nine – Damon

Instead of going to work at Eric and Brandt's clinic, I found myself spending the following morning watching Beck and his former foster sister, Sandy, trying to teach Rex how to shift. I was wearing the thickest winter jacket I'd ever come across in my life, clutching a thermos of hot cocoa while the others were standing naked in the clearing behind Beck's house. They shivered in the cold winter air. Ollie was sitting beside me while his best friend, Brandi, and her girlfriend, Lena, minded his kids inside the house.

Rex had not been impressed with the idea of taking his clothes off in front of an audience, but when Beck and Sandy had stripped without even blinking, the sexy cowboy gave in and did the same.

It hit me that this was the first time I'd seen him naked. When we'd fucked in the bar, he'd been behind me, and the glimpses I'd caught through the grimy bathroom mirror had done the man a great disservice.

Now, I thought his expanse of tanned skin and work-toned

muscle was a sight to behold. Seeing him in daylight made me feel way more self-conscious about my big belly, stretchmarks, and the extra flesh that had made its way to my ass and thighs. Sitting on the porch in a weathered, but sturdy, swinging chair, I wriggled in discomfort.

"He's easy on the eyes," Ollie said, having followed my gaze to the perfect, pert ass Rex had on display, "I'll give him that."

I snorted. Where I had decided to take Rex at his word and forgive him for his freak-outs, Ollie was holding on to his resentment. It was sweet that my friend was so protective of me, but unnecessary.

"We talked last night," I said, keeping my voice low in the hopes that Rex's shifter-enhanced hearing wouldn't be able to follow our conversation. "He apologized. Said he wants to be a part of the baby's life…that he wants to try dating."

"Dating?!"

"Shh!" I glanced towards the others out in the clearing. There was a large gray wolf standing where Beck had been only a few moments earlier, but Rex was still in human form. He didn't seem to be paying me and Ollie any attention, though. I relaxed again and rubbed over my belly, feeling the baby moving lazily under my palm. "Yes, dating," I repeated quietly.

"And you're considering it?"

I frowned at the surprise in Ollie's voice. "Weren't you the one who was all 'ooh, it's a Christmas miracle' and 'fate brought you back together', or was that a different bonded omega?"

"That was before he was a dick to you in front of me."

"He wasn't a dick," I was defending Rex before my brain could catch up to what my mouth was doing. "He thought he was human until six months ago, and he had no idea that knotting me could have knocked me up. Suddenly seeing me like this," I waved my hand over my stomach, "would freak anyone in that situation out."

"He still hurt your feelings."

"I'm hormonal, dude. A toothpaste commercial hurt my feelings last week. I don't see you boycotting Colgate."

Ollie laughed and held up his hands in surrender. "Okay, okay, point taken." He let his gaze drift back over to where there were now two wolves and a naked, shivering cowboy. "I just remember how vulnerable I felt when I was pregnant, and I had Beck doting on me hand and foot, plus the bond."

"Yeah, well, we've established that my experience with mating with an alpha has gone just a bit differently. And, no, before you ask, I don't think it would help us to bond right now, not when I don't know him from Adam."

Ollie was quiet for a long moment and I wondered if I'd offended him, because he and Beck had bonded without knowing each other. Thankfully, that didn't seem to be the case, because he just cocked his head and smirked, "So…dating, then?"

"Yeah. I figure it makes sense. We can get to know each other, see if we're as compatible as biology seems to think we are, and get used to the idea of being together before Junior here makes his appearance."

Ollie observed me shrewdly. "Do you want to be with him?"

What kind of question was that?

I thought back to the previous night, to how sweet and supportive and willing to help Rex had been, and I thought about how much I would like to have that kind of thing in my life. Not to mention how fun it was to banter with him. I just didn't want to give him the capacity to hurt me. Growing up as an omega in an old-school pack, I'd let enough people hurt me over the years.

"I do," I confessed quietly, feeling a lump of emotion lodge in my throat, "but I'm scared."

Before Ollie could reply, Rex's frustrated voice rang out. "It ain't workin'!"

I looked back over to see him throwing his hands up and stomping over to the pile of clothing he'd set down on a large, flat rock. With jerky, agitated movements, he dressed himself. Beck and Sandy shifted back into their human forms with practiced ease, but it was Beck who approached Rex, trying to offer more suggestions to help Rex push past whatever mental barrier was preventing him from shifting.

"How did you do it that first time?" Sandy asked Beck. "Did you just think the wolfy thoughts like I said?"

Everyone seemed to wait with bated breath as Beck considered the question, and I felt my stomach sink when his shoulders slumped and he looked sheepishly towards his mate. "I actually followed the pull from the bond that first time. I could feel how Ollie felt when he shifted and I just let my instincts copy it."

"Well, that's just great," Rex yanked on his sweater, and I couldn't help but think that his ruffled hair looked cute, even as he scowled and pointed at his own chest. "I don't have a bond to follow."

Silence fell, heavy and awkward.

Rex seemed to realize how his bitter complaint sounded, because he cringed and looked over at me. "I didn't mean…" his hands moved about vaguely in the air in front of him. I didn't think there was a way for him to finish that sentence that wouldn't be misconstrued by someone, so I took pity on him.

"I know, Rex. We're doing things differently, that's all."

"It's a pity," Ollie sighed beside me. "If you *were* bonded, you could shift and he could just follow the feeling."

"We're not bonding just so he can trick his body into shifting," I grumbled. "That's an even worse reason than bonding because I'm pregnant."

"Fair point," Ollie conceded, knocking his shoulder against mine. "Except—" I groaned, but he ignored me "—I maintain there's something to Eric's fated mates theory. If nothing else, biology wouldn't kick in unless we were fundamentally compatible with our alphas. Beck and I prove that a solid relationship can be established after a surprise bonding to a stranger."

"You're going to need a wider pool of subjects before you can argue that's the case for everyone," I reminded him. "And I'm not signing up to be a guinea pig on that theory." Rubbing my belly and smiling as I felt my son kicking out at the spot where my palm was resting, I added, "This is enough of a life-changer for me right now."

"Spoilsport," Ollie complained, but his tone was playful.

"So," Beck cleared his throat, "I guess that puts us back at square one." He turned to his mate. "Describe what you feel when you shift."

"It's just instinct," Ollie frowned as he tried to explain it.

I'd never given the sensation of shifting much thought, either. It was something I just did without thinking.

"This is going to sound really airy-fairy, but I sort of reach into my subconscious and follow my inner wolf until I am my wolf?"

From where she was dressing, Sandy nodded her agreement. "My body just knows what to do."

"That's what got you and Rex into this mess, isn't it?" Ollie teased and gave my shoulder a nudge. I snorted.

"You're being really helpful," I replied with a liberal dose of sarcasm. "And it's not like you can talk."

"God bless shifter biological instinct," he grinned back. "I have zero regrets."

"Even when they wake you up all hours of the night?" That was one of my many concerns about parenthood. I didn't know how I was going to handle it.

Ollie's expression softened into something wistful and full of affection. "Even then," he admitted, "they're totally worth it."

Inside me, my son kicked up at my ribs and I grunted at the sharp pain that accompanied it. It was almost as if the little terror knew I was thinking less-than-adoring thoughts about him. Sighing, I rubbed at my belly and addressed it when I spoke, "Hey, you in there, quit being a brat. I'm trying to get all maternal here."

Ollie laughed. "I don't miss those days, though," he said, wincing in sympathy when another internal jab had me grunting again. He lowered his voice and confessed, "I hated being pregnant."

"Yeah, well, you had two of these critters inside you. I'm uncomfortable enough with one."

I didn't know where the admission had come from. Until the previous day, I'd kept most of my whining over my discomfort to myself. Then it was as though opening the floodgates and ranting at Brandt had flipped a switch in my brain. It helped that Ollie was the only other man I knew who would actually understand.

"It's worth it," he repeated, wrapping an arm around me and

squeezing reassuringly, "I promise."

I hoped he was right.

* * *

Rex asked me to go on our first official date three days after his first failed attempts at shifting. As far as I was aware, he still hadn't achieved it when he swung by Eric and Brandt's clinic with a box of chocolates and a request to join him for dinner.

At over six months pregnant and trying to squirrel away every spare cent I could, I wasn't turning down a free meal.

Plus, we'd been texting each other since the night we spent in my apartment, and I had to admit that I liked Rex. I wasn't just attracted to him; I was starting to like the person he was underneath the hot cowboy getup.

Rex was a nice guy. Over texts, I learned that he was adopted after his biological mother died, and he told me about growing up on a ranch in Texas. He didn't say a lot about his relationship with his adoptive parents, and I knew better than to ask, but I started to form an understanding of why he'd never seen himself as the kind of man to settle down. He was used to being transient. He was used to people using him and waving him off when they didn't need or want him around anymore.

I could relate to that.

He also seemed to be making a genuine effort to prove that he wasn't going to run away from our son the way his father had run away from him. Even if he was taking things slowly with me like I'd asked him to, he wasn't afraid to talk about the baby. I appreciated that, even if it chipped away at the wall

I was trying so hard to keep up to protect my heart.

So I agreed to a date. A real date. Even if it had only been a few days, Rex had stuck around and respected my wishes. There was absolutely no reason to turn him down after his obvious effort. At least, no reason that made sense to me. Besides, we were going to be parents together, it made sense to get to know each other properly.

Rex left the clinic with a huge smile on his face and returned at closing time to pick me up.

"Have I mentioned how good you look today?" he asked in his honeyed accent as he grabbed my coat from the coat stand by the clinic door and helped me into it. "It's all I can do to keep my hands to myself."

I snorted and started to do up my buttons. When I'd bought it, the coat had been far too big for me. Even now, it was too roomy in the shoulders and around my chest. But my belly was already straining the buttons' reach around my abdomen, and I worried the coat wouldn't be large enough to get me through the rest of winter.

Feeling ungainly and tired, I could only shake my head. "Are you having issues with your vision now? Shifter sight not as clear as it should be? 'Cause I can ask Brandt or Eric to give you a checkup." I threw my thumb over my shoulder and half turned, as if I was actually going to find one of the doctors.

"Don't play coy with me, kitten," Rex laughed, then bent to kiss my cheek and place one of his big palms over my stomach. We both felt our son kick out at the contact, even through the multiple layers of thick fabric I was wearing. Rex smiled. "You're gorgeous. Besides, I've gotta admit, knowin' that it's my baby in there? I've got this whole primal caveman pride thing goin' on right now."

Three days.

He'd known about his son for three days.

Well, okay, *technically* four.

But still…he'd gone from freaking out to being possessive about my belly? That *had* to be part of our alpha/omega dynamics, right? Especially because, for my part, I was internally preening at his declaration instead of being weirded out.

Rolling my eyes, I asked, "Are you going to feed your baby, then? Because he's starving…and so am I."

"We can't have that." Rex placed his hand on the base of my spine and gently pushed me towards the door. I called out a goodbye to Eric and Brandt as I was ushered outside, instantly pulling my coat tighter around me.

December was brutally cold and, considering I was used to a slightly warmer climate during winter, I was hating every minute of it.

"Let's get you in the truck, kitten."

Rex kept his hand at my back for the short walk to his parked vehicle, then he helped me up into the shiny red cab. I missed the warmth and pressure of his hand when it was gone. My back was getting achier the larger my belly got, and Rex's touch had eased some of that discomfort.

If this date goes well, I might ask him for another massage…

I just about moaned out loud as the thought filtered through my head. At that point, even if the date was a disaster, I would still be tempted to ask him to work on some of the tension in my back. It was the least he could do, seeing as it was his cub causing all the pain.

Rex climbed into the driver's seat and buckled his seat belt. "Now, there's only one restaurant open in town, but if it doesn't gel with your cravings—"

Accidentally cutting Rex off, I let out a loud yawn, the force of it stretching my jaw wider than I felt was humanly possible. My cheeks burned and I ducked my chin.

"Sorry," I apologized, yawning again. It was almost like a switch had been flipped in my head the second I'd gotten comfortable in his passenger seat. My earlier exhaustion suddenly felt bone-deep. My eyes were getting heavier by the second. It didn't matter that I was starving, I was also desperate for a nap. "You mentioned cravings?"

"What are you craving, darlin'?" Rex's tone was soft and patient. "We don't have to go out. Not while you're so tired."

"But…our date…" I protested, though it was a half-hearted effort at best. I did feel guilty for changing our plans, but I couldn't control the oppressive tiredness I was feeling. Apparently it was normal to feel this way during pregnancy, but that didn't make it an easier pill to swallow.

"We can go out another time," Rex assured me. Unlike other men I'd dated, he didn't sound frustrated to have our plans changed. He sounded warm and understanding. "We've got time, Damon."

"That's really sweet," I replied, yawning again. My eyes were drifting shut despite my desperate attempts to keep them open.

The truck rumbled to life and the gentle jostling as Rex carefully drove down the dirt path to the main road was somehow even more relaxing than just being cradled in the warm passenger seat.

I lost the battle and drifted off into dreamland before we even left the property.

* * *

"Mmm," I moaned groggily as my nose twitched to life, scenting bacon in the air. My mouth watered and my eyes fluttered open. "Bacon?" I asked, struggling to push myself into an upright position on my bed.

Rex's answering chuckle came from the direction of my tiny kitchenette, and I swung my legs over the side of the mattress and padded across the room to investigate. "Uh-huh," he answered my query cheerfully, poking at something sizzling in the frying pan. "You said you were craving it the other day. I took a gamble and hoped you still were."

"God, yes," I said as my stomach growled loudly. I could feel myself blushing as Rex turned to grin at me. With his enhanced hearing, there was no way he didn't hear my digestive system demanding sustenance.

"Good. I'm makin' homemade burgers and fries, with some extra crispy bacon on the side just for you."

My stomach growled again, and I smiled sheepishly. "That sounds amazing," I told him, then looked around curiously. "Uh, how'd you get us in here?"

It was Rex's turn to flush pink. "I went fishin' in your pockets for your keys. No funny business, though, I swear." With his hands held up in surrender, spatula and all, I couldn't be mad at him. In fact, I thought he was adorable as hell.

"You're cooking for me," I said, gesturing for him to drop his arms and go back to doing exactly that, "and you let me nap for…" I glanced at the clock on the microwave and almost choked on air, "*two* hours?!"

"Google says that growin' a baby takes a lot of energy," Rex shrugged. "You needed the rest."

"I promised you a date."

"And we're havin' one."

I frowned. "Oh, sure, because me sleeping while you slave away in the kitchen is *super* romantic."

"Our situation's a little different, kitten. For one," he turned around to poke at buttons on an air fryer; an appliance I most certainly hadn't owned when I left for work that morning, "we've already been intimate."

Unable to hide my amusement, I teased, "Oh, that's a pretty word for fucking in a bar's bathroom."

"For another thing," Rex continued, ignoring my snark, "you're six months pregnant."

"No!" I looked down at my giant belly with widened eyes. "Am I?!"

Rex chuckled again, the sound warm and rich and sexy. "So our version of dating just needs to be adjusted accordingly. You're too exhausted to go out? We'll stay in. You're craving pickles instead of whatever restaurant we were going to? I'll buy you pickles and you can eat 'em straight out of the jar. Your back can't handle those uncomfortable seats in a movie theater? We'll find a drive-in or watch movies at home. As long as I'm spending time with you, I'm happy with whatever we do."

The playful mood I'd been indulging in melted away under the assault of his genuine sweetness. It was obvious he was genuinely trying to make things work. He was being thoughtful and considerate of my needs above anything else, and that made my omega very happy. My instincts demanded that I bare my neck and beg him to claim me, but I was thankfully able to ignore those urges.

The other urges, though? The ones I was sure were eighty percent hormonal? Those were harder to ignore.

Slick threatened to pool in my underwear while my heart

hammered wildly in my chest. It was ridiculous how easily I was able to go from neutral to horny-as-fuck. You'd think that being the size of a small house would make me feel less attractive, but nope: my libido knew no bounds.

My silence must have read completely differently, though, because Rex turned off the burners on the stove and guided me over to the lumpy old couch, gently pushing me to sit down. Then he dropped to his haunches in front of me and placed his hand on my knee, asking, "Did I cross a line?"

God, even that was stupidly endearing.

Shaking my head, I knew I had to be honest with him, as uncomfortable as sharing my feelings made me. "No. You've been perfect." With a sigh, I added, "That's the problem."

"I don't follow."

"I just…I guess I wasn't expecting you to follow through when you said all those things the other night. I figured you'd leave, then freak out over everything, then…" I trailed off.

"Run again?" Rex didn't sound offended. If anything, he sounded as though he understood exactly why I'd assumed the worst. Nevertheless, I ducked my head and nodded.

"Yeah."

"Well, I did panic. I've been panicking. I mean, we're havin' a baby in a couple of months and that's terrifying. Especially when it'll be a shifter kid and I can't shift."

I practically gave myself whiplash with how fast I snapped my head back up to look at him. I was surprised by his honesty, though I didn't know why. He hadn't given me any reason to think he'd ever lie to me. Not even during that first evening together in the bar.

Hearing him sound so defeated about not being able to shift also shocked me. I didn't think he'd really wanted to. In fact, some part of me thought he'd be relieved that he was still mostly human.

"You'll get there," I started, but he shook his head, locks of his sandy-colored hair falling into his eyes. He brushed them back with his free hand.

"Doesn't matter if I do or don't. I am who and what I am, and I can't actually control that. All I can do is keep trying. But what I can control—" the look he pinned me with was serious, and I couldn't tear my gaze from his even if I'd wanted to "—is what kind of a father I'll be. What kind of a partner I'll be…if you'll have me, of course."

A small, teasing smile tugged at the corner of my lips. "I said I'd go out with you, didn't I?"

"You did," his blue eyes twinkled. "And I'm hoping that I'll be able to prove myself to you so you'll want more than just dating eventually."

"What, like…marriage?" The word felt foreign on my tongue, and it made my heart do a weird flippy-floppy thing in my chest.

Rex didn't even bat an eye. He nodded. "That…and bonding. Like Beck and Ollie."

That was an even scarier concept than marriage! Bonding was irreversible, as far as Ollie had said. And it was for life. I was afraid enough of dating! I mean, what if we bonded and he realized that it was a mistake? I could imagine feeling his disappointment inside me, and I shuddered. That would break me.

Nevertheless, it was a heady feeling to hear him saying that he wanted it. Nobody had ever wanted to be with me long-term before. And a man like Rex? I didn't deserve a man like him. He was too good for me.

I swallowed hard. "You'd want that? With me? You've only really known me for a few days. How could you—" My breathing hitched, and I stopped speaking as Rex leaned forward slowly, giving me plenty of time to pull away if I wanted to.

Then our lips met, and it was just like that first ever kiss all over again.

Before Rex, I'd never known a kiss to make fireworks explode inside me. I'd never known a kiss to bring my nerve-endings to life, making me hyper-aware of my body and its reactions to my kissing partner. I'd never felt my inner-shifter wake up and take notice of the person I was connecting with.

But, with Rex, all those things happened at once.

The big cat inside me purred at the affection we were sharing. Instinct demanded I roll over and bare my belly, however large it might be, to my mate. It was all I could do to not follow through on those urges.

Instead, I deepened the kiss, pulling Rex closer by the collar of his shirt. Through the sweet press of his lips on mine, my tongue sought his out. He moaned —or maybe it was me; I sure as hell didn't care at that point— and I forgot whatever we'd been talking about. His mouth tasted fresh, as though he'd only recently brushed his teeth or sucked on a mint, and his big arms felt like safety and home as he curled them around my back.

It must have been an awkward, uncomfortable position for him, but he didn't seem bothered at all. Instead, his lips moved with mine as we continued to make out. I have no idea how much time passed before we separated for air, our lips kiss-swollen and our skin flushed from our efforts.

Slick had well and truly pooled in my underwear, making

the seat of my pants damp, and my cock was straining for attention, too. A glance down at Rex's crotch said he was in a similar predicament, but instead of diving back in for another kiss, he sat back on his heels and smiled sheepishly at me.

"Sorry, kitten. I didn't mean to get carried away," he apologized, his voice a little more gravelly than usual. "I just can't help myself around you."

Suddenly, I remembered the catalyst for the kiss, but as I started to speak, Rex shook his head.

"I know it's fast, but my heart wants what it wants…and that's to be with you. Beck and Ollie seem to think it's part of the fated mates deal, and, hell, maybe it is. Doesn't make it feel any less real. But," he gentled his smile and looked me in the eye, "just because my feelings have gotten serious fast, doesn't mean we have to rush things. I promised to do this at your pace, darlin', and that's what we're going to do."

Our son chose that moment to stretch and roll, as if saying 'You're already knocked up, dumbass; it's not as if things between you aren't already serious.' I ignored him and the reminder that my situation was far from normal.

I mean, hadn't I daydreamed about Rex turning out to be a fairy tale prince, saying all the right things and sweeping me off my feet? Now that he was doing that, I had two choices: I could fight it, or I could accept that life for omega and alpha couples was always going to be a little different courtesy of our biological drive to be together. And Rex was still saying that we didn't have to rush things. It made it easier to process, somehow.

Nodding back at Rex, I said, "I can accept that." Then, to lighten the mood, I sniffed the air and rubbed at my belly. "Now, did you say something about bacon?"

* * *

We ate our burgers sitting side by side on my tiny couch while Netflix played the TV show we'd agreed to start watching together. It was a foodie travel show hosted by a comedian, and it was fun to discover that Rex was just as into the whole thing as I was. If the food he'd made for us hadn't clued me in, seeing him pull out his phone to make notes about Googling recipes confirmed that the man who wanted to be my mate enjoyed cooking. He was good at it, too.

"I've had to fend for myself for a long time," he justified when he caught me looking. "I couldn't afford to live on takeout, and eating the same three homemade meals on rotation got boring really quickly. So, I taught myself to cook, and now I find it relaxing."

"Well, you can try out new recipes on us," I patted my distended belly for emphasis, grinning when the kid inside kicked back at me, "anytime you like."

Rex preened at the suggestion. "I have to admit, there's a part of me getting really satisfied and smug at the idea of providing for you."

My omega instincts purred over the same concept. Too content to fight my inherent behaviors over something so insignificant, I could only smile. "That's shifter biology for you."

"I'm starting to realize that a lot of my instincts have always been there," he admitted quietly. "They've just gotten stronger since…well, since that night."

I didn't need to ask him which night, though just the thought of it had my arousal flaring again.

I refused to let every encounter with Rex devolve into sex.

We'd never form a proper relationship if all we ever did was fall into bed together. Not that we had the last time either, mind you, but I'd wanted to.

I still wanted to.

Clearing my throat, I nodded. "That makes sense. You've always been a shifter, but that side of you was locked away for whatever stupid mystical reason."

Rex chuckled. "I'm coming to terms with that, yeah." He pushed to his feet and reached for my empty plate, gesturing for me to stay seated when I awkwardly fumbled an attempt to get up. "Stay. I got this." He grinned, then jutted his chin at the bump housing our son. "Do you have any room left in there for dessert?"

I perked up, everything else forgotten at the mention of sweet treats. "Always."

Twisting in my seat, I watched Rex carefully place our plates in the sink before he rummaged through the fridge, pulling out a foil-covered Pyrex dish. He slid it into the oven, which I assumed he'd been pre-heating while we ate, and then he crossed the room and sat back down beside me.

"It'll be about twenty minutes or so, depending on how well that clunker of an oven works," he informed me.

"Whatcha makin'?" I asked, snuggling into his side when he lifted his arm in invitation.

"It's a self-saucing chocolate pudding," his answer had me moaning obscenely, and he chuckled.

"With vanilla bean ice cream?"

"Uh-huh."

Salivating at the mere thought, I blurted, "Marry me."

Thankfully, Rex laughed and rubbed my upper arm affectionately. "They do say a way to a man's heart is through his stomach." He looked down at my belly and smirked. "Apparently, I'm taking a two-pronged approach to that theory."

The joke startled a laugh out of me and I rubbed at my stomach. "We're joking about this now?"

He shrugged and offered me a sheepish smile. "Humor helps me process, I guess."

Well, I could definitely relate to that. Grinning up at him, I said, "Me too."

It was nice to have something like that in common, and I had a feeling it would help us to deal with issues in the long run, too. If we both relied on humor as a coping mechanism, at least we'd understand the best way to communicate with each other through difficult conversations. Humor usually helped to diffuse tension, as well, so he got bonus points for that.

I wondered what other things we had in common. If I was running with Ollie and Eric's theory that we were fated mates, then it would make sense that our fundamental beliefs and behaviors would complement one another, right?

"Tell me more about you," Rex said. "Obviously, I know the basics now. But…I want to know all the little things, too. Like…how old were you when you had your first kiss? When did you learn to ride a bike? Are you a cat person or a dog person?"

I leaned away from him so I could arch an eyebrow, and he facepalmed.

"Alright," he conceded, "that was a dumb question."

"You never know. I could be one of those hipster cat shifters who says they're a dog person just to be *edgy* and *unique*."

Rex blinked back at me. "Do those even exist?"

"People are people, no matter our species," I shrugged. "But no. I'm definitely a cat person." Frowning, I asked, "Are you a dog person?"

"I like all animals. Raised on a farm, remember?"

"Well, yeah, but…did you feel an affinity for cats growing up? Because I always have." I always put it down to being a big cat inside, but what if being a shifter really didn't make any difference after all? Or maybe, because his true nature had been locked away all his life, things were different for him.

"…no more than any other animal," he replied after seemingly giving it some serious thought. "Even now, I don't really prefer cats over dogs."

I let out a scandalized gasp and clutched at imaginary pearls. "You heathen!" I accused, laughing when the hand that had been rubbing my bicep dropped to my waist and tickled me in retribution. "Stop!" I complained through giggles. "Your kid is on my bladder! I'll pee!"

That was not an idle threat. I'd had more than one close call in recent weeks. Ollie confirmed it was only going to get worse as I got bigger, too.

Rex stopped his tickle assault and smoothed his palm over the side of my belly. "Sorry, kitten."

I wondered if he could tell how much I loved the endearment. Fighting back a smile, I sighed and snuggled back into his chest again. "Are you apologizing for your pro-canine attitude, for tickling me, or for your kid making me uncomfortable?"

"Can it be for all three things?"

I laughed again. "Sure. Why not?"

As we lapsed into conversation again, I marveled at how easily we interacted. He was a veritable stranger, but I felt like I'd known him for years. The texts we'd been exchanging had helped with that, but it was more like we really were kindred spirits. Once we'd stopped and had a calm conversation after our not-exactly-brilliant reunion, our compatibility started to show up in little ways.

We both loved the outdoors and had both lost parents at a young age. We shared a sense of humor and, as we'd just discovered, liked the same types of TV shows. We both seemed to be spontaneous people, living life in a 'roll with the punches' kind of way, too.

Fundamentally, it also seemed like we were on the same page. Neither of us had factored kids into our life plans, but when it came down to it, we shared a vision for our son's upbringing.

I really was starting to believe Eric and Ollie's theories about compatible mates.

The oven timer buzzed, and Rex got up to dish up the heavenly-smelling dessert he had made. My mouth actually watered when he held my bowl out to me, and I dug into the decadent confection with gusto, moaning when the first bite of warm, sweet, gooey goodness lit up my taste buds.

Beside me, Rex shifted in his seat, crossing one long leg over the other while he appeared to concentrate on his own bowl.

The pudding was absolute perfection. There was a bitterness to the chocolate sauce which worked well against the sweetness of the ice cream, and the different textures made every bite a dream.

"This is so good," I mumbled around another mouthful, closing my eyes in my enjoyment. "Mmm. Please tell me there's more."

"I'm glad you like it," Rex replied, but his voice sounded a little strangled.

I opened my eyes and turned my head to find him watching

me intently, his own dessert untouched. The spoon was still in the bowl, lodged inside his melting ice-cream. Frowning, I asked, "Aren't you going to eat that?"

"Hmm?" He blinked at my question, then seemed to come out of whatever trance he'd been in, giving his head a little shake as he looked down at his bowl. "Oh. Yeah. Of course."

Raising an eyebrow at him, I asked if everything was alright. Rex looked sheepishly down at his dessert and nodded. "Yeah," he said, then looked back up at me with a rueful grin. "I was just distracted by the sounds you were making."

"Oh…" I felt myself blushing, understanding that *maybe* I'd sounded a little pornographic. I maintained it wasn't on me, though: it was the dessert's fault.

"Don't be embarrassed, kitten," Rex gave up the pretense of being at all interested in finishing the food he had made, placing his bowl carefully down on the floor at his side. He leaned over and placed his hand on my thigh, squeezing it gently. "I like that you're gettin' comfortable enough with me to relax and make those sounds. And I can't lie: I like that I'm responsible for you making them."

Courtesy of my ever-rampant hormones, I picked up on the arousal in his tone and my body ran with it. Suddenly, I wasn't craving the sweet, gooey chocolate anymore. Instead, I was craving him.

More specifically, I was craving his knot.

Shifting in my seat and praying that my slick wouldn't leave damp patches in my underwear, I swallowed roughly. Being perpetually horny was killing me.

Rex had been nothing but a gentleman over the previous few days, always taking his cues from me. He'd stuck to his word to take things slowly, given that our situation meant we couldn't afford to make things even more awkward between us. He hadn't given me any reason to think that he was only sticking around for the prospect of more sex.

And, really, I was the size of a house: I knew I wasn't the same catch I'd been the night we met. That had to mean he really did have other motivations, right?

When I thought about it, Rex had honestly been doing everything he could to prove that he was serious about sticking around.

Would it really be so bad to follow my urges at that point?

The other night, after he'd massaged my back and I had almost given in, he hadn't complained or called me a tease. Even though I'd felt a little guilty for going hot and cold on him, Rex had rolled with it, reassuring me that he only wanted to do what I was comfortable with.

Ever since I'd come to Shifters Sanctuary, I'd lamented that I'd never find an alpha who would treat me the way Beck treated Ollie…but was that really true? Because the more I interacted with Rex, the more I realized that he was every bit as sweet and honorable as Beck seemed to be. All I had to do was give him a chance.

My instincts told me that he was safe. That he wouldn't mistreat me or consider me his property. All I had to do was let him in.

My puma yowled inside me insistently, urging me to do just that. Even though I liked to think of my breed as a big cat, it was times like this where I understood why scientists classed mountain lions as the largest breed of small cat…because, boy, was my inner feline acting like a needy overgrown house cat!

Tired of fighting my instincts and my hormones, I decided to take a leap of faith.

"You know how you said you'd take things at my pace no matter what?" I asked, biting my lip as my heart rate sped up.

Rex nodded without hesitation, his blue eyes aimed directly at me. "I meant it. I apologize if I made you uncomfortable just now. I got ahead of myself and I—"

"Take me to bed?" Between the horniness I was constantly battling, and my omega urges to reconnect with my mate, the question tumbled out without tact or preamble. I blushed again, embarrassed by how desperate I'd sounded to my own ears, but I didn't apologize or retract the plea. Instead, I gave in to my instincts completely, begging, "Please, Rex?"

His Adam's apple bobbed. "God, kitten, you're such a sweet thing, aren't you? Askin' me so nicely…"

It was a far cry from that first night together, where we'd dragged each other into the ladies' bathroom, desperate to get our pants off. I still felt that same desperation burning under my skin; that same electric connection between us. I needed him, I realized. Not just inside me, but *with* me. The alpha to my omega. My mate.

"Please," I repeated softly, my pride warring with my biological drive. "Not…not to bond," it was hard to say, my puma yowling again at the denial of what he so badly wanted, "not yet. That—that would be too much. But…God, Rex, I'm *constantly* horny. I need…"

"Need what?" Rex asked, with a definite rasp in his voice. He inched closer on the couch, once again squeezing my thigh. It sent a thrill of want through me, and I almost whimpered as I felt my slick building. He spoke gently as he added, "You've gotta tell me, honey."

"I need you to fuck me." I'd wanted the instruction to come out firm and authoritative. Instead, it was almost a sob, whiny and anxious and raw. *"Please,* alpha?"

Addressing him like that seemed to unleash *something* in the air between us: an energy of some kind, not unlike the feeling I'd felt the first time I acknowledged Beck as Pack Alpha. This felt more intimate than that, though. Like my omega was finally acknowledging Rex was *my* alpha. My mate. Electric tingles traveled up and down my nerve endings, and it only seemed to make me more desperate to have Rex inside me.

Thankfully, he seemed to be just as affected. Before I knew it, I'd been swept up in his arms and carried the few steps over to the bed, where he gently set me down on top of the covers. When I protested about the abandoned dessert bowls, he assured me he'd clean them up later. Taking care of me and my needs was apparently more important.

Hearing that made my heart sing, even though I convinced myself that I wasn't going to rush things between us. We were newly dating, after all. Newly dating with a baby on the way, but still only newly dating. My heart didn't need to get too invested yet.

That was easier said than done, though, when Rex took his time getting me comfortable like he had the other evening, sliding a pillow under the bulge of my belly before he spooned up against my back, pressing sweet kisses to the back of my neck that made me shiver with need. My desperation to have him inside me only increased as his hand slid over my hip and under the hem of my shirt, rubbing over the stretched skin of my stomach.

"You're beautiful, you know," he murmured into my ear. "Tell me what you need, darlin'. I've got you."

That seemed to unleash the babble from somewhere deep down inside me as I ground my ass back against his growing bulge. "Rex...*Alpha*, please. I need your knot. I need you inside me. I need...I need...*Yesssss*." I actually sighed as his fingers slipped beneath the waistband of my pants to tease at my slick, desperate hole. "I'm so wet for you, Alpha."

His reply was a low moan of appreciation. "I can feel that." Two fingers slid inside me with ease, scissoring and stretching me in the most delicious ways. I arched my back, trying to encourage him to do more. "Easy, baby. Let me take care of you."

God, was he always so tender and sweet? He was going to ruin me for any other men if he kept that up.

I cried out a protest when he withdrew his fingers and removed his hand from inside my pants.

"Shh," he soothed, pressing a sweet kiss to the side of my head, "I can't get inside you while I'm still wearin' my jeans, can I?"

Ugh.

I was impatient and not in the mood for logic.

"Hurry..."

I reached into my own waistband to fist my cock while I listened to the metallic *tink* of his belt being undone, then the whir of it pulling through the denim loops. I panted as the mattress bounced with his movement behind me, soft thuds signaling his shoes and clothes hitting the floor somewhere near the foot of the bed.

"You still want this?" he asked gently, his fingertips hooking into the elastic at my hips. Never had I been so glad that I'd taken to wearing sweatpants more often than not.

I nodded fervently. "So, *so* badly."

"Okay. You can say stop at any time, alright?"

It was sweet that he was so concerned about my consent,

but I was too far gone to appreciate it. "Get inside me."

Rex shimmied my pants down, tossing them off the bed. Then he stretched himself along my back, the warmth of his chest searing through the cotton of my t-shirt while he lifted my leg and rested it over his muscular thigh. The blood-hot head of his cock nudged at my hole and I rocked my hips, encouraging him to stop teasing me and just get inside me.

I gasped when he finally did, closing my eyes and tilting my head back until it met with his shoulder.

I'd never had sex lying on my side before, but I wasn't the slim twink of six months earlier, either. I didn't think there were that many positions which would work for me anymore, not with my lack of flexibility and the bulge of my belly in play, and those things would only get worse before the pregnancy was over.

With the pillow supporting my bump, and my top leg resting on Rex's thigh, though, this position was surprisingly comfortable.

Rex slipped one arm under me, wrapping it around my chest. The other, which had been gripping my hip gently, slid down to stroke my weeping cock. I had to bite back a shout of ecstasy, muffling it and turning it into another needy whine as he set a gentle rhythm with his thrusts.

"Faster," I urged him, and found myself gripping his toned, tanned forearms with my own.

Rex growled in the back of his throat and tugged me tighter against him. "I don't want to hurt you."

"You won't," I assured him. "Please. *Please.* I need to be fucked properly. I need you to fill me up and knot me. I need you to—" I cut myself off, mildly mortified at the realization that I'd almost told him that I needed him to claim me. Mark me. *Make me his.* Clearing my throat and rocking my hips back to meet his languid thrusts, I said, "I need it harder, Alpha."

He groaned but complied, picking up the pace with his hips and his hand on my dick.

"Yes," I urged him on, "just like that. *Faster.*"

"Fuck," he muttered, snapping his hips into me, "I forgot how fucking amazing you feel on my cock, kitten. So hot and tight and wet."

My orgasm was building, and his dirty praise sent me hurtling closer to the precipice. He hiked my leg higher up his thigh, subtly changing up our angle and *holy mother of God!* I saw stars.

The coil of tension inside me was tightening, my balls sending up warning signals with every brush over my prostate. Precum dribbled obscenely from the head of my cock, slicking up every stroke of his big, calloused palm.

"I'm...I'm gonna come," I warned him. "Don't stop. *Right there.* Fuck me right there. Harder. Faster. Rex! Rex, I need...I need..."

The asshole stopped moving.

"What the ever-loving fuck?!" I complained, my eyes flying open so I could try to crane my neck and glower in consternation.

"Shhh," he crooned, *still* not moving. "I was gettin' too close."

"You're a fucking alpha," I hissed, trying to roll my hips and get myself off, but he pulled his hand off my cock to hold me in place. "You come, you knot me, you come again...and again...*and again.* That's how it works, remember?"

Okay, so we had only experienced it together once, but Ollie assured me that was an ongoing pattern for him and Beck.

Come to think of it, I probably knew way too much about

my new friends' sex life than could be considered healthy. But, as the only other people who had experienced alpha/omega mating dynamics, we'd been eager to compare notes.

Rex snorted and nuzzled his nose behind my ear. It was an affectionate gesture and I liked it. "I wanna make it good for you, kitten."

"I'll tell you a secret," I replied, feeling snarky and still determined to get off, "that will happen if you let me come."

"I've got a lot of making up to do," Rex said, and I wanted so badly to embrace the romance in that sentiment and just let my heart fall for him. However, I knew better than that. Once bitten —or not bitten, as the case may be— twice shy and all that jazz.

"You didn't do anything worth making up for," I replied instead, only for his hand to release my dick and sneak back under my shirt, smoothing over the bump housing my son. *Our son.*

"I could've reacted better to this," he admitted softly.

A lump lodged itself in my throat. "Sure," I agreed with a nod. "Or you could have reacted *way* worse, too. And, anyway, I thought we already talked about this."

"You let me get off too lightly the other night. Besides, you're going through a lot. I'm kind of responsible for it."

It was weird to be having the conversation with his cock inside me, but everything about our situation was weird so I went with it anyway. "I think we established that you're also going through a lot. At least I knew, theoretically speaking, that when an alpha knots an omega in heat, it generally results in pregnancy."

He was quiet for a moment. Then he asked, "In heat, huh?"

I flushed all over again at the gravel in his tone. It almost sounded as though the concept turned him on. Maybe it did. Maybe on some level, it appealed to the alpha side of him. I knew the omega in me was practically clawing the walls of my mind, badly wanting to be claimed and mated by his alpha. What if his alpha instincts were demanding as much of him?

"Yeah…that's, um, that's what Ollie and Eric think happened. I…I remember getting hot all over, needing you to fill me up and breed me." I bit my lip and let out a tiny huff of laughter. "At the time, I thought I was just super horny and having ridiculous omega thoughts."

"Hey now," I groaned as he moved to pull me tighter against him, the action shifting our hips, giving me a hint of the delicious friction I craved so badly, "don't go buyin' in to all that anti-omega stuff, y'hear? Your designation or whatever you wanna call it doesn't make you any less of a man, of a shifter…of a *person* than anyone else."

There went my heart again, thudding near-painfully in my chest. How could anyone *not* fall for a big, buff, sexy man who made impassioned impromptu speeches about self-worth like that?

"Jesus," I breathed, feeling choked up. I didn't know if it was my hormones, or the alpha/omega mating connection that seemed to draw us together, but I was once again overwhelmed by what felt like an insatiable need for him. I bucked my hips. "Fuck me. *Now.*"

Whatever restraint had been holding him back seemed to dissolve. He pulled out until the tip of his cock was teasing my entrance and then slammed back into me when I whined my complaint.

"Yes!" I cried out, not caring who heard. "God, yes, more!"

Rex's hand slid back up to my hip, fingers digging into my

flesh to give himself a bit more leverage with each slam of his hips. I gripped my own dick in my hand and stroked in time with each of his powerful thrusts, once again feeling my balls drawing up. My belly tightened, too, as my impending release built quickly. The intensity of the pleasure I felt as Rex's cock repeatedly nudged my prostate was almost too much to bear. I was a gasping, writhing, babbling mess before the fireworks exploded behind my closed eyelids and I coated my own hand in warm wetness. I wiped it on the sheets.

A low, growly 'Fuck' was the only warning I got before Rex's hips stuttered and warmth flooded my insides. At the same time, his lips found the crook of my neck.

Then, with his knot beginning to swell, I felt the graze of his teeth on my skin and my eyes flew open.

"Don't even *think* about it," I hissed, and I felt him jolt in surprise.

"Shit," he cursed, panting through his ongoing orgasm, his long fingers still flexing at my hip. "Damon. Fuck, I wasn't thinkin'. It…I just felt this…this…instinct…"

My heart was pounding rapidly, from the intense pleasure I'd experienced and the fear that this near-stranger had almost given me a mating bite.

Would it even have worked if I didn't bite him back? There was so little information out there about the whole mating and bonding process that I wasn't sure whether Ollie and Beck's experience was textbook or not. Either way, I didn't want to be bonded. At least, not when I didn't really know Rex.

"I'm so sorry," he continued when I didn't reply. "I wasn't thinking."

"It's okay. Nothing happened."

"*Nothing…?* Kitten, I almost bit you. That's a lifetime of

commitment."

"I mean," I couldn't help but laugh, enjoying Rex's hiss as my body's jiggling teased his sensitive knot, "we're having a kid together, so that ship has already sailed."

Chapter Ten — Rex

Damon wasn't wrong, but I still couldn't believe what I had almost done. I felt like I had let us both down. I promised him that we'd go at his pace and then *bam!* One orgasm later and I had handed my brain over to my alpha side.

Great work, Rex.

It was like I kept taking one step forward and three steps backwards when it came to building a relationship with Damon. Even though I was older, I felt like I was a naïve teenager learning how to date for the first time.

Admittedly, I hadn't ever really had a relationship last more than a couple of weeks, but I wasn't some dumb kid. I was in my forties, for fuck's sake.

That just made my impulsive behavior feel worse. Surely, at forty-two, I should have been able to control myself better than I had.

"Stop beating yourself up back there," Damon chided. "I can practically hear you thinking."

I snorted, trying not to jostle us any more than necessary. Being locked inside him felt good, but the additional stimulation to my knot was starting to border on painful. Slowly, I stroked my hand over his hip and then slipped it back under his shirt, gently resting my palm on the curve of his belly. I could feel the light thumping of our son's little limbs against the walls of his fleshy cell. It was still wholly bizarre to feel, but instead of freaking out, it made me smile.

"I just wanna do right by you," I said after I gathered my thoughts enough to explain them. "We both know bonding right now would be a dumb idea, but I still—"

"I'm just going to go ahead and blame our biological imperative for that," he said, and it didn't sound as though he was angry with me. "My omega is whining at me to bare my neck and demand that you claim me, too."

"But you had the wherewithal to stop me. I—"

"You are still learning how to manage your shifter instincts." He paused, then softened his tone. "Nothing happened. We're okay. I'm not going to kick you out of bed and my apartment as soon as your knot deflates."

"I still wouldn't blame you if you did."

He was quiet for a moment before he said, "And that's how I know you're a good man, Rex."

Even though the shifter side of me was sulking at not having gotten its way, it preened at the words of praise, and I felt relieved that I hadn't undone all the progress I had made with Damon to that point.

"I feel like I hit the jackpot with you, kitten."

He laughed, and I groaned at the movement, trying to enjoy the pleasure/pain as it rolled over me. "Let's see if you're still saying that when I'm even bigger and moodier."

* * *

After the success of our first date, I made an effort to take Damon out again and again, sticking true to my word of changing plans whenever necessary. I also further solidified my place in Shifters Sanctuary, getting a job at a nearby farm.

The family who owned the farm were apparently fox shifters. Sam and Becca were a beta couple with their omega son, Tim, and they were wary of me at first, only giving me a chance because Beck asked them to. However, by the end of my second full day of work, they'd all but adopted me as an honorary member of their family.

It was nice, and I'll admit I got a little choked up when I realized that I actually felt like I belonged. I might have been a cat —and a cat who couldn't actually shift yet at that— but I was still a shifter like them. In their world, being attracted to other men was considered totally normal. I wasn't disappointing them, or any other kind of bigoted nonsense. If anything, they became invested in my budding relationship, and were insanely excited about the baby I'd be having in only a few short months.

For the first time in a long time, I felt good about where my life seemed to be heading.

I even spoke to Eric about buying one of the cottages he owned on the edge of the town's limits. Sitting vacant, it was old and a little dilapidated, but it had character and with a bit of hard work and spit-shine, it would make the perfect home for a little family like the one I hoped to make with Damon and our son.

And by the time Christmas Eve was upon us, I was barely panicked about the prospect of being a father. Watching Beck with his little ones had helped with that. They were cute little things, and he seemed to genuinely enjoy them. It gave me hope that I would feel the same way about my own. I even felt more confident about taking care of my kid, having practiced changing diapers and bottle-feeding Beck's pair on a couple of occasions. I figured, if I could muck out a stable, I could change a diaper. I'd been half right. But, with practice, I'd eventually proven I could do the latter just as proficiently as the former. Ollie had even joked that I did a better job than his mate, much to Beck's bemusement.

Secretly, I thought Ollie was looking forward to redeeming himself with Beck later.

Damon and I spent Christmas Eve together in his apartment. I cooked him a meal based on his latest cravings (creamy pasta with extra bacon) and we snuggled together on his couch watching Christmas movies. I would have happily spent the next couple of days doing the same thing, but he had agreed on my behalf to join him and most of the town at Ollie and Beck's house for the first annual 'Shifters Sanctuary Holidays For Strays' event.

Yeah, apparently Oliver was insane for Christmas and wouldn't let anyone spend the holidays alone. Even though I would have happily spent the holidays with only Damon, I thought it was a sweet gesture on Ollie's part, as well as a smart one. The town was a pack, after all, and I was beginning to understand the nuanced differences between being friendly neighbors and being pack.

Being pack felt like being part of a family, but it also felt like more than that. It was hard to explain why, especially when Shifters Sanctuary's shifters were so eclectic.

Damon had been teaching me how to scent, and it had blown

my mind to realize that the town contained shifters of such varied breeds and backgrounds. Hedgehogs, wolves, tortoises, dragons, rabbits, foxes…hell, there were even a couple of giraffes, which I thought was kind of hilarious. I figured they were able to blend in with the same ease as Brandt, Eric, and Sage (that was to say: none at all).

But, for all their physiological differences, the townspeople cared deeply about each other, even if they didn't always see eye to eye.

Having lived among them for the better part of a month, I was beginning to care, too.

* * *

"I've gotta give it to Ollie," I said, yawning and stretching in my chair, resting my wrist on Damon's shoulder, "this shindig was a great idea."

Under the two marquees they had set up on their property, Ollie and Beck were holding court at the other table, which ran parallel to the one we were seated at. I didn't think I'd seen Rory or Duke set down even once in the playpen that had been set aside for them. Instead, the babies had been passed around what felt like every member of the town, not that either of them seemed at all fazed.

The food had been wonderful, and as we had sat and talked with our tablemates, I'd once again felt that deeper-than-family connection.

Pack, the voice inside me —the one I associated with my inner alpha— said, sounding content, *mine*.

I'd never felt anything like this feeling before. Not really. My adoptive family had been kind and affectionate until I'd hit my teens and my 'proclivities', as my dad had called them, became obvious. But even then, I hadn't felt like I'd belonged. I supposed that maybe some part of me had always known I was different. Not just because I'd been adopted, or because I'd been a boy who liked boys, but because that alpha instinct was always there, simmering just out of my consciousness.

"Mmm," Damon echoed my yawn and leaned into me, resting his head on my shoulder. I slipped my hand down to his bicep and shuffled closer on my chair, soaking in his uninhibited public display of affection. No matter how innocent the gesture, it made my instincts sing. Something inside of me practically purred with satisfaction. "I ate too much," he grumbled, oblivious to the victory dance I was having in my soul. "Now I'm sleepy."

His hand rested over his baby bump and I wondered if our son was also tired after the feast, or if the giant servings of dessert Damon had eaten were going to give the kid a sugar buzz. I knew that drinking cold orange juice made the little thing bounce around like crazy inside his daddy, so maybe all the pudding and pie would, too.

Unable to help myself, I kissed the top of Damon's head. "Sleep, kitten. I've got you."

"You don't wanna come shift with us?" Royce, a teenaged bear shifter asked from beside me. He was all gangly limbs and pimpled cheeks — awkward and stuck in that phase between boyhood and adulthood. He had a sweet smile and had latched on to me from the moment he and his mom introduced themselves.

I'd never really felt empathy towards kids before, and I wondered if the soft emotions I felt when this random kid grinned up at me were my alpha's way of prepping me for fatherhood.

Setting those thoughts aside, I blushed, grateful for the dimming light as dusk turned to night, and I shook my head. "Nah, I'm beat. Ate so much, I think I'd turn into a pie rather than a puma."

Royce rolled his eyes while the other people around us laughed.

Truth be told, I still hadn't managed to shift. Beck assured me that it would happen when I was ready for it, but I honestly *felt* ready. I was settling into the pack. I wasn't panicked about becoming a father. I wanted to be with Damon in every way possible, including our animal forms. I was ready.

Except something inside me wouldn't budge.

It wasn't my inner alpha; I knew that much. He was just as desperate to shift as I was. Maybe even more so. But if I had come to terms with it, and my inner puma had come to terms with it, what was holding me back?

Eric, Ollie, and Brandt had various theories, too, of course. It kept coming back to the mating bond. After all, Beck hadn't tried to shift until after he and Ollie were bonded, so the scientifically-minded members of the pack seemed convinced that the bond must play a part in why I still couldn't shift. Eric even theorized that, even though I scented like a puma, it might take bonding to cement my 'breed' of shifter, as he called it.

With no other alphas —bonded or otherwise— to test the theory, it seemed to make as much sense as any other, even if Beck wasn't convinced that was what was preventing my shift.

"Plus, someone's gotta help me mind Duke and Rory while Ollie and Beck run with the pack," Damon said, making additional excuses for me. He offered me an apologetic grimace. "Sorry: I volunteered us without asking you."

"Making sure your alpha gets more practice before your little one arrives?" one of the women a few seats down laughed with amusement at her own joke. I hadn't met her before, and even though I knew she meant no harm, I bristled at the old 'men are bad with babies' stereotype.

I mean, yeah, okay: I hadn't been great with them before spending time with Beck's kids, but she didn't know that.

"Actually, it's me," Damon told her, and I wondered if I was projecting or if that was a slight edge to his tone. "I'm the one who needs a bit more practice. I'm not the most affectionate type, y'know?" He chuckled and it sounded rueful, but he snuggled in closer to me, the action belying his words. "Plus, Rex has become a pro at changing diapers and calming a cranky baby. Ollie says he's now at the top of their 'Emergency Babysitter' list, right after Sandy, and Lena and Brandi, of course." I delighted in the pride I heard in his voice. For all he said he wasn't affectionate, he had his own love language.

Momentarily, I flashed back to the first time I had seen him. He'd been beautiful, with his long, dark hair tied back at the nape of his neck, telling some sleazy guy that he didn't speak English.

The memory made me smile. His sass and snark had called to me like a beacon.

Whatever language he was speaking now, I was picking up on what he might really mean. Even with his walls up, I understood him. But until he was comfortable letting me in for real, I'd give him time to work it out for himself. English or not, his love languages were enough for now.

Not wanting to focus on the concept of 'love languages' for

too long, I reacted with amusement, "Not Eric?"

Damon snickered. "Eric's a great doctor, but outside of checkups or fixing boo-boos, that man is awkward AF with kids. It's funny." His expression turned thoughtful. "Brandt, on the other hand, is kind of a natural. That surprised me. He looks so gruff and serious, y'know? But Lance Baker brought his triplets into the clinic the other day —they're five, by the way— and Brandt turned into a big kid himself. It was really sweet."

Some immature part of me felt jealous at hearing that. I knew that Damon and Brandt were becoming good friends, but I also knew that Damon had a thing for older men, and Brandt was capital H hot. Omega or not, that dragon was everything Damon seemed to be interested in when it came to other men, and I wanted him to say that *I* was sweet.

I knew that was mostly my instincts flaring up and interfering with my rational thought, but it didn't make it any easier to push the thoughts aside.

Reminding myself that being a possessive, jealous dick about a man Damon was friends with would *not* win me any points, I forced a smile and went back to thinking about how he showed affection without saying the words. He didn't act like that with anyone else, only with me. That meant something.

"Looks can be deceiving," I agreed. Then I blinked and processed the rest of what he'd said. "Did you say triplets?"

"Multiples aren't uncommon with some shifter sub-species," Damon shrugged as though that wasn't a huge deal. "The Bakers are rabbits. It's particularly common to have twins and triplets in rabbit families."

My gaze drifted over to the side of the marquee, where Sandy had one of Beck and Ollie's kids propped on her hip, and Ollie was burping the other on his shoulder.

"I guess it's not that uncommon for wolves, either," Damon added, following my line of sight.

I swallowed roughly and looked pointedly down at his belly. He laughed and patted it. "I promise there's only one in there," he assured me. My elevated heart rate was just calming down as he added, "Mountain lion shifters aren't known for having multiples quite as often as some of the other sub-species, but it's not unheard of. It's the horses, cattle, giraffes…all the larger mammals, really…who generally only ever have one at a time."

"What about the dragons?" I asked, playfully wondering, "Do they lay eggs?"

His expression fell, causing my heart to sink with it. "There hasn't been a dragon alpha in hundreds of years."

Frowning, I tried to work that out. "Well, no, but betas—"

"They're a male-only species," Royce piped up at my side, and I jumped a little in my seat, having forgotten we weren't alone. He cheerfully continued, "So they've only got omegas left, which means they can't have any babies."

"Keep your voice down," his mom admonished him, leaning over her still half-full plate with her cutlery poised in her hands. "I don't think the Weldmans like to think on that a whole lot, and we shouldn't be bringing it up at Christmas. We're s'posed to be talking about happy things."

"Except…" I mused aloud, thoroughly confused, "if the last alpha died hundreds of years ago…" I turned around, craning my neck to try and catch sight of any of the three dragons who had made Shifters Sanctuary their home. My gaze landed on Eric, who looked my own age, and I frowned again. "How do they exist?"

"They're older than they look," Damon nudged me with his

shoulder. "Like…by a few hundred years."

Well damn.

"I'd hate that," I said out loud before my brain could engage the filter between my thoughts and my mouth. "Think of all the friends you'd watch age and pass away…" I shuddered and shook my head. "I'll stick with a normal lifespan, thanks."

Damon blinked at me with wide, horrified eyes. "After Carole *just* said 'don't bring down Christmas', *that's* what you come out with?"

"I didn't mean to!"

At my other side, Royce erupted into a fit of giggles, the traitor.

"Seriously," I scrambled to regain whatever ground I'd lost, "I'm sorry. My big mouth gets ahead of me."

Thankfully, Damon snorted and he nodded. "I know. I haven't exactly forgotten our reunion, remember?"

"So," I grabbed for my plastic cup of water and raised it in a toast, "Merry Christmas!"

* * *

"Jesus H Christ," one of the old bear shifters, Mortimer Drake, growled and glared down at his phone, disturbing the relaxed ambiance of the party.

Night had well and truly fallen, but the dragon-lit bonfires around the marquees were generating enough warmth to keep us all comfortable. Many of the families with young ones had either taken the kids up into Ollie and Beck's house to nap in what I was affectionately calling 'puppy piles', and us grownups had lapsed into long stretches of companionable silence, sated by too much rich food and maybe a little bit too much alcohol for some, too. Chatter had dimmed to low, warm murmurs, and it felt kind of like my very earliest memories with my mama before she'd died.

Well it had, until Mortimer's loud complaint broke the contented air around us.

"Morty," his wife whined at his side, "you're being loud again."

Heads swiveled in their direction, most people wearing amused smirks at their antics. Smirks fell as he held up his phone with a scowl. "Morstein's issued a goddamned call to arms," he groused, and I noticed Beck and Ollie sit up a little bit straighter in their seats.

As the party had dwindled, we'd all moved to one table, and I had been enjoying getting to know even more members of the town. Now I was glad that we were all together because I was able to watch Beckett's reaction to Mortimer's announcement.

"What?" Beck gestured for the phone. "Explain."

I leaned towards Damon, whispering, "Wasn't Morstein that preacher guy? From the cult church?"

"The one that tried to have Beck kidnapped, yeah," Damon nodded, his eyes also glued on Beckett. "He basically controls most of the old-school packs. I'm pretty sure he gets, like, fifty percent of the monthly tithes or something. He's always creeped me out."

I nodded in understanding. I might have grown up human, but even we had our share of evangelical religions and whatnot, particularly down in the Bible belt. Not to mention my long-held personal belief that far too many wars were waged in the name of religion: though it was obvious that social power and money were the real driving forces.

Wasn't there a saying about absolute power corrupting

people absolutely?

Beckett paled as he read whatever it was Morstein had posted online. "Is this guy for real?" he asked, sounding disgusted as he passed the device to his fiance. "Wasn't Moonmusic supposed to be a church? Preaching peace and love and good will to all mankind, especially at Christmas?"

Ollie scoffed and pointed at the screen. "Not when we're clearly *such* a danger to the shifter way of life." He seemed to be paraphrasing the text in front of him. "More like he doesn't want any of the old-school packs getting any ideas about getting out from under his thumb. Our numbers are already growing: that means less tithes headed his way, not to mention a drop in free labor."

"Plus the status of an alpha outranks him, and news is bound to get out that we've got *two* alphas now." Mortimer muttered, accepting his phone back. "Not that Ethel and I have ever cared 'bout status. Came out here for a better life for James, didn't we? Just 'cause he wasn't beta didn't mean he should be treated with any less respect than us. Saved us a pretty penny in tithes, too."

It was a story similar to most of the people living in Shifters Sanctuary, and I could understand why Morstein and his 'church' would loathe the loss of more and more shifters.

"How many people do you really think are going to buy into his lunacy?" Tim, Sam and Becca's son, asked, looking to his parents for reassurance. They'd raised him in Shifters Sanctuary since he was only a couple of months old, because they hadn't wanted to subject him to the kind of life many other omegas suffered. "I mean, with a lot of that older generation, uh," he cringed as he looked over at Mortimer.

"Dying out. You can say it," Ethel waved him off dismissively.

"Yeah, well, with a lot of the older generation dying out, surely less and less people are quite as…zealous." Tim finished his thought. "Like, aren't the younger generations more likely to use critical thinking skills or whatever?"

"If they've been raised with the ability to think for themselves, sure," Damon offered, shrugging. "My pack back in New Mexico made most of our folk homeschool, and only the basics. Critical thinking skills were discouraged. They don't want you to know just how unfair their treatment is."

"Mine were the same back in Virginia," Ollie agreed with a nod. I noticed that he had picked up one of the paper napkins and was twisting it between his fingers. "I applied for every scholarship and grant to get into a college —any college— just to escape it."

"Me too," Damon sighed. "So, yeah, sure…there are a lot of younger omegas looking to escape from the oppression of their packs, but why would the majority of betas in these packs want that? When they get us to do most of their hard labor for free, or toss us into what they see as the most menial roles in their packs and take our tithes out of what minimal wages they allow us to earn…why would they want that to change?"

Beck cleared his throat, and pointed at Mortimer's phone. "Regardless, that diatribe Morstein posted means we're going to have to get a bit more vigilant. I'm not expecting them to attack the town or anything, but they'll probably start sending people to scope us out, find out our weaknesses and whatnot. I'll get the council together tomorrow and we'll organize a neighborhood watch." He rubbed Ollie's back and looked across the table to meet my gaze. "I don't want to freak people out to the point where we all stop going about our daily lives, but we can't dismiss Morstein's ramblings as harmless, either."

I turned to look at Damon as the reality of what Beck wasn't saying out loud hit me.

Despite us not being bonded, my pregnant omega was a target.

Suddenly, I had even more reason to be glad for the Shifters Sanctuary pack. Together, we'd keep Damon safe. We'd keep all the vulnerable people here safe.

Chapter Eleven – Damon

Rex drove me home after the Christmas party became subdued, and it didn't take a rocket scientist to see that his protective instincts were in overdrive. From his eyes darting towards every shadow that moved, to the possessive hand on my back as we walked from the truck to the apartment building, the tension was vibrating within him.

"We're okay," I assured him as he led me into my apartment, even as he turned to lock the door and draw the chain across as well. I placed my hand on his bicep. "Rex, we're not in danger right now."

He spun around to face me so abruptly that I stumbled back a few steps. The expression on his face was the most serious I'd ever seen there. "I don't think you understand what I'm feelin' right now," he said, and I could tell he was choosing his words and tone carefully. He rubbed at his chest. "Just the thought of somethin' happening to you —to our son— because of what I am…" Pausing, he shook his head and took a steadying breath. "We're takin' things at your pace, Damon, but that doesn't change the way I care about you."

I swallowed convulsively, turned on by the steel in his voice. The timing was inappropriate, considering what we were discussing, but damn I did love an older man who could take charge of me…when I allowed it, of course.

"I care about you, too," I admitted, a little afraid to reveal that much. But, honestly, if he hadn't worked it out over the past couple of weeks of us dating, then he was an idiot. "And if those cult people come for you like they came for Beck…" I shuddered.

From what I knew of Ollie and Beck's story, I knew I wouldn't cope if the Moonmusic people got their hands on Rex. He couldn't even shift yet!

"We're gonna keep each other safe, kitten." Rex's answer was everything I needed to hear. I hadn't even realized how tense I was until his firm assurance washed over me.

And, man, it was so stupidly hot that he included me in the equation. It wasn't just the big, macho alpha protecting his helpless pregnant partner. It was that he saw us as equals in this mess, looking out for each other.

I squirmed in place, feeling myself slick up some more.

"You okay, darlin'?" His piercing blue gaze swept over me. Even though we were in the safety of my room, it was obvious that he was still on edge, determined to fight off even an invisible foe.

I smothered a snicker of amusement. The only foe here was my hormone imbalance.

But, fuck, his sudden confidence and possessive vibes were really doing it for me.

"I'm good," the words came out a bit breathy and I squirmed again as he raised an eyebrow in silent question. "Just…

finding this whole..." I waved my hand over his form —back straightened, shoulders broad, expression stony— and sighed, "*alpha vibe* super attractive right now."

Rex's eyes shone with understanding and then turned darker with lust. His voice dipped lower, "That your way of tellin' me you need me right now, kitten?"

It was like we'd been transported back to the night we met. He was confident and assertive back then, too. It was like he had instinctively known which buttons to press and when to back off.

"Fuck yes."

All thoughts and talk about the threat from Morstein and his people ceased to exist and Rex dropped his lips to mine, kissing me hungrily. It was exactly what I needed. Sure, I loved it when he was soft and gentle, too, treating me with a respect and patience that nobody else ever had. But I also needed this side of him: unbridled, dominating, wild.

We moved the short distance to the couch, shedding our clothes with abandon along the way. At first I assumed Rex was going to bend me over the armrest, but he sat down and turned me to face the tv, nudging my legs apart.

"Gonna make sure you're ready for me, darlin'," he said, then gently bent me forward, holding me steady with one big hand while the other parted my cheeks.

I could see us in the reflection of the blackened tv screen, and worked out Rex's intentions only moments before I felt the first burst of his warm, moist breath over my dripping hole.

"So slick for me," he murmured appreciatively, before bringing the flat of his tongue to my rim.

I can't even describe the sound I made, but if Rex hadn't

been holding me in place, I would have fallen forward.

He licked at me with long, firm laps of his tongue until I was almost sobbing, and then he changed tactics and speared the talented muscle inside me, making me cry out in ecstasy. "Fuck, Rex, *more!*"

My hands scrabbled back to grip at his where they were holding my hips, and I rocked back and forth on his tongue, fucking myself on it over and over again to the sounds of his appreciative moans. My dick was hard and leaking, begging for attention, and I knew that I must be practically drowning Rex with my slick. But, the more aroused I got, the more intense the thrusts of his tongue became, and I could only assume he was enjoying himself just as much as I was.

Then, just as I was on the precipice of orgasm, he pulled back. I whined, "*Nooo,*" pushing backwards in his hold.

Rex chuckled. He flexed his fingers on my hips and kissed my ass cheeks teasingly. "Need more, baby?"

"You know I do."

I was pouting and he leaned to the side to grin at me in the reflection of the TV screen. "I've got you, kitten, I promise."

Before I could come up with a sassy retort, he pulled me down onto his lap, keeping his legs spread enough to keep me stable. I could feel the sticky head of his cock at the small of my back, but then in a smooth move I could only attribute to enhanced reflexes, Rex guided me up again, removed a hand from my hip to position his cock under me, and then helped me to sink back down onto him.

We let out matching groans of relief at the sensation of him finally filling me up.

Now that he was inside me, I half expected him to return to being slow and gentle, but I was glad to be proven wrong.

Though he was obviously still mindful of my condition, Rex helped me bounce in his lap at a fervent pace, his desperation seeming to match my own.

"You're so tight, kitten," he muttered into my shoulder, where he was sucking hickies and nibbling at the skin as we moved together.

I wasn't afraid that he would bite me anymore. In fact, some part of me half-hoped that he would claim me after all. Sure, when the lust faded I might regret thinking it, but in that moment, I wanted him to dominate me. I wanted him to make me his. He'd already bred me; a claim was the next logical step between an alpha and an omega.

But he didn't go anywhere near the juncture between my shoulder and neck, just continued to lavish attention on what parts of my back he could reach with his mouth, interspersing the wet kisses and suction marks with filthy praise. "Your slick tasted so good, baby, but it's somethin' else when it's spilling around my cock...*Yeah*, just like that."

I was lost to him, whimpering and begging, feeling heated all over in a way that reminded me of the night we'd met. I was insatiable and dripping for him, and the wet slapping, squelching sounds our bodies were making as I bounced on his cock were obscene.

I loved every moment of it.

"Nnngh," I moaned as one of his hands finally slid around to grip my neglected dick while I continued to ride him, "R-rex..."

"I'm gettin' close, baby," his voice was gravelly and strained. "Gonna need you to come for me. Can you do that? Can you come for your alpha?"

"Fuck!" I shouted, my back arching of its own volition as

his words took me over the edge. I came hard, still bouncing on his cock. I clenched around him in waves of additional pleasure as I felt his knot swelling as he filled me up with his own release.

"God, Damon, you feel so…*ugh*…fucking incredible…"

Slumping bonelessly back against him, I had no idea how he had retained the power to speak through all of that. His cock twitched inside me again, his knot reacting to my movements.

"Still not used to—" he moaned and his cock jerked once more when I snuggled as best I could against his chest "—*that*."

"Mmm," I acknowledged, feeling the soporific effects of the orgasm, combined with the huge meal I'd eaten earlier, taking over.

There was a subtle irony to our position at that moment being almost a direct echo of the first time he knotted me. I couldn't help but mentally catalogue the similarities and differences. I could feel things changing for me emotionally and mentally just by comparing the two situations.

I'd needed this from him.

The question was, now that I'd gotten it, what was I going to do about it?

* * *

New Years Eve was a quiet affair. Some of the townspeople planned on small fireworks displays, but I declined any invitations to attend. With how easily tired I was, I didn't think I'd make it to midnight. Even though I encouraged Rex to go and celebrate, he insisted that all he wanted to do was hang out with me.

Ever since Christmas, he had become more protective, and

I wasn't sure if it was because of the threatening words the Moonmusic leader had posted online, or if it was just because we'd gotten closer.

To be honest, we were pretty much spending any free time we had together by then. Despite my initial resolve, I could feel myself falling harder and harder for him every day.

How could I not when he was so attentive and thoughtful?

He was working hard at Sam and Becca's farm, then taking me on dates and making sure I wanted for nothing in his down time. Somewhere in the middle of all that, he was also trying to buy a property from Eric, and was arranging help from some of the townspeople to help him fix it up enough to make it properly livable. He had to be running himself into the ground, but he did it all with a smile on his face…and damned if I didn't think that was the hottest thing ever.

Not that I liked the idea of him exhausting himself, mind you. But my omega preened at his unspoken attempt to court me. To prove that he was a worthy mate.

I was beginning to believe that he was.

It was a belief that only seemed to cement itself further when we were snuggled up on my couch on New Year's Eve, streaming an old season of *Kitchen Nightmares* and bantering about the drama.

With his nose screwed up watching Gordon Ramsay yelling and swearing at a guy who was convinced his menu was epic, Rex mused, "Y'know, I'm now wonderin' if any of these people he's yelled at were shifters."

Even though the show was no longer on the air, and I had seen all the reruns, I snorted. "Could you imagine a bear or something losing their cool?"

"That would make for some gruesome viewing," he shuddered. "I'll stick to laughing at his creative insults."

I don't know why, but that was the moment something seemed to click for me.

Maybe it was his patience. Maybe it was his lack of expectations. Maybe his empathy. Maybe just the fact that we could have a silly conversation about an old TV show without having to talk through justifications of our opinions.

Whatever it was, I was a goner for him.

But that thought was a double-edged sword, because he was so warm and sweet, and I was…not. I kept my cards close to my chest. I was prickly and moody. I was so terrified of giving anyone control over my heart —of letting them hurt me— that I'd built a wall of snark and sass around myself.

Rex could do so much better than me.

And yet I was selfish and I had fallen hard for him.

When I started yawning, Rex clicked the little red power button on the remote and then helped me off the couch. I waddled into the bathroom to pee for the twelfth time since we'd first sat down, and after washing my hands and brushing my teeth, Rex switched out with me.

"I wish the bathroom was bigger," I grumbled, passing him the toothbrush that now had a permanent spot next to mine in the cup next to the sink.

Rex hesitated before he said, "The one in my cottage will be."

We hadn't really discussed the future beyond agreeing that he'd set up his second bedroom as a room for our son — an acknowledgment that he'd be sharing custody more than anything else. But there was a weight to his words now that I heard loud and clear. He wanted me sharing his bathroom. He wanted me sharing his home.

Deep down, I wanted that, too.

I couldn't deny that, as things stood, Rex had all but moved in with me. Even though he didn't always spend the night, he would come over after work to either take me out for a date or, if I was too tired, he'd spoil and pamper me in my apartment. He would even cuddle me to sleep on the nights we didn't have sex, and then he'd let himself out.

I was getting used to his constant presence. Relying on it, even.

I liked it. A lot. And so did my puma.

Having his scent permeating my home was comforting in ways I couldn't quite explain. Waking up without him was easier to bear when I could scent him in my sheets or on the couch. Ollie told me that those feelings would only intensify after I gave birth, because there would be some primal need to have my mate protecting our cub at my side.

However, even for all of that, we hadn't even been dating for a full month. Things had obviously been accelerated courtesy of the baby in my belly, but I'd only really just started to enjoy my independence from my old pack once I got to Shifters Sanctuary, with the preceding months spent full of anxious energy as I tried to make my way here.

Even if ninety-nine percent of me screamed "Yes!" to the idea of moving in with Rex, there was still that tiny sliver of doubt telling me I needed to slow my roll.

A baby did not mean we had to live together, no matter how convenient having someone to share the load with seemed. Even if my puma demanded that I nest with my alpha, my human brain said it was too soon. Or maybe that was my fear talking.

Rex held his hands up in the universal sign of surrender and offered me an easy, lopsided grin. He also gave me the out I was looking for, saying, "Just for those nights you come to my place, I mean. Once it's properly livable, we can alternate runnin' up the utility bills between both our homes."

He didn't seem hurt or disappointed that I'd quite obviously hesitated over his real meaning, and I kicked myself for worrying that he might. Over and over, he assured me that he would take things at whatever pace I needed, and yet I always got all up in my head about how to let him down gently.

I knew that was a carryover from the way I'd been raised, but I still hated that I did it. I trusted Rex. I had fallen for Rex. I wanted him to know those things. I didn't want him to think he needed to always walk on eggshells around me.

I wanted to give him a reason to stay with me. Not with our kid, but with *me*.

Meeting him halfway, I bit my lip and replied, "It will be nice to not feel like I'm sleeping in the living room and kitchen every so often."

My studio apartment had its pros and cons, after all. I liked it because it was the first place that had ever been my own space, not governed by anyone else, but it was tiny, and I knew it wouldn't work in the long run. Not once the baby got too big for his bassinet. But those were future problems.

"Less convenient for midnight snacking, though," he said thoughtfully, but then he shrugged and added, "but I'll be happy to walk down the hallway and get snacks for you anyway."

And there went my heart again, beating rapidly inside my chest.

I was *such* a goner for him.

* * *

"So…" Ollie's tone was suggestive as he sat on the edge of my desk in Eric and Brandt's clinic. He waggled his eyebrows and leaned forward for privacy, though there weren't any people in the waiting room at that moment, not that it would have made a difference with shifter hearing anyway, "tell me: how's Rex with rope? Inquiring minds want to know."

I blinked at him from where I was trying to make sense of the note Brandt had left for me. Did that say Mrs. Peterson wanted an appointment for Thursday? Or was it his lunch order? Pepperoni on rye, maybe?

"Huh?" I asked, bewildered as my brain tried to process far too many conflicting concepts. "Ropes? Why?"

"I mean, he's an honest-to-God cowboy," Ollie answered, as if that explained anything. "Please tell me his roping skills carry over to the bedroom."

It was a testament to how exhausted I was that I hadn't explored this theory already. I had actually thought about it once or twice, but I'd never brought it up with Rex. Not even after I'd mused about how much I'd enjoyed him taking charge and being more dominant.

However, despite my near-constant fatigue and aching back, my cock perked up at the flood of images suddenly whooshing through my brain, encouraged by my friend voicing those same previously glossed-over fantasies.

I shifted in my seat and swallowed. "We, uh, we haven't really gotten kinky yet."

Ollie looked horrified, dramatically clutching non-existent pearls as he gasped, "That's a crime, Day. An actual crime."

I pointed at the basketball I appeared to be smuggling under my sweater. "Do you remember being like this?"

"Yeah," Ollie shrugged, "and I was horny all the time. Like… *all* the time. I needed Beck's knot practically lodged in me permanently."

It was strange to think that we'd only known each other a month, considering how candid we were with each other. But being the only two omegas to turn up pregnant in a few hundred years made for a unique bonding experience, I supposed, and I'd never exactly been prudish.

I nodded. "Yeah, I can relate to that. But I'm also the size of a house and I can't lie on my front…" Letting out a huge sigh, I lifted my hands at my sides in a 'what can you do?' kind of gesture. "What's he gonna do? Hog tie me sideways?"

Even though I was joking, I did feel another thrill of pure arousal shoot through my veins at the idea of being tied up and completely at Rex's mercy.

"Or break out the shibari patterns? Get on your knees on the mattress and experiment. Build up a wall of pillows to support the bump if you have to. Oh!" Ollie whipped out his phone and tapped at the screen with a manic energy before he let out a quiet "ah ha!" and then turned the device to face me.

Staring at the picture on the screen, it took me a moment to work out what I was looking at. It was like one of those inflatable pool loungers, quite thick, with a large hole in the middle, a rectangular hole just above that, and then another face-sized hole near the top of the device.

"You stick your belly in the hole," Ollie said with excitement, as though I hadn't just cottoned on to his idea, "and then you can lie on your front again. "Lena said she bought one for her sister-in-law for Christmas." He turned his phone back around and looked at the screen wistfully. "I wish I'd known about these things when I was pregnant."

"Maybe next time, then," I teased.

Still looking at his screen, he nodded. "Maybe I'll just borrow yours."

"I'm not—"

"Too late; I'm clicking buy now."

"—buying one." I finished lamely, shaking my head. "Where are your rugrats, anyway?"

"Beck's got them." Ollie grinned. "He's got a council meeting and he's convinced that he can use their cuteness to distract the others from going off on their tangents or arguing over nonsense. I'm imagining total chaos."

"Which is why you're hiding out here instead of hanging out in your own house?"

His grin turned wicked. "How else will he learn?"

I was still laughing when the front door opened and a stranger walked in. Ollie and I seemed to scent him at the same time, both of us straightening as the now-familiar scent of dragon registered.

The man walking across the room to come and stand in front of my desk was completely unassuming at first glance. He was tall and lean, with short brown hair and a smattering of freckles over his long face. His eyes were a murky sort of blue, and everything about him seemed sharp, even his smile.

"Hello," he greeted us stiffly. "I'm looking for the Weldman family. I was told I'd find them here."

Ollie climbed off his perch on the side of my desk and turned to face the guy properly. He smiled back but jutted his chin upwards in challenge. As the Pack Alpha's mate, he was more defensive of our town than almost anyone else. "This is the best place to find them, yes. And you are…?"

The stranger's lips twitched with a hint of amusement. "Forgive me, my manners are always shocking after a long flight." He held out his hand, "Dexter Burnside."

Ollie's defensive countenance changed to excitement in a blink as he took Dexter's proffered hand. "Oh, the infamous Dexter! Welcome to Shifters Sanctuary. I'm Ollie."

"Ah, yes, the one bonded to the first alpha in centuries," Dexter cocked his head, looking Ollie up and down. "You bounced back well after the baby?"

"Babies," Ollie corrected, seemingly completely unfazed at what I thought was a kind of rude appraisal. "And yeah, I think I have." He shrugged. "Mostly."

Dexter nodded and then his attention drifted to me. I watched his eyes widen when his gaze landed on my sizable bump. "Another one?" He looked between me and Ollie with incredulity. "Another alpha?"

There was no use denying it, so I inclined my head. "Yeah. One more and I'll call it an epidemic."

The dragon laughed at that, and some of the weird tension in the room melted away. "I'll kick Sage's ass for keeping that tidbit to himself. He'll tell you Eric is the attention whore, but Sage is just as bad. He likes a bit of drama."

"We've had enough drama to last us a lifetime," Ollie told him. "Evil religious cults, kidnappings, surprise pregnancies…I'd just like to settle into a normal existence now, please."

Holding up my hand for a high-five, I said, "Amen to that."

Ollie slapped his palm against mine and then tapped at his phone screen again before bringing the device to his ear. "Hey," he spoke, presumably when the person on the other end of the line picked up, "are you working right now?" He looked over at Dexter and smiled. "There's a surprise at the clinic for you."

* * *

Watching Sage and Dexter reunite was fascinating. The redheaded dragon stood in stunned silence in the doorway for a moment before he stomped forward and slapped the brunette hard across his cleanshaven cheek, then wrenched him in for what appeared to be a bone-crushing hug.

"You asshole," Sage hissed, but he was squeezing Dexter tightly, "you took your time getting here! And not even a phone call, or an email, or even a text!"

Dexter just laughed. "Consider it payback for not telling me there was another alpha in this hick town."

"Hey," Ollie cut in, "we're standing right here."

Dexter didn't seem at all apologetic. "You're not hicks. You're the alphas' mates."

Ollie, I had learned, was particularly protective of Shifters Sanctuary. He folded his arms and raised an eyebrow. "Nobody living here is a hick, Dexter. We're all outcast shifters. We're a pack of good people who care about each other."

"Uh-huh," Dexter waved a dismissive hand, and I was back to thinking he was a bit of an asshole, "And you've all chosen to settle down in the middle of God-Knows-Where, Iowa. Why not a city, or an idyllic town in Europe or something?"

"He's just stirring you up," Sage cut in before Ollie or I gave in to the temptation to hurl a stapler or something at his dragon buddy. "Pushing boundaries is kind of his thing."

I didn't see it as pushing boundaries so much as being a jerk, but I held my tongue. Ollie made a non-committal sound that suggested he and I were on similar wavelengths.

"Anyway," Sage was perceptive enough to catch on to the vibe in the room, "I'll get Dex out of your hair. We've got a lot of catching up to do."

Dexter smirked at me and Ollie as he was dragged back out the door, calling over his shoulder, "Nice meeting you! We'll talk about what it's like to be knotted later!"

When we were certain he was well and truly out of earshot —even for shifter hearing standards— Ollie and I looked at each other and laughed.

"That dude is *so* bringing more drama," I told my friend, who groaned.

"Which dude?" I looked up to find Rex leaning against the doorframe, his head cocked in curiosity.

Just seeing him made me smile. I probably looked deranged.

"New dragon," Ollie answered, shaking his head. "He's a friend of Sage's, apparently, and a real smartass."

"Oh, so Dex has finally shown up?" Eric interjected as he led his last patient out of his office. The elderly hedgehog shifter nodded and waved at us all as he ambled past and out the door, but I was more focused on Eric. "He's not a bad guy. He's...well," he sighed and shrugged. "One of those people who'll soften once you get to know them."

"Right, well, Beck's going to love that," Ollie rolled his eyes and tapped at his phone. "I'll call and give him the heads-up." Before he pressed the call button, though, he looked at me pointedly. "Aren't you going in for your ultrasound?"

I'd completely forgotten about that! No wonder Rex had turned up; he'd been excited about getting to see our kid on the screen.

Ollie snorted before I could answer. "You forgot, didn't you? Why did you think I came down here? I'm taking over reception while Eric gets his jollies treating you like a lab rat."

"And here I was thinking you just wanted to chat," I feigned hurt as Rex crossed the room, before I dropped the act and replaced my pout with another goofy smile when he kissed the top of my head, murmuring a sweet, "Hey, darlin'."

Channeling the big cat in my soul, I rubbed the top of my head against his jaw.

Ollie just rolled his eyes and pointed towards the hallway. "Get your ass in the consultation room. Your cowboy looks like he's about to combust."

Sure enough, when I stopped snuggling and actually looked at Rex, it seemed that he was practically vibrating with anxious energy. It was cute, and the urge to keep bantering with my friend evaporated.

Instead, I turned to Eric. "Are you ready for us, doc?"

Chapter Twelve — Rex

Feeling our son moving around inside Damon was one thing, but seeing the little guy on the ultrasound screen was something else entirely.

I don't know why, but seeing the distinctly shaped small person —with his large head, curved spine, and perfectly formed fingers and toes— moving around on the two-dimensional, black and white screen made the whole situation feel even more real.

That was an honest-to-God baby.

That was *my* baby.

"Little guy's measuring on track for thirty-four weeks gestation," Eric told us cheerfully, bending over a notepad to jot the information down. "Well, that's sticking with the timeline and the theory that omega pregnancies run for roughly the same forty weeks as humans or betas. It held true for Ollie, and it seems to be the same for you."

As I understood it, Eric was documenting the similarities and differences between Ollie and Damon's experiences at the same stages, and theorizing on whether the differences were due to the nature of multiples vs singular fetuses, or because the men were different breeds of shifter.

Eric spun back around on his wheeled stool, bringing the transducer wand back to the lubricated, exposed skin of Damon's belly. The smile he shot me was warm and understanding. "Want to hear the heartbeat?"

Beck had already warned me that this was Eric's favorite part, but I was keen to hear it anyway. I nodded with enthusiasm and leaned forward in my chair, which was situated next to the examination table. I'd been unable to tear my gaze from the screen across from me for very long, and I'd been fixated on the flickering in the middle of our son's chest, bewildered by just how fast his tiny heart seemed to be beating.

"Yes, please," I answered redundantly, because Eric was already reaching with his left hand to flip a switch on the complicated machine attached to the transducer wand.

A fast *whoosh-whoosh-whoosh* came through the speakers, the sound in time with the fluttering on the screen.

Holy shit. That's his heartbeat.

My own heart picked up pace, seemingly thudding in tandem with the baby's. I was glad I was sitting down. Emotion lodged itself in my throat and my chest felt tight. Hell, tears even welled in my eyes. I blinked rapidly against them.

"Wow," I croaked, startling as Damon threaded our fingers together.

"Roughly six weeks to go, and he'll be here," Eric continued blithely, oblivious to just how overwhelmed I was.

Six weeks.

That sounded like no time at all.

"You can still run," Damon teased, and *that* got me to tear my blurred gaze away from the screen. When I looked at him, he lifted the corner of his lips. "I see you panicking, babe."

Babe.

Huh.

While I used a number of endearments on Damon, it was new to hear him flipping the table and using one on me. New, but welcome. So damn welcome. I loved his fire and sass, but those moments where he dropped the façade and let me see the softer, vulnerable side he kept hidden kept me coming back for more.

We were still taking things slowly, but he had started dropping his walls and letting me in. I cherished that trust more than I could say.

My panic began to recede and breathing came easier again. I shook my head and smirked, "I've told you, kitten; I ain't goin' nowhere."

Damon's expression softened and became warmer as he squeezed my hand. "You always get more country when you're emotional," he murmured. "It's really cute."

"You only get to call me cute 'cause you're carryin' our kid," I pretended to grumble. Meanwhile, on the inside, I was doing a happy dance over his assessment.

He thought I was cute.

"Newsflash," he snarked back playfully, unable to stop himself from smiling, "I thought you were cute the night we met, too."

"Liar. You thought I was hot as sin."

"Cute."

"Sexy."

"Cute."

"A silver fox."

"Cute."

"Gentlemen…" Eric interrupted our silly little game, sounding both exasperated and amused. He gestured to the screen and said, "I'm going to print you off some photos, but we're otherwise done here. We'll do another scan in four weeks and, at that time, I'll also scan to check on the progress of your birth canal, Damon."

Damon cringed, wrinkling his nose. "Can't you guys just do a C-section? Ollie's description leaves a lot to be desired."

"Brandt and I have discussed omega caesarians," Eric's tone was gentle, and I knew before he said anything that Damon's request was about to be carefully rebuffed, "and we're of the agreement that, with the exception of emergency situations, it's not worth the risk. As omegas, our bodies are constructed slightly differently to human or beta females…and there are enough inherent risks in a traditional C-section without adding the difference in physiology that being an omega brings to the table."

Damon pouted as Eric wiped the lubricant from his belly. "Well that sucks. Ollie said there's a fuckton of pain…and that I'll shift to grow a new hole…and did I mention the pain? Oh, and the post-partum bleeding? Because *ew*, Eric. Ew."

The dragon wasn't swayed. He just rolled his eyes. "Human and beta females go through something similar, including the pain and post-partum bleeding. Even those who have C-sections recover from birth the same way. I suspect your body would still form the birth canal to release the blood from the–"

"I can't hear you," Damon covered his ears, but Eric ignored him, finishing calmly.

"—open blood vessels which form after the placenta comes away from the uterine wall."

Even I cringed at the description. Why couldn't it be like the movies? A little bit of pushing and yelling and then hey presto! Clean, chubby baby and none of the medical gore. I was glad I was the alpha in this situation, even if I also felt a bit guilty that I'd inadvertently been responsible for what Damon would have to experience.

Damon groaned, shutting his eyes. "We're never doing this again," he muttered, and the words made my stomach flip-flop.

Yet another confirmation that he saw a future for us.

"I'd never ask you to," I answered honestly.

Cracking an eye open, he squinted through it. "Is this because you didn't want any kids?"

Danger! Trick question!

Even Eric cleared his throat and busied himself with his notes, the coward.

"I want this baby," my reply was firm and without any hesitation. "But I'm already forty-two. I don't think I'm young enough to start a whole brood. However," I added carefully, "you're my mate, kitten. If you wanted more babies, I'd think about it."

At the end of the day, his happiness meant more to me than my hangups. Besides, didn't shifters have a longer lifespan than humans?

"Relax, cowboy," he gave me a little smile, "I don't think I want more, either. I mean, we can always see how this one goes, but…well, my vision of the future kind of stops at one kid."

It didn't escape my notice that he hadn't refuted my calling him my mate.

"Whatever you want, darlin'," I grinned, unable to contain my happiness.

"Now help me up," he demanded, "I've gotta pee."

* * *

Over the course of the next five weeks, I spent every free moment I had getting my cottage finalized. The mountain lion inside me was becoming more agitated as our son's due date loomed, and I suspected he was just as anxious about Damon still wanting to live in his poky apartment as I was. I knew he was anxious about the most recent feedback from the neighborhood watch Beck had set up. Shifters Sanctuary hadn't seen any suspicious newcomers at all. None. That felt wrong. My alpha agreed.

God damn, but it felt weird thinking of my inner alpha as a separate entity.

We were one and the same…and yet somehow different. I couldn't fully explain the sensation, just that my shifter side felt like his own person at times. Or, rather, his own cat.

But back to the original point. It wasn't that I didn't respect Damon's wishes. I just had this deep-seated urge to protect my mate and cub. How could I do that if we lived on opposite ends of town? Especially when we had no idea what Morstein was planning, or when he and his kin would act. And they would act, I was sure of it.

Still, I knew better than to push Damon just because I was feeling overly protective the closer we got to his due date. We had been making good progress on our relationship since I'd arrived in town. I wasn't dumb enough to undo it all by giving in to my mildly irrational shifter urges, especially when all signs pointed to things being quiet on the cult-y front.

Besides, I was a shifter who couldn't shift. Just how much protecting did my inner puma think he could do while he was stuck on the inside, anyway?

Instead of voicing those thoughts or wallowing in my concerns, I reveled in Damon's increased displays of affection. The more he seemed to understand I wasn't going to leave, the more he opened up. He was still sassy, but less prickly with me. And, on one memorable occasion, possessive as fuck. *That* had been hot as sin.

He'd brought lunch to Sam and Becca's farm during his first week of forced leave from his job, and had stumbled upon me mucking out the stalls. It was an unseasonably warm day and the labor-intensive job had seen me removing my shirt only fifteen minutes before his surprise arrival. His hungry gaze had swept over my body and his Adam's apple had bobbed tellingly…and then he'd caught sight of Tim.

Tim, Sam and Becca's *barely* legal at nineteen-years-old omega son.

Tim, who I'll admit seemed really quite interested in learning about alphas.

Tim, who might have been giggling at my antics as I regaled him with tales from the farm I'd grown up on as we mucked the stalls together.

I hadn't made it to almost forty-three without some sense of what *might* seem like a compromising situation under specific circumstances. I had opened my mouth to try and head off any potential misunderstanding, but Damon had raised his chin, offered Tim an incredibly frosty smile and greeting, and had pointedly stared the younger omega down in an unspoken challenge. Damon may as well have shifted and pissed on my leg, marking his territory in every way possible.

At that point, if he'd been shifted, I assumed Tim would have literally fled with his tail between his legs. As it was, he'd turned pink and made a swift retreat in human form.

Damon's smile had turned into one of smug self-satisfaction before he'd closed the distance between us and kissed me with more heat and passion than I had been braced for, rubbing against me, covering me with his scent.

I'd had an erection that wouldn't quit for hours after that. My inner cat had felt claimed, and my feelings had never felt more reciprocated.

Then, as his due date seemed to rush at us, Damon nested, for lack of a better description. Eric and Brandt had made him completely stop working at his thirty-sixth week, which came as a relief — or at least it did for me. His belly had grown to a point where I knew his back and hips ached more often than not, and staying put in his bed or on the couch was preferable to walking around town. Even so, he had turned his nose up at the strange inflatable *thing* Ollie had bought him to supposedly ease his sleeping woes. Instead, Damon's bed now housed a mountain of pillows to support his back and bump, and I was pretty sure he had shifted into his mountain lion form and curled up to sleep among them on more than one occasion. (I kept finding fur in his bed.)

But, during his thirty-ninth week of pregnancy, when I arrived at his apartment with a bag of takeout from the town diner after a long-ass day on the farm, I was not greeted by the sleepy, uncomfortable Damon I'd become familiar with. No…instead, I was greeted by a version of the man similar to the one I'd first met in a bar.

His eyes were bright and his smile was sultry as he tugged

me into his apartment by the collar of my gingham shirt. I barely managed to get out a 'hey' in greeting before his lips were on mine, his talented tongue begging entrance into my mouth.

It had been *weeks* since Damon had had the energy to do more than cuddle, and my cock was more than happy to go with this sudden —but entirely welcome— change of pace.

Deciding that the burgers I'd bought would be just fine eaten cold, I dropped the paper bag on the couch as Damon manhandled me towards the bed.

"I'm so horny I could die," he declared between kisses, moments before he shoved me backwards onto the mattress.

"Well, we can't have—*oof!*" I landed among the pile of pillows and barely had time to get myself situated properly before Damon was crawling over my body, his belly grazing my thighs and cock, then stomach. My hands moved to his hips, supporting him as he wriggled and maneuvered his shirt over his head, tossing it to parts unknown. In my jeans, my own dick strained under the unintentional lapdance, and it only got harder as my eyes drank in my lover's exposed skin. "That's it, kitten," I praised, smoothing my hands up his sides, "take what you need from me. I've got you."

He undulated his hips, more graceful than I would have been if I'd been nine months pregnant, closing his eyes and sighing with delight. But then he crawled back off me to rummage through his bedside table drawer, and I wanted to whine.

I had no idea what he was looking for, considering we didn't need lube or condoms, but I didn't have to wait long.

"Ah ha!" he declared triumphantly, turning to show me his find.

My eyes bulged from their sockets and I scrambled to sit up

against the headboard. "What are you plannin' on doin' with that?" I gestured to the bundle he held in a loose fist.

Rope.

It was red and had a shine to it, and even though I hadn't reached out to touch it, I knew it would be silky beneath my fingertips.

Biting his lip, my kitten turned shy. "I was hoping you'd be the one doing stuff with it," he answered.

My heart hammered. *"Now?"* Holding up my index finger, I took a moment to breathe, aware that my question had come out sharp and incredulous. When I looked back at him again, I was careful to soften my tone. "Darlin', you're due to give birth next week…"

"I Googled," he insisted, crawling back onto the mattress, still clutching the figure eight of soft red rope. "And, yeah, there are some positions that we should avoid, but some that are still safe. We just have to err on the vanilla side this time, that's all."

This time.

"I mean," he continued before I could get hung up on the implications of those two little words, "you're a cowboy. You said you were good with ropes when I asked."

I couldn't deny that. Weeks earlier, the topic of rope play had come up seemingly out of the blue, and I'd admitted that I did have some experience with the kink, and that I did enjoy it. Damon had nodded, humming thoughtfully, and the conversation had moved on. I'd thought that maybe —just maybe— we might revisit the topic and negotiate a scene one day, but never in a million years would I have thought it would happen before he gave birth. Especially not so close to his due date.

But Damon was impulsive. I'd known that about him since the moment we met. I liked that about him.

Still, doing any kind of BDSM without pre-negotiations made me uncomfortable.

"I'm not sayin' no," I told him gently, reaching out to splay my hand over his rounded belly in the hopes that my touch would be reassuring. "But we can't just launch into somethin' like this. Now, I've got a fairly good idea of your physical limitations at the moment, but what about your emotional ones? You ever been tied up before?"

He shook his head and I hated seeing the tears welling in his eyes, as well as the pink flush of embarrassment on his cheeks. His expression was chagrined and he kept his gaze averted.

"Kitten, look at me," I insisted, and he did, once again bestowing that absolute trust in me. I wouldn't break it. Not now, not ever.

I smiled softly. "If this is somethin' you really wanna try tonight, we're gonna do it real slow and basic, okay? No elaborate shibari all over your belly, nothing too tight or restrictive, and I'm not putting you in a position that could hurt you or the baby. Not even accidentally."

Damon nodded enthusiastically. "I was thinking—hang on, let me show you." He grabbed his phone from the nightstand and swiped at the screen before turning it to face me. "Something like this?"

I scanned the webpage he had navigated to, realization dawning on me. He'd been researching. He'd ordered the rope online. This wasn't just a spur of the moment idea: this was something he had wanted for a while.

I flashed back to Christmas, to how wet he'd gotten at the tiny show of dominance I'd put on, and everything seemed to click into place. Damon, for all of his prickly-as-a-cactus outer shell, wanted someone to take charge of him.

Well, I could do that!

"Okay," I agreed after a long moment of consideration. "We can do that." I cocked my head. "Where are your shears?"

My kitten practically scrambled back off the bed, digging through his nightstand again. He pulled the shiny new shears out and showed them to me before setting them down on top of the same bedside table, dropping his phone next to them.

"Need help getting your pants off?" I asked. Bending had become an issue for him, and I enjoyed helping him dress and undress.

"Nah," he stretched out the waistband of his loose pajama bottoms and slid them down over the curve of his ass. Gravity took care of the rest, leaving him completely naked.

I thought he was the most gorgeous thing I'd ever seen.

"Aren't you stripping, too?"

His plaintive question shook me from my ogling, and I grinned. "Want me to put on a show for you, kitten?"

"Please."

We switched places, with him on the bed and me standing in front of it. I hummed the tune of Joe Cocker's 'You Can Leave Your Hat On' as I performed my impromptu striptease, moving my hips in the best Magic Mike impersonation I could manage. I felt silly, but the heat in Damon's gaze kept me going.

By the time I was shirtless and had pulled my belt free from its loops, cracking it in the air like a whip before I dropped it to the ground, Damon was stroking his dick and making the sweetest whimpering sounds.

I turned around and faced the bathroom door as I popped

the button over my fly, then unzipped, hooking my thumbs into the waistbands of both my jeans and underwear. Still humming, I swayed my hips and inched the fabric down, exposing a hint of my ass cheeks.

Damon whined low in the back of his throat. Glancing over my shoulder, I grinned.

"See somethin' you like, darlin'?"

He nodded and swallowed roughly. "Stop teasing, Rex."

That got a laugh out of me. "But you wanted a show."

"I've changed my mind. Please. I need…" he squirmed, his hold on his dick tightening on his next upstroke. I was worried he was going to hurt himself.

Abandoning the act, I dropped my pants and stepped out of them, making a beeline for the bed.

"Still want the rope?" I asked, "Or just my knot?"

The pun, lame as it was, wasn't even intentional. It went over his head anyway. Or maybe he was just so horny he didn't care for my silly jokes at that point.

With his eyes shut, he tilted his head back and sighed, as though my proximity had eased some of his desperation. "Tie me up, Alpha. I'm yours."

Whoa.

That was a headrush.

Tingles swept through me, and my shifter side purred with satisfaction.

Whether Damon had intended it or not, it felt like he had completely accepted me as his alpha. Not just as a Dom to his submissive side, but as the Alpha to his Omega. I knew deep in my bones that we would both still cede status to Beckett as the Pack Alpha, but this felt like he had still chosen me as his. Almost like the way Beck had described bonding, but without the mind-link.

Coupled with his increased displays of trust and affection, and the possessive display with Tim, I wanted to shout from the rooftops that I loved him and I was pretty sure he felt the same.

"And you're mine, kitten. My omega. My mate." I had no idea what had spurred me to reply that way, so strangely formally, but it made the tingling sensation beneath my skin hum with additional pleasure.

Fuck, but I needed to get inside him.

Damon whined again. "Rex, *please…*"

Right. The rope.

I unfurled the twin lengths of silky, smooth bondage rope and got familiar with the weight and tension of it. As a benefit of my profession, I considered myself somewhat of a rope aficionado. I could tell you the difference between a head rope and a calf rope, could explain why not all ropes are lassos, could go into the necessity for breakaway ropes…and I could tie knots more proficiently than a sailor. As Damon had rightly assumed, that carried over to my skills in the bedroom. Bondage, while not an everyday thing for me, came naturally. Especially rope play.

The rope I held in my hands as I got Damon into position, his back supported by half a ton of pillows, was high quality. It was going to be gentle on his skin, regardless of how tight I tied it. Not that I had plans to go hard on him when he was so heavily pregnant. I knew his blood flow was increased and that he'd had some fluid retention issues. I wasn't going to risk any circulation or nerve damage problems if I could help it.

The image he'd shown me on his phone was of a frog tie

position, which I agreed would be the most comfortable this far along in his pregnancy. It involved tying his ankle to his thigh in what was called a 'double column' tie, using a couple of variations of knotting styles.

I decided he'd be more comfortable reclining against the mountain of pillows with his legs splayed, able to plant his feet on the mattress for stability, rather than resting on his knees with his thighs and ankles tied behind him. After checking that he'd stretched and that he was okay with my plan, I asked him to tell me his safe word before we got started.

His eyes widened. "I need a safe word?"

I swear to the Gods, I almost called red then and there.

But he was so excited to try this, so I took a deep breath and asked, "Is this your first time tryin' anythin' kinky, sweetheart?"

His cheeks flushed pink and he shrugged a shoulder. "Maybe. I mean, I've been cuffed before…"

"Without a safe word in place?" It was hard to keep the horror out of my voice. Was this our age gap finally showing itself? Or was it just his inexperience with kink? Could it be both?

He shrugged again. "It was just cheap aluminum cuffs from a silly cop costume. I've got shifter strength. I could have broken them if I wanted." He shook his head. "But I get that's not the point. I was dumb and, like, nineteen at the time. All I remember is that I enjoyed giving up a little control."

"Okay, well, for us…you're gonna need a safe word. I need you to understand that the second you say it, I'll cut the ropes and end the scene." I was grateful that he had at least done enough research to have the shears on hand. "If it helps, I usually use the traffic light system."

"That works for me," Damon smiled sheepishly. "And I'm green lighting this right now."

"And if you want me to stop?"

"Red light, Alpha. I promise."

There was that tingly feeling again. I *really* liked that.

Reassured, I nodded. "Okay. Good. Usually, I'd tell you not to speak unless asked a direct question, but tonight we're goin' easy, okay? So I want to know what you're feeling, especially if it's too uncomfortable."

"Okay, that's fair." He wriggled. "Can we start now?"

I snorted but got his legs into the position I wanted. To get us both back into the mood, I ran my hands over his skin, from his toes all the way to his gently stubbled jaw and then back down again. He closed his eyes and tried to lift his hips towards me, and I watched as a droplet of precum dribbled down his renewed erection. I could also see his slick shining off the curve of his ass, and I couldn't wait to have his legs restrained so I could dive between them and enjoy that part of him while he writhed.

I doubled the first length of rope over and then took my time wrapping it around his thigh and ankle, bending forward to press kisses to Damon's belly as I worked. I created the first part of the Lark's Head knot, slipping the end of the rope through the loop I'd created when I doubled it over, and then tugged it back down, reversing the tension of the knot. I slipped two fingers between the rope and his skin, wanting to make sure I wasn't cutting off his circulation or, worse, creating an opportunity for irreversible nerve damage.

When I was happy with the degree of constriction, I wrapped the rope around his limb again and again, keeping the lines of rope uniform and maintaining the same tension. Then I slipped the tail end of the rope through the bight from the original knot and tied off with a Surgeon's Knot.

"How does that feel, kitten?" I checked in with him softly, glancing up into his lust-blown eyes.

"Still green light," he breathed back. "I can't move much—" he gave his tied leg an experimental stretch, still able to jostle it side-to-side "—but that feels really fucking exciting."

"Good. It's not too tight? Too loose?"

"Nope. It's just right."

Grinning, I moved to the other leg to repeat the process. "Is this the part where I call you Baby Bear?"

"I was thinking Goldilocks, actually."

I laughed. "Careful, or the nickname will stick, darlin'. Then you'll have to explain how you got it, and it ain't got nothin' to do with your hair." He'd cut his hair to make it more manageable, but it was still shoulder length, smooth and dark. Nothing like the blonde curls belonging to the character from the fairytale.

He smirked. "What about the gold in my eyes, hmm? You like that. At least, you always say you do."

I finished tying the Surgeon's knot on his second leg and rested my ass on my heels, shaking my head. "Except the 'locks' part of 'Goldilocks' refers to her hair, so that don't make sense. Anyway, how does that feel?"

Damon did the same experimental movement, trying to pull his ankle away from his thigh. He let out a cute, excited squeal. "Perfect. I can't move them." He bit his lip and cocked his head. "I'm completely at your mercy now, Alpha."

Oh, but how I loved the coy act. His hands and arms were still free, and we both knew that he had the ultimate control of the scene, but I played along happily.

I crawled forward and spread his thighs apart further, diving between them just as I had fantasized I would.

He cried out and squirmed, unable to wrap his legs around my back as instinct likely demanded of him.

"Oh, fuck," he all but sobbed as I flattened my tongue and licked him from his slick-covered rim all the way up over his balls and up his shaft in one swipe. Then I sank my mouth down over his cock and took him to the back of my throat. "Rex! *Fuck!*"

He'd already been so worked up before we even started, we both knew he wasn't going to last long.

"Rex…A-alpha…please…I can't…I don't want…not yet…"

His blissed-out babbling was music to my ears as I sucked his cock, lessening up on the intensity to hopefully extend his pleasure.

"Need your knot, Alpha. Please. *Please.*"

He sounded close to tears.

I released him with reluctance before I kissed my way back down to his hole.

"Better make sure you're ready for that, hmm?" I asked him, and he practically yowled as I followed through by spearing him with my tongue.

I loved the taste of his slick. I didn't know if it was because I'm an alpha and I'm designed to want it so badly, or if it was just a me thing, but tasting him was guaranteed to get me harder than I thought was physically possible. My dick ached to be inside him, to mark my territory in the most primal way, to knot him and fill him with more lifegiving seed.

What the hell was that about, anyway? Damon was already heavily pregnant with my kid. It wasn't like I could get him *more* pregnant.

I couldn't — I'd already asked Eric. And Beck…*And* Brandt. So sue me: I was paranoid about these urges. Who knew what shifter biology and magic could achieve.

Damon whined and mewled and writhed as I alternated between lapping at his rim and tongue-fucking him. When I started adding fingers to the equation, he was beyond begging. I pulled back with a smug smile, faltering at the sight of tears trickling down his cheeks.

"I need you in me," he said plaintively, and I was done torturing him.

"I've got you, kitten, but we're swapping positions."

A few moments later, I was propped up against Mount Pillow and I was pulling him onto my lap, careful of his still bound legs. I had my hands bracing his back, my innate shifter strength making it a lot easier to help him ride me, even in his semi-reclined position. We made matching sounds of relief as he sank down onto my cock, enveloping me in his slick heat.

I was never going to get enough of that feeling.

"Darlin', you feel so damn good…*ungh*," my breathing hitched as he clenched around me. "Yes, baby, just like that."

We took it slow, and I relished every second of sliding in and out of his perfect ass. I wished I could kiss him, or worship his beautiful body with my hands, but it wasn't going to work in our current position.

"I…I need to come," he whined, his face contorted as he hovered on the edge of orgasm.

"Touch yourself," I ordered. "Come for me, kitten."

Taking a shaking hand to his leaking dick, which he probably couldn't see straining beneath the bulge of his belly, he did as told. My balls drew up tight as I watched him. With his head thrown back, he tugged at his cock and bounced on mine, managing maybe five strokes before his ass was clenching around me and his warm cum was splashing my abdomen.

"Fuck, yes, darlin', that's it…" I praised him, trying to hold off coming myself.

"It's not enough," he sounded wrecked. "I *need* your knot."

"Not like this." How I had the presence of mind to understand that getting locked together while his legs were still bound was not a great idea, I'll never know. I put it down to those protective alpha urges. "Gotta untie you first."

"Hurry."

I couldn't quite understand the urgency in his tone. Not when he'd just come. But it got me moving. He leaned back, bracing his palms on the mattress, while I quickly worked at undoing the knots holding the ropes in place.

As his impatience climbed, he began to bounce his hips, which was fucking distracting considering I was still inside him.

I freed his left leg with an exultant cry, then moved to his right, throwing both lengths of rope over the edge of the mattress once I was done. I felt a sense of loss as Damon climbed off me to shift onto his knees, but then he was grabbing my shaft by the base and sinking down onto me again with a groan.

Now he could lean forward and, even though we were still mildly impeded by his belly between us, we could kiss. My fingers threaded into the silken strands of his hair, holding him in place as his tongue plundered my mouth with desperation.

He mewled as he bounced in place, his hands scrabbling at the back of my shoulders, but he never stopped kissing me, and there was something special in the way his passion seemed to match mine.

We panted and moaned and grunted as we picked up speed. We smelled like sex and clean sweat and something that was uniquely *us*.

"You gonna come again?" I murmured against his lips, and he whined long and low, nodding his answer. The next kiss I gave him was chaste and I nuzzled my nose next to his in a move I could only describe as feline. Then I slid my hand beneath his belly, gripping his dick as I urged, "Come for me, baby. Come for me, and you'll get my knot."

"Fuck, Rex!" Damon arched his back and came for the second time that night, the contractions around my cock tearing my orgasm from me. I couldn't have stopped it this time if I had tried.

I rode out the wave of ecstasy, then groaned as my knot began to swell. "*Nngh*. That's it, darlin', take it all."

Damon undulated his hips, stimulating my knot. He smiled lazily as I came again. "God, I love it when you do that," he admitted. His eyelids were getting droopy, his expression finally sated. In the yellow light from the bare bulb above us, and with a thin sheen of sweat on his skin, he practically glowed. He bit his lip, and in a soft voice added, "Thank you."

Grunting through the waves of resulting pleasure-pain as I moved and tugged on my knot, I slid us down onto the mattress until we were lying together on our sides, his belly and back supported by pillows while I curled around his front, locked inside him.

"I don't know why you're thankin' me," I eventually replied, kissing the top of his head sweetly, tasting the salt of his sweat on my lips. "I should be thankin' you. A few months ago, I had nothin'. Now..." I placed my hand on the swell of his belly and swallowed an unexpected lump of emotion. "Now I've got everything."

Chapter Thirteen – Damon

"Rex."

Silence.

"*Rex.*"

A grunt.

"Rex, seriously, you need to wake up."

"Hmm?" He was groggy, but at least he was finally responsive. I took a deep, calming breath.

"I'm about ninety-percent sure I'm going into labor."

Hours after Rex's knot had deflated, I'd gotten out of bed to use the bathroom. After doing my business, I noticed tenderness in the stretch of skin between my balls and my ass. Ollie had warned me that it was a precursor to labor. Sure enough, mild cramps started to ripple through me not even half an hour later, as though my noticing the painful patch of skin had given it permission to begin.

Have you ever seen a six-foot five naked cowboy startle awake so abruptly that he fell out of bed?

I have.

Rex picked himself up quickly and rushed to my side, his eyes scanning me over intently. "Are you feelin' okay? Do I need to call Eric? Brandt? An ambulance? Shit, do they even *have* ambulances out this far?"

"The nearest hospital's about an hour away," I replied calmly, my heart tripping at his worry, "and, yes, they do have a fleet of three ambulances. But, no, I don't need one." I paused and grimaced through another belly cramp. They were painful but reminded me of gas pains more than anything else. Manageable.

I wasn't naïve enough to believe they'd stay that way.

Still squinting at me with concern and mild panic, he asked, "How the hell are you so calm right now? Shouldn't you be screamin' about me never gettin' to touch you again, or somethin'?"

I couldn't help laughing at that, feeling marginally guilty at the pang of hurt in his eyes, which he blinked away as I answered, "It's still super early right now. The contractions aren't regular, and…the *you-know-what* hasn't formed yet."

"Birth canal?" he hazarded a (correct) guess. I cringed.

"Shh! Don't say the words!" I was still really uncomfortable with the concept of developing a whole new orifice. Even though I couldn't stop my body from going through with it, I didn't want to think about it.

While I shuddered through the thought, Rex located his discarded clothes and started to re-dress.

"Uh…what are you doing?" I asked, cocking my head.

He froze. "Getting dressed?"

I shook my head. "Nope. Strip."

"*What*? Why?"

Frowning, I wondered if he'd paid any attention to any of

Brandt and Eric's prenatal advice. Slowly, as if talking to a toddler, I answered, "I need you in the shower with me."

"Uh…"

His bewildered expression would have been both adorable and comical if I wasn't starting to give in to the discomfort of the cramps and *the thing* developing between my legs.

"Eric and Brandt said that the warm water will help with the pain from the contractions later on," I reminded him. "And it makes more sense to be naked for that."

"But," picking up on my rising irritation, Rex seemed to do his absolute best to speak calmly and carefully, "aren't we going to the clinic to have the baby? You know, where they have all the medical tools and things?" He was smart enough to leave the 'in case something goes wrong' unspoken. I heard it anyway.

I hated to admit that he actually made a valid point. But… this was my home. I'd gotten comfortable in my apartment over the past few weeks. I'd gotten my bed all cushy, and the whole place smelled like me and Rex. It felt safe. Warm. Welcoming. The perfect location to welcome our cub into the world.

"Plus," he added even more cautiously while my head warred with my shifter instincts, "your shower is, uh, kinda' tiny, darlin'. I barely fit in there on my own."

Damn him and his logic.

My lower lip quivered. Rex's expression immediately softened and, before I knew it, he'd closed the short distance between us to wrap me in a hug. I clung to him like a life-raft. He really was my safe place.

"It's gonna be okay, kitten, I promise," he soothed as the first sobs escaped me. "It's okay to be scared. It's okay to change plans. It's okay to cry and scream like all those laboring people in the movies do."

Through my tears, I snorted, but I really appreciated him saying 'people' and not 'women'. Like, I knew that I was only the second documented pregnant male omega in a few centuries, but it was nice not to feel like it made me different. Really, it was likely that most omegas *could* get pregnant…as long as they came across their fated mate or, as I kept thinking about it, a compatible alpha. With two of us going through this so close together, I wouldn't have been surprised if it started becoming more common across the world. Like evolution had kicked into overdrive or whatever.

Anyway, I was thinking in circles, mostly to avoid facing the fact that I was actually *having* a baby.

The sense of calm which had settled over me only an hour or so earlier seemed to evaporate into thin air.

I was going into labor.

I was having a baby.

In a handful of hours, I would officially be a dad.

I didn't know *how* to be a dad.

Why, during all those weeks of prenatal care, had Eric and Brandt not prepared me for that part?

"You've been helping Ollie with the twins," Rex reminded me gently, and I realized belatedly that I must have blurted all of my thoughts out loud. "You know how to hold babies. How to feed 'em, and how to change 'em. Pretty sure you know how to bathe 'em and dress 'em, too. The rest is all trial and error, darlin', and we'll learn together."

Once again, he was right. Between the way he was rubbing my back, and his steady heartbeat beneath my ear, I started to calm down again. "Sorry," I apologized sheepishly, but Rex gently pushed me back, holding me at arm's length as he shook his head.

"You're allowed to feel whatever you need to. I can't imagine how terrifying what you're going through is. But you're not gonna be alone. I'm here. And I'm still not goin' anywhere."

A handful of months earlier, when I'd arrived in Shifters Sanctuary, I'd thought there was no way the alpha who had knocked me up and run away could ever compare to the way Beck was with Ollie. However, in that moment, I had even more proof that I hadn't given Rex a fair chance way back when.

He was perfect. Or, at least, perfect for me.

I knew that telling him as much while I was in labor would be a mistake, though, so I kept the revelation to myself. I didn't want him thinking that it was my panic and insecurities talking. When I finally told him, it would leave no doubt as to my sincerity.

"What do you need me to do?" he asked, pulling me from my musings.

"I don't…I don't know." I hated not knowing, but I was suddenly struck by indecision. Rex was right: it made more sense to go to the clinic and have access to medical supplies, but I was scared. Life had finally settled into a routine that felt good, and it was about to be upended all over again.

Plus there was the immediate fear of the pain and uncertainty of labor. I was only the second male omega in however many hundreds of years to experience childbirth from this perspective, after all. We were all pretty much going in blind, save for Ollie's recent experience. What if something went wrong?

"Okay," he gently guided me over to the bed and sat me

down, "how about we cuddle until your contractions are more regular or something changes, uh, *downstairs*…and then I'll call Eric and we'll let him decide whether stayin' here or goin' to the clinic is the right choice?"

Perfect.

* * *

Eric wasn't lying when he said that the hot water from the shower would work wonders on my labor pains. It was almost noon and Eric had shut the clinic so that he and Brandt could give me their undivided attention. Like Rex, they had both thought that it made more sense for me to have the baby where they had access to all of their supplies, so that's where we ended up.

Thankfully, because the clinic was housed in Eric's cottage, I had access to his surprisingly generous bathroom. He must have had it renovated in recent years, because it was more modern than the rest of the cottage, and large enough to comfortably fit both Rex and me in the shower stall.

"Gods bless the inventor of the handheld shower head," I moaned, arching as Rex aimed the spray to the achy spot at the base of my spine. When the next contraction hit, I got him to move it to my tightened belly while I braced my hands on the tiled wall and breathed through the pain.

It was also nice to be under the water to wash away the blood from when the…*ugh*…birth canal had formed (which had been just as freaking painful as it sounds – like shifting, but only partially, and with pressure and stretching of parts that should not exist). My water had broken not long after, but Eric had examined me and declared that I wasn't dilated enough yet.

With all the pain, I was convinced he was wrong, but I was just shoved back into the shower and told to try and relax.

Relax? Ha!

Apparently, this wasn't even the worst of it. Eric had sounded *far* too cheerful as he informed me that active labor was going to be worse. I couldn't help but hope that he found an alpha and got to experience this for himself. You know, for research. Science and all that jazz. We didn't want him to miss out on the magic of childbirth, right?

Please note, what I was going through could not, under any power of imagination, be considered 'magical', and I would strangle the next person to use that description within my enhanced earshot.

"Ow ow ow *owwwww*," I whined as the cramping intensified. Squeezing my eyes shut, I fought the sensation of building panic. "I've changed my mind," I told Rex, "I don't wanna do this."

"Aw, kitten, I wish I could fix it…" He really did sound apologetic. "But there's no goin' back now, baby. I'm sorry."

I was not going to be a cliché. I was not going to tell him that this was all his fault and that he'd better be sorry.

But I *was* going to petulantly think it.

So I did.

I thought it *so* hard.

Rex rubbed my back, not seeming to care that he was getting as wet as I was. Where I was naked, he was still wearing his boxer briefs, but I thought they'd be drenched by now.

Another contraction built within a minute of the previous one ending. This one seemed even more intense, or maybe I was just tiring, but when it crested, I cried out…and then the urge to *push* made my knees buckle.

Rex's reflexes were thankfully super quick. He caught me before I crumpled, wrapping one strong, tanned arm across my chest as he held me to his body, shutting the shower off with his free hand.

"What's wrong?" he demanded with concern. "Talk to me, Damon."

"I…I have to push…" I couldn't explain beyond that. My body was working on instinct.

A strangled sound came from the back of his throat, and he leaned out of the shower, pulling me with him as he shouted, "Uh, a little help?!"

Eric and Brandt were at the open doorway within seconds.

Usually, I'd be a little uncomfortable being completely naked in front of the men who were also my employers unless we were all preparing to shift, but they'd seen everything when they'd been monitoring my pregnancy, and I was in too much pain to care who saw me naked at that point. Hell, they could invite half the town in and, as long as they were helping me survive this experience, I wouldn't care at all.

"What's happening, Day?" Eric asked me as he walked into the room, grabbing the towel he'd set aside on the closed toilet lid. He carefully helped dry my skin and gestured to Brandt to swap places with Rex so he could also get dried off.

I immediately missed being in Rex's arms and I whimpered. "I need to push."

Eric nodded, not at all surprised. "Gravity has done its job, then," he smiled up at me from where he was drying my legs. "I'd like to check dilation before you follow those urges, okay?" He nodded at Brandt again. "Can you grab the shower chair? And a mirror?"

"What, are you planning on some kind of magic trick?" I

snarked as Rex stepped back in to support me. I didn't need it now that the contraction had eased, but I relished his presence. My puma relaxed, too.

Brandt disappeared down the hall and returned in less than thirty seconds, carrying what I called the 'old people seat' — a plastic seat with a hole in the center, not unlike a rudimentary camping toilet. All you needed was to put a bucket under it or dig a hole in the earth and…that was *so* not what they were planning on using it for.

Eric gestured to the seat. "Sit down and we'll check you out, okay? This is going to be easier than getting you onto a bed if you're planning on squatting to deliver."

"Squatting?" Rex sounded horrified as he helped me to follow Eric's instructions.

Eric just nodded, but he was focused on the square mirror he had just slid under the chair. "Or kneeling braced over the side of the bed. It makes gravity work in your favor as opposed to pushing against gravity in a reclined position." He looked back up at us and smiled again. "You're fully dilated, Day. It's showtime. How do you want to do this?"

I could feel another contraction building and I groaned and gripped the plastic arms of the chair, pushing without even thinking about it. Eric got me to breathe through it, but he was once again focused on what was happening underneath me.

"Okay," he coached as the contraction eased, "good. Now, we're not staying in the chair for this. That's not an option. So, squatting, or kneeling, or on the bed?"

In the end, I chose the bed. When Rex and Brandt helped me up, I felt too wobbly to trust myself squatting or even kneeling. They guided me from the bathroom and into the same treatment room where I'd gone for scans and other prenatal care. The bed was no longer a narrow medical exam bed, but a proper hospital bed, complete with waterproof mattress and adjustable side rails. The back had been raised, ready for us.

"Rex, up on the bed behind him with his back against your chest," Eric instructed, then helped me up onto the bed after Rex was settled, getting me positioned between his legs. "Okay, I want you to bring your knees up as close to your chest as you can. Rex will help hold them there."

Another contraction was starting up and I was suddenly terrified, but I did what Eric told me to, automatically bending forward to push as the pain built.

Eric nodded. "That's it, just like that. Good. Well done, Day. Now relax."

"Stop telling me to relax," I snapped. "I can't relax. I'm… *ohhhh* why is there another one already?"

He didn't need to tell me to bear down through it. My body was determined to boot the kid out as quickly as possible.

"Every birth is different," Eric answered my question, even though it had been mostly rhetorical. "You're doing great."

Rex kissed the crown of my head. With his chest pressed to my back, I could feel his heart beating wildly. For all his calm demeanor, he was as panicked as me. I appreciated that he wasn't giving in to it, though. He was soldiering through for me. For our son.

That realization made me determined to do the same.

"You've got this, darlin'," he murmured into my ear as I braced for the next contraction.

His reassurance fortified me.

I bore down and screamed.

* * *

Two hours later —including a lot of tears, bargaining with the universe, and telling Eric to shut the ever-loving fuck up and just *help me*— Eric held a wriggling, bloodied, tiny humanoid up for us to see.

"Congratulations, guys. Meet your son," he declared as the pitiful wailing started. "All ten fingers and toes accounted for, and a healthy set of lungs, too."

My heart ached.

Our son.

Rex and I had made that weird looking, loud little thing… and he was *perfect*. My eyes tracked his movement from Eric's hold to Brandt's as Eric guided me through delivering the afterbirth. It was nowhere near as painful or traumatic as delivering a baby, and it wasn't long before Brandt was cutting the cord and the squirming, ick-covered baby was nestled against my chest, already rooting around for food.

And how weird was it that I could provide that food?! I hadn't really thought about it before, but as he latched on to my nipple and suckled, it made sense. Early shifters hadn't had access to formula or anything, so of course our bodies were designed to nourish the lives of our young. It would definitely be weird to carry and birth them and not have a means to keep them alive, wouldn't it?

I reclined against Rex with an exhausted sigh, and his arms moved around me to help cradle our son as he nursed.

Our son, the thought struck me all over again. *Wow.*

"Look at that hair," he murmured sounding every bit as awed as I felt. "Little guy's gonna take after you, huh?"

Sure enough, the baby had a thick mass of dark hair, wet

and matted with blood and vernix as it was. It inspired mixed feelings inside me. On the one hand, I thought he was absolutely perfect. On the other, I'd kind of been hoping that he'd come out looking like his daddy.

I watched him snuffle and suckle for a few long moments before I said, "I think he's got your nose. Maybe your eyes."

"It doesn't matter who he looks like, darlin'. He's his own person."

How the hell did he always know the exact right thing to say? "You're right. And he's perfect."

Rex nuzzled my cheek with his own. "That he is." He waited a beat. "He's gonna need a name."

We had been tossing suggestions back and forth for a few weeks, but had opted to wait until we met him, thinking that we'd get a better idea of what kind of name would suit once we did.

We were wrong.

I looked down at him and drew a blank.

It was bad enough we were going to saddle him with the hyphenated Richards-Murphy surname. What the hell kind of first name worked with that?

"What was your dad's name, kitten?" Rex asked me when all I could do was flounder in silence. "He sounded like a good man. It'd be nice to honor him, wouldn't it?"

A lump lodged itself in my throat. "Campbell. Everyone called him Cam."

"Campbell Richards-Murphy," Rex tested it out loud. I could hear his smile when he followed it up, "I like it."

"It doesn't sound too…I don't know…snooty?"

"Nah," I was jostled lightly as Rex shrugged. "Specially not if we're callin' him Cam for short."

"I think it's cute," Brandt agreed, bringing a clean hospital blanket over and laying it over us. He smiled, his mottled European accent sounding stronger than usual, "little Cam. A strong name for a strong cub." If I wasn't mistaken, that was a look of yearning in his eyes, but he blinked it away before I could comment on it.

I was totally going to corner my dragon-shaped friend when I was more awake and alert. I'd call it payback for all the times he'd made me vent to him over the past few months.

Rex kissed the top of my head, distracting me. "What do you think, darlin'? Cam?"

I looked down at the baby again. He'd fallen asleep with my nipple in his mouth. It was insanely cute.

"Yeah," I smiled, feeling overwhelmed with emotion. "Cam it is."

Chapter Fourteen – Rex

Some part of me had been convinced that I would shift when my son was born. I'd imagined that my alpha would be so overwhelmed with pride and joy that he would break through whatever invisible barrier had been preventing the change.

I was wrong.

The joy and pride were there, of course. I had never loved something —someone— as quickly or as intensely as I loved Cam. It was different to the feelings I'd developed for Damon, though I'd realized I loved him, too.

I'd burn the world to keep both of them safe, but the instant attachment I'd felt to that baby had made me almost dizzy. It was a fierce love; animalistic and raw. Instantly unconditional. Damon and I would be his world until he was an adult, and even then, I'd always be there for him in every capacity that I could.

And still I couldn't shift.

I was afraid that I was broken. That maybe I was more

human than shifter after all.

How would I be able to properly bond with my son if I couldn't shift when he finally learned to do so?

Eric and Beck both seemed to think those fears were unfounded. Ollie maintained his theory that bonding with Damon would finally unlock my shifting ability. Damon seemed to think that the more I focused on not being able to shift, the more I was preventing myself from doing it.

Whatever the reason, I was beyond frustrated with my stunted abilities.

Two weeks after Cam's birth, the town assembled for a pack run. It was an initiative Beck and Ollie had implemented for pack bonding, and everyone seemed to love it. Beck had explained that there was something magical about connecting with everyone in shifted form, and I couldn't help being jealous that I still couldn't experience it.

Instead of even trying to attempt it, I told Damon to go have fun. He was still recovering from childbirth, but Eric had already assured him that historical accounts suggested shifting would help accelerate the process. And, as it had been so long since the last time he'd been able to run and leap around while shifted, Damon was excited to give it a go.

So I found myself with the other childminders in Beck and Ollie's house, with a veritable herd of small children who were all too young to shift. At least I could be a little useful, even if I felt like an impotent alpha. I couldn't even properly compel the older tykes to behave when I tried to do the 'magical compulsion thing' Beck said he could do.

"It's nice havin' an alpha here with us," one of the middle-aged women said as she jiggled a set of toy keys over a grizzly baby. I'd already forgotten her name, but she scented like a rabbit.

I had, at least, been getting better with being able to scent things.

"I know we haven't seen hide nor hair of any troublemakers in a while, but I can't help always being on edge. My old pack was really violent when it came to keeping omegas in line. That's why we left: my parents didn't want my little brother suffering." She huffed and rolled her eyes. "They'd been perfectly content to stay there until he was born."

I nodded sympathetically. "Some people don't like to rock the proverbial boat, is all. But they looked out for you and your brother when it counted."

Rocking Cam in my arms, I knew that I would have done the same thing as her parents. His crescent moon birthmark marked him as an omega, just like his papa, but it didn't make any difference to me.

Well, no, that was a lie: I'd be brandishing a shotgun at any potential alphas when the time came…at least until Damon could talk me out of it.

"I s'pose," she agreed with a sigh as Lena, another rabbit shifter, came down the stairs. She had just put Beck and Ollie's twins to bed, and looked like she'd been through the wringer. Nevertheless, she smiled at me and plucked Cam from my arms, taking him upstairs to be put down in the bassinet Ollie had provided. The hair on the back of my neck stood on end as he was carried out of my sight.

You're being paranoid, I told myself, almost chuckling out loud at how the voice in my head sounded just like Damon. My kitten found my protective instincts 'adorable', or so he said. *Lena's got him. He's fine.*

"Still can't help feeling like they were complicit in the

mistreatment of others, though." Bringing my attention back to the conversation, the woman I'd been talking to looked down at the baby on her playmat and smiled more genuinely than she had earlier. "Thankfully, my kids and grandkids aren't growing up like that. And Beckett's turning this town into a proper pack, the way it used to be in the olden days. Well," she paused, "maybe a bit more eclectic given the different breeds we've got living here. But I'm glad these babies are going to have that."

"Me too," I agreed wholeheartedly. "I didn't have much of a family growing up. I'm happy that Cam's got a huge adoptive family."

"With dragons for godfathers and all," Sage's friend, Dexter, joined the conversation, sauntering in from the kitchen. He carried a tray of snacks and drinks and placed them carefully on the coffee table before gingerly sitting on the couch by the window.

"Speaking of dragons," I arched an eyebrow at him, "I'd have thought you'd go stretch your wings with the others."

For all that Ollie and Damon had believed that this guy would stir up problems, he'd actually been a bit of a hermit, hiding out at Sage's house and barely appearing at any town events. Sage had been remarkably tight-lipped about the whole thing, too. It just made me more curious.

As if thinking the same thought that filtered through my brain, Dexter's lips quirked and he 'tsk'd. "Curiosity killed the cat, Rexxie."

"Seriously, though," I pushed, sitting down in one of the armchairs. "Why aren't you out there?"

"Why aren't you?" he countered, raising his eyebrow in challenge.

My inability to shift was not common knowledge. I wanted to keep it that way. "Damon hasn't been able to properly enjoy a shift in months."

"Well, let's just say there's a lot of that going around."

That was a cryptic response if ever I'd heard one. I opened my mouth to tell him exactly that, when a strange scent caught my attention.

I sniffed at the air, frowning.

What the hell was that?

"Weasel," Dexter got to his feet, also scenting the air. He bared his teeth. "There aren't any weasel shifters in this pack." He turned to face one of the other childminders, "Right?"

She shook her head, frowning.

"Isn't that cult-leader-guy a weasel?" Lena asked, her foot hovering over the final step from the staircase, then she muttered, "Which, y'know, is a bit clichéd if you ask me...and I'm pretty sure weasels get a bad rap because of it, too. I mean, weasels are actually really cute."

Ignoring her nervous rambling, I felt anxious. Cam was out of my sight, and there were strange shifters nearby, and the coincidence of them being the same species as the guy who had tried to have Beck kidnapped was even more unnerving. Especially when that same guy had been strangely silent since posting his diatribe to his followers at Christmas.

"Are the kids safe up there?" I asked, tilting my chin in the direction Lena had just come. There was a baby monitor on the coffee table —one of those fancy ones with a video feed— and a glance down at it showed all three babies were fast asleep.

Still, unease tugged at my gut, and I'd learned to trust my instincts. "Go back up there. Dex, you go with her."

Neither of them argued.

I looked at the others still seated around the living room, on the floor or in the additional chairs Beck and Ollie had bought, most cuddling their children close, and I did my best to smile reassuringly. "I'm just gonna go see if these newcomers are lost, or if they've just got really bad timing."

"Uh huh," the woman I'd been chatting with only minutes earlier arched her eyebrows, holding her granddaughter to her chest. "*Sure.* That's why you've sent the dragon to guard the Alpha's kids and yours, huh?"

"It's just a precaution," I insisted, trying not to sound too frustrated. I was a new dad, and I was pretty sure Damon would castrate me if I didn't think about Cam before I went outside to investigate the strangers who still hadn't come to introduce themselves. Hell, I'd castrate myself. "And if there's a problem, Dex and Lena will get everyone into one place. There's safety in numbers."

As I said it, I scented the air again, a feeling of foreboding bubbled in my gut.

If the strange shifters were here to cause trouble, they'd also understood that concept. They must have been waiting for an opportunity to strike, because it seemed far too convenient that they'd arrived when most of the town's defenses were down. And if they were smart, they would have also come in force.

The faint scent of weasel was gone, but the air felt *wrong* somehow. Instinct told me they were still out there.

Hadn't Eric mentioned something about scent blockers once?

Shit.

For all that Beck, Eric, and Brandt had said they were expecting the Moonmusic people to regroup and come at the town again, it felt as though they had become complacent. Where was the security on nights like this one, when the pack was dispersed and running Gods-only-knew where?

Glass broke overhead and Lena's shout had me launching into action. As much as I wanted to race up the stairs to protect my son, I knew I needed to make sure the group gathered downstairs with me were safe as well.

"Change of plan: get into the downstairs bathroom," I demanded, pulling the adults up from their seats as I spoke. They clutched their little ones to their chests and bustled down the hallway. "It'll be a tight fit, but at least you can lock and barricade the door. Don't come out until one of the pack confirms it's safe." I had no idea how much of that they paid attention to, given that they were already halfway down the hallway while I was making my way up the stairs.

I stopped short in the doorway to the nursery, terror speeding through my veins. I felt sick, and my heart hammered at the sight of the overturned bassinet. My knees threatened to give way when I saw that it was empty, as were the twin cribs.

Lena's limp form was slumped against the wall to my right. I almost hadn't noticed her. When I bent to check on her, she had a pulse, but she was out cold. On the floor, Dex was sprawled on his stomach, bleeding from a pretty significant head wound.

Something inside me *snapped*.

One second, I was a terrified man —a new father whose two week old newborn had been snatched out from under his nose— and the next I was shifting, my bones and organs rearranging, fur sprouting from my limbs. It didn't hurt, per se, though I wouldn't call the process comfortable. My clothes tore and I lashed and kicked to get out of them.

Then the world was in sharper focus, somehow. Scents, sounds…even my vision was all so much more intense.

As I became used to my new form, I could hear my son crying. In fact, I could hear all three of the missing babies crying.

I didn't stop to think, just leapt out of the window, landing on the pitched roof of the wraparound porch. My claws instinctively dug into the tiles to slow my slide, but when I focused on retracting them to leap from the roof to the ground, it worked.

I followed the sounds and scents of our abducted pups and cub, still unable to catch more than just the faintest whiff of the strange shifters. Someone was muttering, though, making demands to get the babies to shut up.

They were in human form, then. At least some of them were. It made sense: it would be hard to carry children off in animal form, especially for creatures as small as weasels. Who knew how many wolves or other predators were with them in shifted form, though. There was no way —especially after their attempt to kidnap Beck— that they wouldn't bring enforcement.

As much as I wanted to rush after them, I knew the smarter thing to do would be to stalk from afar. I needed to get a better idea of how many there were. I couldn't let them leave town with our children, but I also knew better than to run into unknown danger. I wouldn't be any good to Cam, Duke, and Rory if I got myself caught, or injured, or killed.

It struck me that Eric or Brandt would still be at the clinic. One of them always stayed there in case someone needed urgent medical attention. Unfortunately, the kidnappers were heading in the opposite direction to the clinic. I was a mountain lion, and my phone was presumably still somewhere in the tattered remnants of my clothes back in the nursery.

Casting one last mournful glance in the direction of my baby's wails, I made the soul wrenching decision to head to the clinic.

At least in this form I was fast.

All four limbs worked with effortless, feline grace as I raced towards the clinic. I scratched at the front door, yowling until Brandt swung it open with a scowl. The expression slackened into surprise when his gaze landed on me.

"Rex?" he asked.

I opened my mouth to explain the situation, but all that came out was a series of feline yowls and growls.

Fuck, I couldn't speak.

Panic overtook me.

How could I communicate with him?

"Shift back," he instructed calmly, but there was obvious concern in his tone.

I hesitated. If I did shift back, would I be able to turn into a puma again? I needed to. Cam's life was at stake. Instinct told me that I'd be able to do it, if only to save my son.

Wasting precious seconds on concentrating, I thought about what it had felt like to shift and considered how it would feel in reverse. Sure enough, my fur receded, and my bones and organs shrank and morphed back into my biped form.

Before Brandt could say a word, I launched into my panicked explanation. Tears rolled down my cheeks, but I couldn't care less.

"You need to shift," I told him. "You need to shift. Fly and find the others. I'll keep following the babies..." my voice broke, but I wasn't going to break down. "Then you find the assholes and track them from above and…do whatever you need to."

Eat them, I thought viciously. *Eat them all.*

"Sounds like a plan." Brandt didn't hesitate. He ushered me out the door and I focused on shifting back into my mountain lion form again. It came easier, this time. More fluid. Still uncomfortable, but it felt more natural. I felt *right* in my cat form.

I didn't wait for Brandt to shift, pelting in the direction I'd last scented the kids. Later, I would be sure to think about how amazing running in my puma form was. How aerodynamic and sleek I felt. How fast and powerful and graceful I was. But at that moment, I was too focused on finding the assholes who had broken into the Pack Alpha's home and taken our young.

I had the urge to claw them all to shreds.

Thankfully, I caught up to them within a minute or so of running. I considered myself lucky that they didn't have any vehicles on Beck's land, likely having kept their mode of getaway distanced to ensure that their approach went unnoticed.

I clung to shadows, keeping downwind from the large group of wolves and bears and — was that a freaking *tiger?* The shifted predators surrounded the human contingent: a group of ten men, three carrying the babies while the four surrounding them carried heavy weapons. Three others carried cases which looked large and military-like in nature. I shuddered to think of the kind of weapons that necessitated large cases like that, but it explained their slow progression, at least. I'd been so afraid that my detour would have given them enough of a window to leave with the kids.

Suppressing the urge to growl, I stalked the group and hoped that the dark sky was enough to conceal Brandt when he came looking for the group. I knew he wouldn't be able to blast them with fire —not while they had the kids hostage— but if they managed to get the babies into a van or something, we'd need him to be able to follow them.

Not that I was planning on letting them get that far.

I hated that I didn't have a plan, and that I was so terribly outnumbered. I did my best to ignore the human part of my brain, because I was beginning to feel like the worst kind of parent. Cam was only two weeks old, tiny and helpless, and I hadn't been able to protect him.

If only I had kept him with me downstairs. If only I had thought about better security during events like the pack run. If only—

A blur of gray fur sped past me, the large wolf growling and snapping as it launched itself at the strange shifters. A smaller blur followed it, then a sleek feline form, and a bunch of foxes. Realization struck me that this was my pack and I threw myself into the fray with them, surprised that my senses helped me to distinguish the difference between enemies and foe.

Human voices shouted and then the sound of gunfire burst through the air, making my sensitive ears ring. I flinched, but kept clawing and biting.

The beating of large wings overhead was also a relief, until a glance showed that the humans with the big cases were stopping to assemble large weapons. Somewhere in the human part of my brain, I knew the word for the tubular-looking giant guns, but I was too far gone in my cat form to care for the label. All I knew was that those things would wreak a lot of havoc.

The strange wolves and bears provided a furry blockade, making it impossible to get to the cluster of humans in the centre of their circle. I hissed and shrieked the loudest, most intimidating sounds I could get my vocal chords to manage, swiping deadly claws to try and break through the furry barricade.

The ground shook as a large dragon landed heavily in the field nearby. His scales were such a dark red that they were almost black, especially when the only light was coming from the stars and moon above us. He stomped forward, lashing his tail to send a number of the unwelcome shifters flying. The humans with guns fired as rapidly as they could at him, but his scales seemed impenetrable. He tilted his head to the sky and roared.

Within moments, another dragon landed at my back, the impact of his landing just as jarring. When I turned to catch a glimpse, I noticed that his scales were a brighter red, the difference noticeable even in the darkness. He was smaller than his brother, too, though he looked just as menacing.

The bright red dragon —Eric, I determined through scent— reached forward and wrapped his clawed hand around three of the attacking wolves, picking them up and flinging them aside with ease. He repeated the action with a bear and a literal handful more wolves, thinning out their defensive line. The bigger, darker dragon (Brandt) did the same where he stood his ground, evening out our pack's odds significantly.

Until the large-barreled weapons were raised.

I yowled in warning, watching in horror as one of the men fired at Eric. The weapon let out a very sharp, loud *bang*, the blast from the back of it tearing into the earth behind him. A spray of dirt and grass flew at the people around him, but I swivelled my head to watch the rocket —there was no other word for it— sail towards Eric.

A single, terrible thought filtered through my mind.

He's going to die.

Chapter Fifteen – Damon

There weren't enough words to describe the tangle of emotions coursing through me as I scratched and fought the strange shifters.

They had my baby.

Above all else, the terror and anger kept my adrenaline pumping in my veins. I was going to claw and maim and destroy every single one of these assholes.

Underneath that, though, was a heaping serving of parental guilt. I'd gone out for a run —gone out to enjoy myself— and my helpless newborn had been abducted while I ran and frolicked. What kind of selfish father was I?

The yowl of a fellow mountain lion caught my attention, and if I'd been in human form, my breath would have caught in my throat.

Rex.

He was beautiful. Much larger than me, with sleek tan-colored fur and strong, muscular limbs. He radiated alpha power, much like Beck did in wolf form. But instead of fighting viciously, as I was certain he had been if the bloodied stains around his muzzle and claws suggested, he was frozen in place, his dark eyes wide with a very human expression of horror.

The epic *bang* that followed his yowl made my ears ring and I flinched against the sound, then understood exactly what had caught Rex's attention so terribly.

Eric's reflexes were sharper than I would have imagined a creature of his size's would be. He hunched in on himself and dropped to the ground, letting out a grunt as the giant-ass bullet —was it a rocket?— caught his folded wing on its way over him. In the distance, it crashed to the ground in the open field with an explosive effect.

Rex yowled again and sprang forward off his strong hind legs, tackling one of the humans with the bazookas.

At least, I thought they were bazookas. Rocket launchers, maybe? I'd never really been much of an expert when it came to weapons. Anyway, technicalities didn't matter. What did matter were the guns now being aimed in Rex's direction.

With Eric down, and the other two bazookas being readied for action, I acted on instinct. Using feline wiles, I raced between the fighting clumps of wolves and bears, weaving past snapping jaws and lashing claws. I found the gap Rex had taken advantage of and launched into the fray, biting and screeching and trying to take out the threat to my mate.

Even if we hadn't bonded, that's what Rex was to me. He was my mate, and he was in danger. I needed him whole…and then we needed to rescue our cub.

I could only imagine what Rex was feeling. If I felt guilty for not being there, he must have been tearing himself apart inside. The first thing I resolved to do once we were human again was to assure him that it wasn't his fault. The second would be to demand our pack rethink its security. We'd gotten complacent, even knowing that Morstein was out to get us, and this was the price we were paying.

In defending Rex, my ears picked up the sound of Cam's cries and something inside me snapped.

I'd heard stories of human parents accomplishing extraordinary feats when their kids were in danger. Lifting cars, fighting off far stronger attackers, walking through flames; that kind of thing. The odd mixture of adrenaline and calm which overtook my body and mind had to be similar to what they had felt. It was as though I saw everything in slow motion and in even sharper focus than before, and I knew I was going to get my son back.

Gnashing my teeth against anything and everything in my way, I fought harder and with more purpose than I knew I was capable of. At my side, Rex did the same, and I knew when the tides had changed in our favor, because Ollie and Beck joined us in the fight to corner the humans holding our kids.

I was dimly aware of Brandt's ginormous dragon muzzle snapping up the guys who had been trying to get their bazookas up and aimed his way. I couldn't help but think that they deserved the painful, terrifying ending. When I was human, I might be more concerned by my complete lack of empathy, but in my puma form, I was just pleased that the threat was taken care of.

The other gunmen were incapacitated by our pack's shifters. In the end, all I could focus on were those three shifters in human form. They wore scent blockers, which had a mildly chemical smell up close. But through that, I was able to still scent their fear as we approached, baring our teeth and growling.

At my side, Rex shifted back to human, his skin filthy and his hair matted. He was scratched up and visibly bruising already, but he stalked over to the now cowering men, practically radiating his alpha power.

That was new.

Sure, since he had come to Shifters Sanctuary, Rex had scented like an alpha: a vaguely electric scent that tingled in my sinuses and made me instinctively want to submit to him. But he hadn't radiated the same dominating vibes as Beck did. Not until now.

"Give me my son," he demanded of the man cradling our screaming, tiny newborn. The words sent a shudder through me, and I realized with a start that he was channeling the same kind of alpha compulsion that Beck was able to wield.

If I'd thought Rex being naked might lessen the impact of the growled command, I would have been wrong. The guy holding our baby handed him over, though I could see he was trying to fight the instinct to do so. As soon as Cam was cradled against Rex's chest, relief swept through me.

But it wasn't over yet. I hadn't noticed Beck shifting a few paces away, but he crowded in and added his own command in his gravelly, angry voice for his children to be returned, and another wave of that intense power rolled over us.

The two men holding Rory and Duke hesitated, but when Rex and Beck barked, "*Now!*" in unison, it was as though the men became robots, unable to fight the commands at all.

Fascinating.

I wasn't as interested in the science-y history stuff like Ollie, Eric, and Brandt were, but even I was curious to see the alpha powers at work. It had to be more than just biology. There was something magical here, too.

Which, yeah, okay; considering we were people who could turn into animals —including *fire breathing* dragons— at will… that shouldn't have surprised me as much as it did.

Still, how much magic (there really wasn't a better word for it) was out there in our world, undiscovered and untapped? Could it be accessed by more than just our alphas? It was worth asking Eric and Brandt, anyway.

Shit. Eric!

With the fight over and the remaining men subdued before they could shift and run away, my limbs became wobbly as the adrenaline faded, but I still turned to look over at the crumpled dragon in the field. I was torn between checking on him, and making sure my mate and cub were okay.

A whine burst from the back of my throat, and Rex was at my side almost instantly.

"Are you hurt, kitten?" he asked, crouching beside me, Cam tucked against his chest. Our baby was no longer screaming, but I wanted to get him out of the cool night air and into the safety of our home.

Our home.

Somewhere in the past couple of weeks, I had started thinking of Rex's cottage as ours, even if I hadn't officially moved in. Our combined scents permeated the space, and it truly had become the setting where I imagined raising Cam.

I shook my head and then concentrated on shifting back to my human form, ignoring my aches and pains in preference of throwing myself at Rex. I nuzzled Cam and then my mate, finally letting the tears come.

"I'm so sorry, Damon," Rex held me tight against him, but I could hear the strain of emotion in his voice. "This is my fault.

I should have been upstairs with the babies. I—"

"Stop it." As much as I wish the protest had come from me, I was beaten to it by Beck. The Pack Alpha's expression was grim as he closed the distance between us. Ollie was pressed to his side, holding their son, and Beck himself was cradling their daughter to his chest. He frowned. "You should have been safe in our home. Everyone should have. I...*we*...should have considered that they'd come after the kids. After last time, we thought they just wanted an alpha. We should have realized that they might use the kids as bait. Or...God, I don't know." Ollie rubbed his back.

I nodded, then pulled away so I could look my mate over. "Are you okay? Are you hurt? I should have been there with you." Once again I was afraid of losing him, but now it was a fear that he could be taken from me. That he almost was. That our baby was almost taken. My voice wobbled as I continued, "The thought of something happening to you...God, Rex, I was so scared. I can't believe none of us thought they might come for the kids."

"We were short sighted," Ollie sighed, leaning into Beck, visibly drawing comfort the same way I was with Rex. "We got lulled into a false sense of security. All of us did. This isn't anyone's fault."

It felt surreal to be surrounded by death and destruction, standing naked as our pack regrouped. It hurt my heart to see that some of our own people had been hurt —some even killed— in the struggle. They were innocents in all this mess.

Those who weren't hurt were corralling the survivors from the attacking group, herding them into a small group guarded by Brandt's looming dragon form. I had no idea what we were going to do with the handful of bad guys, but I figured that was something Beck and the council would need to decide. Maybe hand them over to the authorities? That didn't seem the greatest idea, when these guys were shifters and the human police had no way to manage that.

Anyway, that wasn't going to be my problem, and I didn't feel guilty in washing my hands of them. Even in human form, I thought Brandt eating them might be the best course of action. I mean, they'd taken my baby. They couldn't possibly redeem themselves from that.

Thinking about Brandt reminded me about Eric again.

"Eric," I gasped, taking a stumbling step out of Rex's grasp in the other dragon's direction. Only, the dragon was gone, replaced by a curled up, human form. I hurried over to him, understanding that he was the person I would call for to give medical assistance, and Brandt —our dragon guard— was the other.

"Where the fuck is Sage?" I demanded of Beck and Ollie. "Or even Dexter?" We could use another dragon right now. One to threaten the remaining bad guys so Brandt could see to his brother.

Beck frowned, passing Rory to Ollie as he hurried over to help me with Eric. "I don't know."

"Shit. Dex is at the house. He was with the babies. They knocked him out somehow," Rex explained as he joined us, hovering anxiously as he still cuddled Cam. "And the others are locked in the bathroom downstairs. I should go check on them."

"But Sage?" I repeated, frowning. "He wasn't running —*flying*— with the pack?"

Beck shook his head. "I assumed he was with Dex."

On the ground, Eric groaned. "He's…out of town."

"Stay down," I told him, eyeing the epic open wound over his shoulder blade. "Don't move. We're going to need to get you an ambulance."

He groaned again and attempted to push himself up, shaking his head.

"Stay down," Beck issued the command using his magical power, and Eric flopped back to the ground.

"That's cheating," he complained weakly. "Asshole."

My lips twitched. Eric and Beck had a funny sort of friendship, and it was a reassuring sign to hear Eric falling back into banter.

Beck snorted and relaxed a bit, too, probably thinking the same thing I was. "You love me, Weldman. Stay put. We'll get you help."

"Come back to Beck and Ollie's with me," Rex all but pleaded, and I would openly admit that there was no way I wanted to be separated from him, either. "I need to check on Lena and Dex. And let the others out of the bathroom."

"I've just sent Sandy to grab our phones and stuff," Ollie told me, awkwardly trying to readjust his hold on his kids. I took Duke from him and he sagged with relief. "Thanks. Anyway," he tilted his head in the vague direction we'd been frolicking in before we'd heard about the attack on the house, "our stuff will be here soon. Brandi and the others were already heading to the house before we came this way. As she put it, she's more menacing as a woman than as a rabbit."

I snorted. Ollie's best friend, Brandi, was dating Lena, and she was a riot. But she was also fiercely protective of her friends, and I imagined that she could do a whole lot of damage if she wanted to. I definitely wouldn't underestimate her, even though she was a petite blonde woman and a rabbit shifter to boot. With a veritable herd of equally determined smaller species shifters at her side, I assumed she would be okay.

"Good," I said, nodding. "Then we'll head over to the house and see if she needs a hand."

I felt bad leaving Eric behind while he was injured, but it made no sense to have both alphas out in the fields when half the town were probably going insane with worry at the Pack Alpha's house. Besides, I was exhausted and felt grimy, and I just wanted to wash up and snuggle up with my mate and cub. Cam was due for a feeding anyway.

It was funny how even with all the drama, my instincts were still attuned to his schedule.

Biology. It was wild.

As expected, the half of the town who were smaller species shifters were crammed into Beck and Ollie's house when Rex and I got there. Jazz offered to hold Cam while Rex and I washed up, but neither of us were willing to let him out of our sight, so we took turns showering. We also borrowed clothes from Ollie and Beck's closet before we headed back into the crowded living room. There, Rex hovered over me while I fed Cam, and he answered as many questions as he could, assuring the townspeople that we'd neutralized the threat for now.

Dex and Lena were among the assembled group, too, which was a relief. Brandi had Lena's head in her lap as they sprawled on the floor, her expression dark. Dex was slumped on the end of one of the two couches, nursing what appeared to be an epic headache. He looked grim and defeated, which was unsettling considering his usually smarmy, snarky personality. But they were otherwise okay, and there had been no further attacks on the house.

But I was officially once bitten, twice shy, and I hoped that the pack would behave that way going forward, too.

Chapter Sixteen – Rex

In the weeks that followed the attack on our town, I found myself roped into helping Beck deal with the fallout. It was rough for a while, with people mourning the six shifters who had died and calling for us to retaliate. There was no point reminding the townsfolk that our dragons had done far more damage to the attacking side at the time, either.

I also thought that we had gone vigilante enough when we held the contingent of seven Moonmusic shifters against their will, questioning them for hours about the motivations for the attack. As much as I hated them for trying to take my kid, I didn't think we needed to devolve into our own cult-like mentality. Perhaps that was the part of me who had been raised human, but I believed in the justice system.

Thankfully, in the end, Beck sided with me and we reached out to nearby law enforcement. Imagine our surprise when the cops who turned up were also shifters! They assured us they weren't sympathizing with the old-school packs —especially when one of them was an omega himself— and we were more than happy to send our hostages off in the backs of their trucks.

On top of that, we began discussing the need for proper pack security. More and more strangers were visiting the town, and I couldn't help but wonder how many were staking us out for our weak points. I felt ridiculously paranoid, but at the same time, I couldn't help feeling justified in those feelings. Our kids needed to grow up safely.

"You're doing the 'burn the world' face again," Damon said, shaking me from my musings. He switched off the bedroom light and sauntered towards the bed, backlit from the nightlight in the hallway. We left the door open, and even though we both had enhanced shifter hearing, we kept a video baby monitor on my bedside table, too. "We're safe, babe, I promise."

If anything good could have come from the whole abduction saga, it was the closeness Damon and I now shared. Maybe it wasn't healthy that we had clung so tightly to each other in the fallout, but I'd been in love with him beforehand, and I was even more in love with him after watching him fight to save our kid and the pack from further harm.

But I hadn't said the words yet. Firstly it was because I'd promised to let him set the pace. Then it was because I didn't want him to think I was professing my love just because he'd given birth to our son. Then it was because I didn't want him to think it was a trauma response.

I swear to the Gods, I wasn't making excuses. I was turning forty-three soon: I was adult enough and mature enough to face my feelings.

I was.

Except, alright: maybe I was a *tiny* bit afraid that he'd still find it too much, too fast. I mean, he'd just been through something traumatic, too. Was it wrong to give him some time to process that first? I didn't think so.

As it was, I was almost afraid to point out that he had all but moved into my place in the weeks following the attack. At first, I thought he was silently humoring my desperate need to keep him and Cam in my sights as often as possible, but then I paid a little more attention and realized he was making himself at home. My inner cat preened with smug satisfaction. My mate was settling into the home I had provided!

Some part of that felt mildly patriarchal and outdated, but I didn't care. I wasn't forcing him to be there, and he seemed happy to settle in my home. If he was happy and I was happy, there was no problem, right?

"Seriously, you're starting to freak me out." Damon sounded mildly amused beneath his concern and I blinked, smiling sheepishly.

"Sorry. I was thinkin'."

He laughed and shook his head. "Yeah, I got that. I was giving you a damn strip tease and you were *not* reacting the way I wanted."

Those words had my attention. I focused on what he was wearing —or, rather, what he wasn't wearing— and my mouth went dry.

"That's more like it," he practically purred, giving an enticing swivel of his hips as he dropped his underwear.

My heart hammered. It had been almost seven weeks since Cam's birth, and we had done little more than cuddle. I obviously hadn't been pressing the issue, knowing that Damon needed to take as much time as necessary to recover from pushing an entire person out of his body, but we'd both also been kind of wiped after working and then looking after a newborn. Whoever coined the expression 'slept like a baby' has obviously never spent time with an honest-to-God baby. They don't sleep. At least, not for extended periods of time.

Where was I?

Oh, yeah. Sex.

Sex with Damon.

Fuck, had I missed sex with Damon.

"The baby…" I protested, looking at the monitor as though our beautiful —but potentially evil if his sleep schedule was any indication— child would wake up at any second.

Damon laughed and climbed onto the bed beside me, sliding beneath the covers before reaching for my hardening cock. "I just put him down. He'll be good for a couple of hours."

With his hand squeezing me through the thin cotton of my underwear, I caught maybe five words of that. Not that I had any plans to argue with him. "Fuck, kitten…" I bucked my hips. I flashed back to the last time we'd had sex and almost whined. "Please don't tell me you need me to tie you up tonight. I don't have the patience."

I'd promised him we'd experiment more with rope play after the baby was born, but there was no way I'd hold out to do it right. Not at that moment.

Damon chuckled and the sound went straight to my dick. "We'll need to get Beck and Ollie to babysit if we wanna do that," he said, and I ignored the stab of anxiety at the thought of handing our son over to someone else for a night. "Tonight," he continued, whispering sensually and mouthing at my neck, "I just want you inside me. I need your knot, alpha."

I've never scrambled to get naked so fast in my whole damn life.

"On your back, darlin'," I instructed, having a very clear idea of how I wanted this to go down, so to speak. "Let me take care of you."

With the exception of that last time, where his legs had been tied and splayed out, or the few times he had ridden me with his belly in between us, we'd never made love face-to-face before. That was what my alpha was demanding I do, and I was going to take my time worshipping Damon the way I should have when I first met him. I'd thought he deserved more than a quick bathroom fuck at the time, and now I was going to make up for that.

The heat in Damon's gaze softened into affection, even though his eyes still burned with lust, and he lay back on his pillow. "Yes, alpha," he answered teasingly.

Fuck, but he had to know that it went straight to my cock when he did that.

I kissed him deeply, showing him with my actions how I felt for him when I still couldn't quite say the words.

"Rex…" he breathed my name against my lips when we parted for air, and the words tumbled out anyway.

"I love you."

There was a moment of stunned silence and then he grinned, grabbed my face in his hands and tugged me down for another deep, delicious kiss. "I love you, too," he whispered afterwards, the confession ghosting over my skin in the scant space between us. "Now, please, get inside me."

"Not yet."

"Wh—"

I cut off his question with another kiss, then pulled back to pepper more down his cheeks, his neck, his chest, and his abdomen. His breathing hitched when I got to his leaking erection, and I didn't waste any time sucking him into my mouth from tip to root.

His ecstatic cry was cut off and muffled as he grabbed for my pillow and held it over his face, making me chuckle around his dick. That made him moan and writhe some more. It was glorious.

While he mewled and complained into my pillow, I continued to suck, then brought my fingers to his slick hole. He was almost as wet at the day we'd met, practically dripping for me, and I moaned to find him so ready and aroused.

"Mmphk mmmmee," he begged, still trying to keep his sounds muffled with the pillow over his face.

I smirked and slowly pulled off from his cock. "What was that, kitten?"

He yanked the pillow from his face and hit me with it. "I said fuck me, damn it."

"Ask nicely, darlin.'" I pumped my fingers in and out of him, watching as he threw his head back and bit back another moan. "Say 'please, alpha' like a good boy."

The gush of extra slick coating my fingers told me that he liked that as much as I did.

"Please, alpha," he repeated, rocking his hips. "Please. I need your knot."

"Good boy," I repeated as I withdrew my fingers, sucking the slick from them while he watched, open-mouthed. I crawled into position over him, then froze as the baby monitor caught my eye.

"He's still asleep," Damon huffed impatiently.

"Yeah, but…should I…should we maybe use a condom?" It was *probably* something I should have thought about earlier. I didn't even know if the ever-present condom in my wallet was still in date.

Damon shook his head vehemently. "The chances of you knocking me up off-heat while I'm still feeding him from my body is slim to none."

It was cute the way he avoided saying 'breastfeeding' wherever possible. I made a mental note to tease him about that later.

"You sure?" I asked.

"Rex, I swear to God, if you don't get inside—*oh, fuck, yes.*"

I was just as impatient as he was, even if some part of me had wanted to hear his idle threat in full.

Sinking inside him was complete, utter bliss. His body gripped mine like a glove, and we moved together in a well-practiced rhythm, kissing and sighing as our bodies got reacquainted. We pressed our foreheads together and rocked slowly, neither of us wanting to rush to the finish line. Not this time, anyway.

"I love you," he gasped after one particularly well-aimed thrust of my hips.

"I love you," I repeated back to him, thrilling at how easy it was to say now.

"I'm…I'm super close," he warned me after another thrust. "Me, too."

Then he tilted his head to the side. "Mark me, alpha."

My hips stuttered along with my heart. *"What?"* I could hardly bring myself to hope that I'd heard him right.

He didn't hesitate to reply, "Bite me. Please, alpha. Bond with me. I'm yours."

"Fuck," I cursed as his words pushed me over the edge and my orgasm rocketed through me, "fuck, kitten…"

He arched off the mattress as my knot began to swell, then tugged me down for what I thought was a kiss as I continued to come. But instead of pressing his lips to mine, he sank his teeth into the juncture between my shoulder and neck. The pleasure I felt from his mark was instantaneous and almost indescribable. Instinct told me to bite him back, so I did.

Suddenly, the bond between us opened in a rush. I could feel his physical and emotional bliss almost as though it was my own, and I knew that he could feel mine. It became a feedback loop, and the tightening of his slick flesh around my sensitive knot almost made the ensuing continued orgasms too much to bear.

Almost.

It was amazing. I was wrung out in the best ways, but simultaneously energized. Everything about this moment felt right and perfect. My inner alpha was beyond satisfied with this turn of events.

I rolled us to our sides as I collapsed in a sweaty, sated, ridiculously sappy heap on the bed, my cock firmly locked inside Damon by my knot.

He cuddled into me, with his head tucked beneath my chin and his leg slung over my hip. A strange '*prrrr*' overrode the erratic thumping of my own heartbeat in my ears, and it took a moment to realize that it was purring.

We were purring.

Together.

Considering how much other crazy shit I'd seen since I'd met Damon in that bar, nothing surprised me anymore.

"Holy shit," Damon murmured after a while, careful not to move or disturb my slowly deflating knot. "We're bonded."

I could feel his elation through the bond, and I was relieved that there wasn't even a hint of regret.

Kissing the top of his head, I said, "Mmhmm." Then, because

I needed the reassurance to be verbal, asked, "No regrets?"

He gently leaned back so he could look me in the eye. "None. I'm yours now. Forever. And you're mine."

If someone had asked me a year earlier whether I liked the idea of being committed to someone for life, with a newborn baby and all, I would have laughed them off and run for the hills. But since meeting Damon, I couldn't think of anything I wanted more.

"Forever sounds good to me, darlin'."

And it really, truly did.

Epilogue — Damon

"On your knees."

They were my favorite three little words, especially when drawled out by my sexy mate. I scrambled to obey.

Ollie and Beck were looking after Cam overnight, with the trade off being that Rex and I would form part of the guard for the kids and other vulnerable shifters during the following night's pack run, and I was taking full advantage of a childfree night at home.

Kneeling naked on the bed, already gagged and blindfolded, and holding a bell in my hand in case I needed to safe word, I was practically vibrating with desperate excitement already.

I could hear Rex's quiet movements around the side of the bed, but I couldn't see him. Through the bond, I could feel his answering enjoyment of this scene, though.

There was something equal parts arousing and relaxing in letting Rex tie me up. Sometimes, we went with basic bondage, but when we got the chance, I loved letting him decorate my body in intricate shibari patterns before rendering me immobile and fucking me senseless.

With Cam staying at Beck and Ollie's, this was one of those times.

The silken shibari rope caressed my heated flesh as Rex began the first tie of the night, wrapping around my chest. I tried to follow his slow, deliberate movements, picturing the design in my head. As he crisscrossed over my shoulders and around my pecs, weaving decorative knots, I guessed it was a diamond chest harness – one of my favorite shibari patterns to look at.

Once finished with my chest, he repeated a similar pattern around my waist, down over my abdomen and then framing my crotch. I was leaking slick down the insides of my thighs, but with the tightening rope surrounding my cock and balls, I was achingly hard and leaking precum, too.

Through it all, I kept as silent as possible, made easier to achieve with the gag in my mouth. But, even so, I was still vibrating out of my skin with the need to see Rex's artwork. He was a master with rope, after all.

Cowboys and rope, I thought happily, *a match made in heaven.*

"Good boy," Rex said when he finished tying the last of the knots. "I think you deserve a reward."

I whimpered as he removed the gag from my mouth, but instead of taking away my blindfold, he ran the sticky, blood-hot head of his cock over my lips. I sucked him into my mouth greedily, delighting in his resulting moan, and in the way his fingers carded through my hair, holding my head in place.

"That's it, kitten. Fuck, just like that."

I sucked and licked and bobbed my head as though this prize would be taken from me at any second. Knowing Rex, it just might.

I could feel more of my slick trickling down the insides of my thighs, my arousal incited by the pleasure I could feel through the bond. Rex's pleasure, which I was responsible for.

When he pulled away, I whined in protest.

He chuckled. "Hold on, darlin'. I want you to see how beautiful you are."

The fingers in my hair moved to pull the blindfold up and off my head. I blinked a bit to adjust to the low light of the room again, and then looked towards the mirrored wardrobe doors, directly across the room from the foot of the bed.

He was right; I did look damn good all trussed up in his decorative bondage.

"I'm not done with you yet, baby," he murmured, then took hold of my wrists and brought them behind my back.

My cock jerked and dribbled with anticipation.

Yes.

I closed my eyes and enjoyed the feeling of completely submitting as Rex tied my wrists together, then my ankles, then the two separate ties as one. I was hogtied while kneeling, and I couldn't even be bothered snarking about a cowboy's choice to hogtie his partner, because it felt too damn good.

Then it got *better*.

After reclining on the bed, Rex used his alpha strength to manhandle me until I was straddling his lap, the latex-covered tip of his cock teasing at my slick hole. He held me steady by my hips and thrust into me, causing us to both cry out at the sensations of ecstasy zipping through the bond on feedback loop. He held me in place as he rocked up into me, and soon the room was filled with the sounds of our lovemaking.

Flesh slapping flesh, the wet sound of my slick squelching

around his cock, our panted breaths and quiet groans…it was nothing short of perfect. I couldn't move my hands or legs, and my head was floaty from just how cherished I felt.

"I'm…I'm gonna come…" I warned him as the building pleasure became almost unbearable. I knew he could feel the tightening coil of pending release through the bond, but I couldn't help babbling anyway. "Rex…please…right there…" I tried to bounce in place and *oh, God, yes!*

I practically whited out as my orgasm crashed over me, with the answering echo of Rex's own following directly afterwards. Smaller jolts of bliss came next as I clenched around Rex's knot and he came again and again, weaker but still just as pleasurable.

He groaned and pushed himself up into a seated position, grimacing through the additional stimulation to his knot, reaching around me to release the tie binding my hands and feet together. With a look of concentration on his handsome face, he also undid the ties on my wrists and ankles, so we could fall to the mattress more comfortably.

Sated, I began to drift to sleep, lulled there by the way his fingers were gently trailing over the remaining ropes over my torso.

"You're perfect, kitten," he murmured, sounding awed. "I still can't believe you're mine."

"I'm glad." I yawned and closed my eyes, smiling softly. "You're kind of stuck with me, cowboy."

Then I drifted off to sleep, thinking about just how perfect he was, too.

* * *

"And you're sure you don't want to trial the birth control Eric and I have created?" Brandt asked, bouncing Cam on his lap while Duke and Rory tumbled around on the rug, fighting over a stuffed toy wolf. They had two of the things, of course, but like most siblings, each one wanted whatever the other had.

I felt the stab of sheer panic coming from my mate through the bond and I snickered, shaking my head, not even bothering to look over at him, where he was rolling around in his puma form, entertaining a bunch of older kids, who were still too young to shift. I didn't care what he said, he was a natural dad.

"No, Brandt. I'm not being a guinea pig. What if they fail?" More of that panic raced through the bond. I sent back a wave of exasperation, still looking at Brandt as I gestured to the brawling toddlers. "I don't need that in my life, thanks."

We were on guard duty during the monthly run. There were additional security sweeps around the property, and Sage was still investigating my theory about tapping into magic to create magical protections, too.

In the year or so since the attempted abduction of our children, our pack had not only become far more security-conscious, but had also grown significantly. We had yet to connect another omega with a 'hidden alpha', as Eric was still calling them, but people were leaving their cult-minded packs and coming to us for sanctuary on a weekly basis.

Unsurprisingly, Morstein's rants about the 'Neo-Shifter Movement' had increased in answer to his gradually dwindling flock. Some of the newer shifters had even reported that their packs were reconsidering their structure and ties to Moonmusic, which was probably also making Morstein mad. However, if enough packs pulled away from him, he was just one man and he'd do less damage without their support.

I'd also had the shock of my life when Brandi had stopped wearing scent blockers and revealed that she was also an alpha. A female alpha. My mind had been blown, but Beck and Rex had been relieved to have the additional alpha backup as the pack continued to grow.

Due to the expansion of our pack, the human townships in the area had also become aware of our existence. However, Beck and Eric worked overtime to make connections and prove that we weren't all that different to them. That had meant that they'd had to warn the humans about the *other* kinds of shifters, too, but they were both convinced that we were making allies among our neighboring towns and that would only benefit us in the long run. I was on the fence about that.

Some of the local scientists and doctors had also offered their help and equipment towards Eric, Ollie and Brandt's research, and many businesses were willing to employ the new shifters moving into the area, too.

Where we had started as a fledgling, mottled pack, we now felt far more substantial and powerful. With three alphas at the helm, most teething issues as we expanded were dealt with efficiently and quickly. But that also meant that we needed to be even more vigilant against attacks from the old-school cult-y shifters.

I really needed to think of a better way to describe them.

The Moonmusic sect, maybe?

Either way, the more they lost followers, the more tithes they were losing. Their bid for not only financial control, but social power would only become more desperate over time. Eric was having a larger building built for town meetings, but also for times like this, where the most vulnerable members of the pack were even more defenseless and exposed.

Still, none of that detracted from my personal happiness.

Brandt pretended to be affronted. "You believe my calculations are off?"

"I believe that no birth control is one hundred percent effective."

"Amen to that," Lena huffed and dropped into the seat beside me, rubbing her hand over her heavily pregnant belly. "A word to the wise: the implant can fail during a heat."

I laughed, while Brandt sighed and told her, "Your implant was due for replacement. If you hadn't left it so long, you and Brandi would still be pretending you were happy just dating."

"You're a town doctor," she complained at him, "you're supposed to be professional and impartial."

He shrugged. "I've been here since the beginning. I'm your friend, too. If you want impartial, switch to one of the new doctors."

Yeah; the town had expanded so much that we had a proper doctor's clinic in the main street and everything, but I still worked for Eric and Brandt in what they had rebranded to their fertility and birth center.

Lena rolled her eyes and pouted. "I don't wanna."

"My, how the tables have turned," Ollie teased her as he wandered into the room. He seemed to take great pleasure in his friends' situation. I assumed there was a story there, but that was their business. He sat beside her and placed his hand over her belly, smiling when one of the babies inside kicked. "Weren't you the one placing bets that it would be Beck and me having more babies?"

"Shut up," she batted at him, but she was laughing. "Mark

my words, Smith, that alpha of yours will knot more babies in you yet."

Ollie had taken Beck's surname after they'd gotten married in a very elaborate ceremony in front of the whole pack at the last Christmas parade. He shrugged and looked over at his kids, his eyes lighting up with yearning. "I wouldn't mind," he admitted.

Over on the mat, Rex groaned and sent me a look —and accompanying feelings through the bond— that told me not to go getting any ideas.

I rolled my eyes at him.

As if my feelings would have changed from three minutes earlier.

"Anyway," Ollie said, redirecting the conversation, "Beck and Sandy's friend and former housemate is finally coming to stay for a while. I've only met Micah a few times, but he means a lot to Beck, so can we all please play nicely?"

As Brandt became unusually silent, I gave Ollie an insulted look. "Since when do I not play nicely?"

Ollie pointed at me emphatically. "You fight with Dex every time he comes into the clinic."

"That's because he's an ass—" the growl from the mat reminded me that there were little ears listening. *Damn it.* "—ssssassin."

"An assassin, huh?" Ollie repeated with amusement.

I glared. "You know what I actually wanted to say."

"Not that it's an excuse," Brandt cut back in, sounding a little *off*. I supposed that he had actually been there during Dexter's formative years centuries earlier, so he knew him far better than we did. "But Dexter is…going through some things. He's not usually quite as abrasive."

I couldn't exactly say I couldn't relate, could I?

Back when I'd met Rex in that bar, I'd been sarcastic and dismissive, too. I'd been miserable in my pack, and if he hadn't come along and upended my life, who knows where I would have ended up.

Probably still miserable, sneaking out and turning down sleaze-bags in random roadside bars.

With a bit more empathy, I nodded. "Maybe Dex and I just need to have a proper conversation."

"Speaking of," Ollie gave Rex a pointed look and my mate let out a sigh before pushing to his feet and trotting out of the room. When he came back, he was fully clothed.

He took my hand, nodded at Ollie, and then walked me out onto the porch.

"What's going on?" I asked him.

We were bonded, but I couldn't get a read on his feelings. They weren't masked, exactly, but it almost felt like he'd worked out how to muddle them across the connection between us.

He looked out into the darkness and took a deep breath before he turned back around to face me…and then dropped to one knee.

My eyes widened.

"Rex…?"

"I've been thinkin' about the best way to do this for a while now," he started, then pulled a square ring box from his pocket, which made my heart stammer, "and I'm still nervous as hell." He paused and chuckled, then, looking up at me with amusement and adoration. I felt those emotions clearly through the bond. "I'm pretty sure I fell head over heels for you when I caught you tellin' some guy that you didn't speak

English just to turn him down. And even though we're bonded together already, I still want everything with you, darlin'. Even if that's more rugrats at some point down the line, or if you decide you want to leave this pack and move to Aruba, I want us to do it all together. So," he opened the box, while I stood there gaping, the cool breeze and twinkling stars the only witnesses to this magical moment between us, "will you marry me, Damon?"

Nodding, I thought back to that life-changing night as well, and remembered what I had told him then. "Just so you know," I let all the love I felt flow through the bond to him, and repeated the words I had spoken, setting off a chain of events neither one of us could have predicted, but that I didn't think either of us would take back. "For you? I'll speak any language you want."

As we kissed in joyful celebration, I hoped that the same words would bring just as much unpredictable happiness to us in the future, too.

The End

Thank you so much for reading *His Prodigal Alpha*. This one was a real journey for me, but I'm so excited that the boys got there in the end, haha. I also can't wait to explore *Shifters*

Sanctuary further from here.

I'd love it if you could leave a review on your retailer of purchase or on Goodreads.

Reviews not only tell the algorithms that our books deserve attention, but honest feedback also encourages and inspires me to keep writing. Even a star rating helps, and I greatly appreciate you making time to do so.

Speaking of my writing, if you want a glimpse into Book Three of the Shifters Sanctuary world, titled *His Unicorn Alpha*, keep turning the pages because Chapter One is waiting for you.

And if you'd like to see Ollie and Beck (from *His Alpha Unlocked*) enjoy themselves in a 3,700 word additional steamy scene where they explore the sharing of sensations through their bond, you can find that by signing up for my newsletter at:

https://annasparrows.com/newsletter-subscription/

If you're already signed up and still want a copy, email me at:

annasparrows.author@gmail.com

I'd love to hear from you!

Love,

Anna

Sneak Peek: His Unicorn Alpha

Chapter One – Brandt

"You're okay with doing the fertilization tests today?" Eric asked as I wandered into our shared clinic.

My life had both changed significantly and also not at all since I had moved to Shifters Sanctuary roughly two years earlier. I had always been a doctor and a researcher, honing my skills over my centuries of existence, but when I had moved to the town my younger brother had established with the then-only known alpha in existence, I had been drawn into assisting him with his research into alpha/omega dynamics and omega fertility.

It had been the focus of Eric's research since the last known dragon alpha —our father— had vanished, presumably killed by dragon hunters, though his remains had never been found. Eric was determined that we could save our species from extinction.

We were an all-male race, dependent on the existence of alphas to impregnate our omegas. Without alphas, there was no longer any way for our omegas to have babies.

When Eric had called me, excitedly announcing that he had discovered an alpha —albeit a wolf shifter and not a dragon— his hope was infectious. For the first time in centuries, I imagined that maybe our race had a chance after all.

Beckett Smith had grown up entirely human until he had met his omega mate and they had been thrown into a whirlwind mating heat and bonding experience. What followed was a series of events which upended a great deal of the shifter community, causing an even deeper divide between the 'new age' of shifters, who believed in social equality, and the 'old-school' faction, who appeared to be led by a cult-like religion called Moonmusic, whose reasons for keeping things the way they'd always been seemed to be driven purely by financial greed and a lust for power.

Because alphas, it turned out, were just as powerful as legends suggested.

They radiated it, in fact. Their very scents were electric, buzzing and energizing. And, as we had discovered, they had the ability to compel and control betas and omegas through commands alone if they so chose.

I imagined just how terrible things could go if the wrong sort of person had those abilities and I shuddered. No wonder the Moonmusic-founded sect had wanted an alpha of their own.

So, to cut a long story short, I was working for Eric in the hopes we could save our species, as well as find answers to the questions raised by the existence of all the new alphas.

"Yes," I replied, making my way to our private lab, though I was convinced the task would be just as fruitless as with every other round of testing.

In the couple of years since Eric settled here with the first of the new alphas, people had been arriving in the hopes that they, too, were potentially affected by 'hidden alpha syndrome' or 'locked alpha syndrome', as Eric had called it. However, as time continued to pass, we were all losing hope that we would find more alphas.

From the start, I had been skeptical that we would find any dragon alphas. Eric's theory that the locked alphas had some genetic throwbacks to shifter lines made the likelihood of finding someone with dragon genes even slimmer. After all, our father had been gone for hundreds of years: even if he had sown his wild oats in the human community, those lines were likely far too diluted by now. Additionally, I didn't believe that Eric, Sage, or I would be fated or compatible mates for someone within our genetic line. Yet, we still worked in hope. It was that or resign ourselves to extinction.

Eric and I had spent months working out the science on inducing egg production in omegas without being able to incite mating heats. In the end, it involved using similar chemical hormones to the birth control we had devised for Ollie, Damon, and Lena – mates to the town's alphas. Not that Ollie or Damon felt confident in relying on our science to prevent future pregnancies, much to Eric's frustration, and Lena was pregnant and unable to be our test subject for at least another six months.

With mild desperation to prevent our research from stalling, Eric convinced the Pack Alpha, Beck, to host social events between the growing numbers of potential alphas and the omegas in town, but none had sparked the kinds of connections that Beck, Rex, and Brandi had reported.

Through a meticulous documentation process, we had

decided to attempt blind insemination attempts in the lab, using sperm donated from multiple potential alphas and even the town's betas, and ovum from omegas who had been willing to undergo the invasive procedure to donate them to science.

Eliminating the combinations of omegas and potential alphas who had interacted at the social events left us with possible combinations of ovum donors and sperm. The plan was ultimately to alert any potential matches should any of the insemination attempts become successful and allow the parties in question to make decisions on how to proceed from there.

We believed that, under controlled circumstances, potential mates could meet and ride out the initial mating heat while simultaneously avoiding pregnancy.

It was beginning to feel like we were throwing things at a wall in the hopes something might stick, though. There were too many variables, even if Eric was convinced that fate and magic would be on our side.

My youngest brother had always been the dreamer of our family.

* * *

Two hours after walking into the lab, I was staring open-mouthed at successfully fertilized eggs. Three of the four in the petri dish were viable. My heart hammered wildly. This meant that there was another potential alpha among us after all. Eric was right.

I checked the numbers on the petri dish and pulled up the records to see whose samples had matched so spectacularly. Chances were, I would be on a first name basis with the omega, given the ovum-retrieval process was run out of our clinic. I had less to do with the potential alphas than Eric, who conducted all their interviews and collected their samples, but I might have crossed paths with them in town.

My mouth went dry and I felt dizzy when I saw my own name staring back at me from our records.

It can't be, I thought. But, when I double checked the records, there was no doubt left.

They were my ovum. My eggs. The petri dish in front of me held *my* potential children.

Dragons.

I didn't rush to look up the potential alpha, too shocked at the realization that I had three viable, fertilized dragon eggs —from my own dusty womb— sitting right in front of me.

Eric, Sage, Dexter and I had all undergone the ovum-retrieval process out of a sense of desperation to save our species, but I had never imagined that one of us would find a match, especially not me. I was one-hundred years older than Sage and Dexter, and almost two-hundred years older than Eric. I was practically middle-aged by dragon standards!

The urge to ensure the safety and continued viability of my test-tube created young rushed over me in a wave of overwhelming determination.

Even if they weren't inside me, they were my babies. I had technically even made them.

But who was their other father? Who was my potential alpha?

After carefully returning my petri dish of hope back to the specialized, protected storage Eric had had manufactured for his lab, I turned back to our records and looked for the corresponding number for the sperm donor.

I blinked, then frowned deeply as the name registered in my brain.

Micah Hawthorne.

Beck's friend and former roommate.

A *beta.*

How is that possible?

Sitting back in stunned silence, I mused over the discovery. I'd never met Micah. Even at Beck and Ollie's wedding in front of the entire town, our paths hadn't crossed. But from what I knew of the man, the contents of that petri dish should not be possible. Firstly, he was a beta. Secondly, unlike Beck, Rex, and Brandi, he had grown up knowing he was a shifter and he had the ability to shift. Finally, he was a horse shifter.

Beck and Ollie were both wolves. Rex and Damon were both mountain lions. Brandi and Lena were both rabbits.

I was a dragon. Micah was a horse. How could we possibly be compatible?

If we were, and if the fertilization of my ovum wasn't a fluke, this discovery would throw all of our theories to that point into the wind.

And, assuming Micah was also affected by locked alpha syndrome, did that mean inter-species breeding was possible between alphas and omegas after all, like it was between betas of different species? And, if so, would those fertilized eggs be dragons, or would they be horses?

I decided that, on that last question, I didn't care either way. They were still my babies, made from my ovum — something I'd honestly thought was a daydream at best. They were precious, regardless of their species.

However, another realization hit me like a punch to my solar plexus.

Eric and I did not have the facilities to freeze the embryos. After a few days, they would need to be frozen or disposed of.

I felt sick at the idea of disposing of them.

Especially when Micah didn't live in Shifters Sanctuary. He traveled all over the world for work. Even if I contacted him, would he want to uproot his life to be saddled with a man he'd never met, or to have children simply because I was desperate to try to save my species and, if I was being honest, because I desperately wanted to be a father?

I'd wanted it for centuries, but had never imagined it possible.

The petri dish called to me, speaking to those desires like a siren.

I knew it was unethical. I knew it would be a breach of my Hippocratic oath as a doctor…

But I *really* wanted to be a father. As far as I could tell, this was my only shot. It was fate, as Ollie would say.

And so, under my brother's nose, I prepared to break laws and oaths and ethics in order to fulfill that dream and potentially ensure my species would continue.

What was the modern saying? Seek forgiveness, not permission?

Well, I hoped I'd be forgiven for my next actions, because they were going to change history.

About the Author

I've been writing* for as long as I can remember. I started with silly short stories as a kid, moved on to fanfiction in my teens (and still write it now when the mood strikes).

I have been an avid reader of MM romance my whole life. Ask me about my beginnings with *Buffy* fanfic, haha! I wrote a sweet and kinky MM romance novel in 2022 and the reader response changed my life. From there, I knew I had found my niche.

And thus Anna Sparrows was born.

*All of my writing is 100% my own. No part of it is generated by Artificial Intelligence (AI) software of any kind. Yes, that means that it's sometimes flawed, but I'm okay with that.

You can connect with me on:

🌐 https://annasparrows.com

f https://www.facebook.com/AnnaSparrowsAuthor

🔗 https://www.instagram.com/annasparrows

Subscribe to my newsletter:

✉ https://annasparrows.com/newsletter-subscription

Also by Anna Sparrows

I write ridiculously sweet & steamy MM romance with guaranteed HEAs…and sometimes with a side of kink.

Littles & Lace Series
The Littles & Lace series is an MM Age Play series, following a group of like-minded friends in the BDSM community. You'll find mild ABDL, light Pet Play, Femme Play and more here.

Book 1: Asher's Answer

Book 2: Matteo's Mettle

Book 3: Ted's Temerity

Book 4: Spencer's Satisfaction

Book 5: Chance's Choice

Book 6: Josh's Jackpot

Dads & Adages Series
Visit Australia's sunny Gold Coast where an assortment of single dads find love and even learn a few life lessons along the way.

Book 1: Where There's A Will

Book 2: You Don't Know Jack

Book 3: A Match Made In Evan (release TBA)

Shifters Sanctuary Series
In a world where alphas are thought to be extinct, a number of men are about to have their worlds rocked.

Book 1: His Alpha Unlocked

Book 2: His Prodigal Alpha

Book 3: His Unicorn Alpha (release TBA)

9 781763 664616